THE LAST CHARGE

Roderick broke into a run with the rest of his command lance flanking him. He was in the suburbs of New Edinburgh now, and the buildings were concentrated enough that he had to stick to roads for the most part. He pounded forward, closing on defenders that had been guarding the artillery emplacements until they were wiped off the planet. They were already retreating, but on the scanner their movement looked random and disorganized. Roderick edged west, cutting across a broad parking lot and zeroing in on a *Ghost* that was reeling away from the fire behind it. Roderick fired his autocannons and watched the rounds bore holes in the *Ghost*'s torso. The narrow body of the 'Mech looked unsteady, but its sturdy legs kept it upright.

Roderick charged forward, now relying on his laser as the *Ghost* tried to get off shots of its own. Its lasers fired, passing in front of Roderick, who had slowed down to draw a better bead on the Silver Hawk 'Mech. He hit the *Ghost* with his pulse laser, and the 'Mech stood still. He left it standing in the middle of the street, looking like a statue, a ready-made memorial to the battle raging around it.

Tanks surged forward in front of him, doing some of the street-level grunt work that urban fighting required. Roderick laid down autocannon fire to drive back some Silver Hawk vehicles and clear a path for his tanks.

The confusion of the Silver Hawk Irregulars was already dissipating. They were too well trained to stay disorganized for long, and Roderick saw on his scanner that their pullback was becoming faster and more cohesive. That was fine. He'd gotten what he wanted.

MechWarrior
DARK AGE

THE LAST
CHARGE

A BATTLETECH™ NOVEL

Jason M. Hardy

A ROC BOOK

ROC
Published by New American Library, a division of
Penguin Group (USA) Inc., 375 Hudson Street,
New York, New York 10014, USA
Penguin Group (Canada), 90 Eglinton Avenue East, Suite 700, Toronto,
Ontario M4P 2Y3, Canada (a division of Pearson Penguin Canada Inc.)
Penguin Books Ltd., 80 Strand, London WC2R 0RL, England
Penguin Ireland, 25 St. Stephen's Green, Dublin 2,
Ireland (a division of Penguin Books Ltd.)
Penguin Group (Australia), 250 Camberwell Road, Camberwell, Victoria 3124,
Australia (a division of Pearson Australia Group Pty. Ltd.)
Penguin Books India Pvt. Ltd., 11 Community Centre, Panchsheel Park,
New Delhi - 110 017, India
Penguin Group (NZ), 67 Apollo Drive, Rosedale, North Shore 0632,
New Zealand (a division of Pearson New Zealand Ltd.)
Penguin Books (South Africa) (Pty.) Ltd., 24 Sturdee Avenue,
Rosebank, Johannesburg 2196, South Africa

Penguin Books Ltd., Registered Offices:
80 Strand, London WC2R 0RL, England

First published by Roc, an imprint of New American Library,
a division of Penguin Group (USA) Inc.

First Printing, December 2007
10 9 8 7 6 5 4 3 2 1

Copyright © WizKids, Inc., 2007
All rights reserved

ROC REGISTERED TRADEMARK—MARCA REGISTRADA

Printed in the United States of America

PUBLISHER'S NOTE
This is a work of fiction. Names, characters, places, and incidents either are the
products of the author's imagination or are used fictitiously, and any resemblance
to actual persons, living or dead, business establishments, events, or locales is
entirely coincidental.
   The publisher does not have any control over and does not assume any responsibility for author or third-party Web sites or their content.

To Kathleen,
who deserves a book dedicated to only her.
That, and a whole lot more.

ACKNOWLEDGMENTS

The following people played a role in shaping this book, whether they like it or not:

- As always, Sharon Turner Mulvihill provided expert guidance with an ever-positive spin. It's good to have someone who keeps pushing for the book to be better.
- Randall Bills also provided advice, continuity help, guidance, and, of course, the dashing good looks for which he is known worldwide.
- Kevin Killiany was fun to conspire with, despite his tendency to work the word "Niops" into every sentence. He's fast, talented and responsive—like a sports car, only sleeker.
- Thanks must go to the other writers who set up the characters and situations I played with in these books. In addition to already named people, Mike Stackpole and Blaine Pardoe deserve particular thanks.
- This book and anything I do would not be possible without my parents.
- And here's a list of names: Iris, David, Lindy, Elissa, Megan, Gretchen, Katrina, Jenica, Steve, Cindy, Rob, Bill, Tamara, Geri, Bill, Ann, Dave, Beth, Joe,

Hugh, Patti, Fritz, Meg and Lisa. These are various siblings, in-laws, and spouses of in-laws who in various ways have been excellent people and deserve to be acknowledged. So there they are. My brother, who shall remain nameless for my own purposes, is naturally not named here, but still deserves the same acknowledgment as the rest. Only without a name.

- And my wife, Kathy, and son, Finn, are kind and supportive and let me type when I need to. They rock.

Mountain Retreat
Paltos, Atreus
Marik-Stewart Commonwealth
13 February 3138

The words were there. Anson Marik could feel them, hovering around his head like angry bees. But they were elusive, staying out of his reach, out of his thoughts. It should be easy. He should be able to just take a deep breath and have them come to him. Then he would let them free, and the fury that would follow—it would be beautiful.

"Who the hell . . . ? Confounded . . . bloody . . . Of all the . . . arrogant, useless . . . Shove a *tree branch* up . . . blast!"

He exhaled. It still wasn't coming as easily as it was supposed to. This shouldn't be.

He stomped on the wooden floor; outside, snow fell from nearby branches. Someone, who knows which of his ancestors, had built this room to be cozy, like a cabin high in the mountains, right down to the knotted pine floors. A cabin built on the edge of the massive lump that was the rest of the retreat. All Anson could see, though, was a room that would be easy to tear apart if he set his mind to it. The floor would splinter if he just kept stomping hard enough. Then he could pick up a loose floorboard and smash the desk, the chair, the bookshelves, the electronic screens and their useless information. They would smash up nicely.

Then he'd shatter the picture window, leap outside and set about tearing down the whole thrice-damned mountain.

His fists clenched and unclenched. Then again. Then they stayed unclenched. His breathing slowed.

"Bloody hell!" he shouted. He shouldn't be getting calm yet. He needed his anger. He *trusted* his anger. He wasn't about to let it go.

Heat returned to his face, and he knew the skin beneath his brown beard was turning red. He was ready.

He didn't bother to push the button on his intercom. "Tell Daggert to get the hell in here!" he bellowed.

He didn't have to wait long, but even in those few seconds, Anson felt his heart rate slow a touch. His back sagged, and he briefly thought about sitting down.

Then he straightened up and took five solid, heavy steps across the room. *Damn it, what's the matter with me?*

The door to his office opened and Cole Daggert walked in. A dark man from head to toe—from the tight black curls of his hair (with gray at the temples) to the shiny black pointed tips of his shoes, he looked like an undertaker. An arrogant, stubborn undertaker.

"Daggert," Anson bellowed. "What in the hell is the matter with you?" Then he grimaced—the words just weren't echoing around the room like they should. They weren't filling his chest properly.

Daggert waited a moment before he spoke. When he did, his tones were low and level. "Perhaps, my lord, this is a conversation we should have when you are calm."

"When I'm *calm*?" Anson shouted. "You know what's going on out there. You know, better than anyone but me, the shit we're in. From every damned side. You tell me—when exactly do you think I'm going to be *calm*?"

Daggert's eyes did not waver. "Your guess is as good as mine."

Anson slammed a hand on his desk. "You're not getting insolent, are you, Daggert? I could throw your ass down the mountain for that remark. I've done worse for less."

"Yes, my lord. You would be within your rights to dismiss me."

"Don't tell me what my rights are!" Anson thundered, and he enjoyed it. It felt natural. Maybe he'd just been out of practice, but the words were coming easier, the air rushing out of his lungs like the winds through a mountain pass. "I bloody well know what I can and can't do! And I'll tell you what I can and can't do, just so you know." He stepped forward until his nose almost touched Daggert's. "I can do *whatever the hell I want*!" he bellowed.

Again, Daggert didn't flinch. "Of course, my lord."

Anson took a step back. Daggert wasn't making this easy. Shouting matches were much easier to sustain when both sides were angry.

"Now that we've cleared that up, I'm going to tell you what I'm going to do. I'm going to take your letter of resignation and shred it. Then I'm going to throw the shreds into the fireplace. Then I'm going to take the ashes and *rub them in your thrice-damned face* if you ever try anything like this again!"

"My lord, may I just say—"

"No! You can bloody well keep your mouth shut until I tell you to speak! We are in the worst emergency the Commonwealth has ever faced—frauds and pretenders, Lyrans and Wolves and Falcons and who knows what else closing on all sides—and it's only going to get worse. What makes you think this is the time to get out? I can't afford to lose any of my senior staff, especially my *chief bloody tactical adviser*! I don't have to explain how bad the situation is—*you're* the one who keeps explaining it to *me* every morning. My head, the head of the whole

Commonwealth, is on the line here, and if my neck is in danger, then your neck better damn well be sticking out next to it!"

"When you put it that way, I can't see why I'd want to step down," Daggert said.

"This isn't a time to be *clever*," Anson said with a sneer. "This is what you signed up for! You don't just step down when things are getting difficult. You gut it out! Win me this war, get all our enemies running away with their tails between their ass cheeks—*then* you can retire. Not now."

"With all due respect, sir, I think it would be best if you accepted my resignation now. I think it would be best for you, for me and for the Commonwealth as a whole."

Anson prepared to let loose another gale of anger, but his lungs didn't respond. They didn't fill up enough for a full roar. He had to say something, though.

"You think that would be best? Why?" That last word had an oddly plaintive note to Anson's ears. He didn't like the sound of it one bit.

"In a time of crisis such as the one the Commonwealth is facing, a nation needs leaders who are ready and willing to give their entire selves to the nation's defense and to act in concert against the looming threats. At this time, I feel your office would be better served by an individual who could offer the complete dedication and effort this crisis demands. I believe I should step aside so you may find that individual."

Anson glared at Daggert. The tactical adviser remained stiff and straight, eyes focused on something beyond Anson. He was ready for another torrent of words from the captain-general. So Anson decided to take him by surprise.

He smiled. Then he laughed. It wasn't a merry sound—it was the laugh of a victor gloating over his vanquished rival—but still, it was clearly not what Daggert expected to hear. His eyes flickered, and it may have been that the dark skin on his cheeks grew a trifle redder. That,

Anson knew, was as much as Daggert would ever let his composure slip.

"Damn it, Cole, how many times did you stand in front of a mirror rehearsing that little speech?" Anson said between guffaws. "You did the words okay, but did you ever think about moving your damn arms when you talk? You look like a mannequin."

"My lord, whether my words were practiced or not—"

"Yeah, yeah, just because you practiced 'em doesn't mean they're not true. Fine." Anson's laughter trailed off. He couldn't sustain it. "It doesn't matter. I wasn't going to make this decision based on your delivery or your pretty words. You can talk and talk and say everything just right and it doesn't matter. I need you. So you're staying."

"I must ask you to consider—"

"You can ask me to consider whatever the hell you want, but at the end of the day I'll decide you still work for me, so you might as well stuff it."

"My lord, I feel the demands of my family—"

"Oh, screw all that! This 'family' nonsense. Every time a politico steps down, they talk about being with their family. It's all bullshit. You got as far as you did because you like what you're doing, because you like the power you have, and that's not something you just stop doing. You never, ever, stop wanting power if you've made it this far. It's like not wanting water. You may have your reasons—maybe you're scared of this war, maybe you just don't like me. Who the hell cares? There's only two things I know about your reasons for resigning—first, it's not about your family. Second, whatever your reasons are, they're not good enough."

"I have to say I don't think you are being—"

"Of *course* I'm not being fair! Since when was it—"

"Would you have the courtesy of at least allowing me to finish a sentence!" thundered Daggert.

Then there was silence. Snow thudded softly outside as the two men stared at each other.

"Well," Anson finally said, his voice gravelly. "This

may be the first time you've ever come in my office and brought your balls with you."

There was something in Daggert's eyes, some fire behind the deep brown Anson had never seen before. And Daggert's body, which usually seemed stiff, was now taut. Ready to jump, though Anson didn't know which way he'd leap. He decided to find out.

"How long has that outburst been coming?" Anson said. "How many times have you yelled at me when you're alone because you didn't have the guts to do it to my face?"

"Never," Daggert said, his voice still thundering, "confuse a respect for decorum with a lack of courage."

Daggert moved, but he didn't pounce. He turned toward the door, took two steps, then whirled back on Anson.

"I'm done with you," he said, quieter but with no less fire. "I've had it. Fight your wars. Keep living life as an overgrown schoolyard bully. I'm done. I'm leaving. You may do as you wish." He turned again and walked toward the door.

"What I wish," Anson said, "is to throw you in a deep, dank dungeon if you try to walk out on me."

Daggert froze in his tracks.

"Yeah, you *should* stop. You know it's no bluff. I've got what I need right here. It's a benefit of being old nobility—everywhere you go, your ancestors seem to have built a dungeon. One of the perks of power."

"Or one of the perils," Daggert said without turning.

Anson waved his hand dismissively. "I'm not playing word games. This is your choice. Retire to the dungeon or keep working for me. Shouldn't be a tough decision."

Daggert still stared at the door. "Why?" he said. "Why not just use someone else?"

"Because you're the best I have. And even if you weren't, I don't have time to bring anyone else up to speed. We have decisions to make, and we have to make them now, and I don't have time for your weak stomach. Turn around and let's get to work."

Daggert remained where he was, just long enough to show a trace of defiance. Then he did the only thing he could and came back to Anson.

"You are a bastard," said Daggert. His voice was empty.

"Right," Anson said. "Look, this works out pretty good for you. You can call me names and know I won't have your head. You know I need you too much. What more do you want?"

Daggert didn't reply. The fire that had briefly flared was gone.

"Good," Anson said. "So—work. There's plenty you need to do for me. You should find Daniella Briggs—I don't know what happened to her on Marik, but we need every level head we've got. The pony express is working well enough that we should have heard from her by now. So someone needs to *find her* and *tell me where she is*! We've got plenty of work for her here, what with almost every faction in the damn Inner Sphere coming to our borders, playing their damn games. We need to tell them to go back to their own sandboxes and leave ours the hell alone."

He took a breath. "You need to look at Gannett. Some of them damn Clanners, the Wolves this time, are doing the Lyrans' work for them. They've demanded surrender of our forces there. You need to come up with a way to tell them to shove it up their asses."

Daggert nodded.

"Take a look at troop positions, then get back here in an hour. We'll talk."

Daggert left without a word.

Anson picked up a glass as Daggert went through the office door. As the door swung shut, Anson cocked his arm and aimed the glass at the heavy door.

Then he stopped, dropped his arm and put the glass back on his desk. He'd handled Daggert okay, but, damn it, he still didn't feel right.

2

"I think that covers everything. We'll deploy according to your instructions." Hauptmann Denis paused. "Are there any standing orders of which my troops should be aware?"

Duke Vedet Brewster snarled and deep, familiar grooves furrowed across his face. "Yes. Stay the hell out of my way."

Denis saluted briskly, then left the duke's quarters as soon as his salute was returned. Vedet did not bother to stand. He wouldn't stand for his next visitor either.

There was a list of names on the screen in front of him, a list continually updated by his aide-de-camp sitting on the other side of the metal door that helped keep the duke separate from the rabble and their annoyances. None of the names on the list were people Vedet had any real desire to talk to.

The business of war, he'd discovered, had even more administration than the business of 'Mech production, especially when it involved occupying hostile territory. The Silver Hawk Irregulars, who were operating more as a guerilla force than as a real army, caused him enough trouble; the bullheaded citizens of Breckenridge, who were either too dumb or too stubborn to acknowledge that they were now Lyrans, were almost as bad. He generally ended his days by wondering aloud why he and his forces didn't just raze the whole town to the ground, which meant he had to listen to halting lectures from a collection of aides about why such an action might not be a good idea.

Each day, Vedet thought their explanations sounded weaker and weaker.

The door to his office had not opened, even though Vedet saw a long list of names on his screen. Someone was wasting his time.

"Krieg!" he bellowed into his intercom. "Next!"

The door opened. Krieg worked hard to keep the duke appeased.

Holden Barnes walked in, spine straight, uniform pressed, eyes firm. But he had a tell. Vedet always looked at his knees the minute his security chief walked into the office. Whenever Barnes had bad news, he always went a little weak in the knees. It was barely perceptible—unless you were used to looking for such things.

Vedet was talking before Barnes was done saluting.

"Barnes, I assume you're here to tell me that you've made no progress rounding up the dead-enders."

Barnes' long face did not change, but Vedet noticed an additional small tremor in the left knee.

"Sir, as I've mentioned before, the task you've assigned me is significantly more complicated than a normal criminal—or even military—operation. It's possible we might arrest the people behind the bombings and attacks, but doing so wouldn't change anything."

"Judging by the fact that you've made well over a hundred arrests and nothing in this damn town has changed, I'm inclined to agree."

"Yes, sir," Barnes said. "What this means is that making headway is difficult. Unless we start arresting virtually every townsperson . . ."

"Right. Do that."

Barnes faltered. The shaking in his knee was now visible. "Sir?"

"Do that. Arrest them all."

"Sir, we don't have the capacity—"

"Then *develop* it. Build some camps, lock people down in their homes, I don't *care*. I want the bombings to *stop*! If it means locking up all these people, lock them up!"

Barnes fumbled for words, but Vedet silenced him with a wave of his hand.

"Go. Put a plan together. The curfew didn't work. Martial law didn't work. So take it one step further. I'm done trying to send these people messages. Just keep them away from me, and maybe I won't be forced to blow up the whole town."

"Yes, sir."

"I want to see your plan in six hours."

"Yes, sir." Barnes saluted with clear relief, then darted out of the room.

Vedet watched the door close, knowing it would open again soon. There was a book—an old book, ancient Terran—that told the story of an officer who snuck out his window to avoid meeting with his subordinates. Vedet had never read the book, but he'd heard people talk about that story when he was at Defiance Industries. He'd always broken into those conversations to assure his workers that his door was always open, and he'd always be sitting in front of that open door. Here in Breckenridge was the first time Vedet had ever been tempted to not be where he was supposed to be.

Which meant he was more determined than ever to stay.

He turned on his intercom. "Next, damn it," he said. "Next!"

Breckenridge proved to be a refiner's fire, the sort of test that melts lesser men but from which a true leader emerges, purified and hardened.

No. No, no, no. It wasn't an original metaphor to begin with, and he was straining it far beyond the breaking point. It would never do.

Vedet erased the sentence on his screen. He could do better than that. He turned his mic on, then off, then on again. Then he spoke, taking long, firm strides across his office as he did.

"The best leaders are individuals. A committee never led any group, any nation, to greatness. True leadership is solitary, which also makes it lonely. A leader must make his own decisions, make his own mistakes—which only paves the way for his greatest triumphs."

He stopped and leaned over his screen to read the transcription. No. Still not right. That part about loneliness sounded self-pitying, and the rest of it just went on and on.

He looked out the window. Gray mist, a regular sight in this mountain town, hung low in the night sky. For once, though, the mist was not illuminated by flashes of explosives, and Vedet had not heard the crack of gunfire all night. That didn't mean the new crackdown was going to be a complete success, but it was a good start.

He found the mist oddly comforting. He couldn't see the stars. He could tell himself that the quagmire he was in here couldn't be seen, that the curtain on this operation wouldn't pull back until he was good and ready to have outside observers look in, when everything would be clean and orderly.

He could also ignore the fact that one of those stars was the system where Clan Wolf troops would be carrying out the archon's bidding.

He hadn't meant to think about that. He turned back to the screen—his memoirs-in-progress were something worth paying attention to. He decided to give the opening of his Danais occupation chapter a final try. He took a deep breath and a long step.

"Danais was tougher than expected, defended by Marik-Stewart forces who did not have enough honor to fight like a real army. It would be dishonest of me to pretend there were not dark days on that planet—I would not be human if the slow pace of conquest did not drag on my soul. It was a trial, though, that proved instrumental to the events that followed, and Anson Marik, the self-appointed captain-general of his small Commonwealth, would eventually personally repay every drop of blood shed by his forces.''

He leaned over his screen again. There. That was it. That felt right. It had, of course, the slight handicap of not yet being true, but that mattered little. What he knew of memoirs told him that the intended truth of one's life—the truth that should have been, if not the truth that actually was—played a vital role in shaping the life of the writer, and thus needed to be told. Vedet was completely dedicated to making sure that paragraph would eventually be true, right up to and including the moment he wrapped his hands around Anson Marik's neck and extracted his revenge.

He could almost feel Anson's flesh, pliable and warm, under his fingers as he reread the sentence. It was a keeper.

3

Scripps, Gannett
Marik-Stewart Commonwealth
15 February 3138

Alaric Wolf could feel the other 'Mechs even though he couldn't see them. He did not have to look at his scanner to know where they were. They were his, and they were following orders. He could sense their movement the same way he could sense the weapons on his 'Mech. He did not need to touch them to know what they could do and how he could use them. They were his natural extensions, his tools. His hands.

He moved forward slowly. He was the solid base of a circle that stretched up and out from him. A circle that was tightening.

"Alpha One, report," he said.

"We have subdued their fire," Star Commander Zuzanna said. "The breakout attempt has been quashed. They are pulling together."

"They will make another attempt soon. Close the circle slowly."

He could afford to be patient. The outcome of the battle had already been decided, the fate of the planetary militia 'Mechs was already determined. The only matter left in doubt was how much this victory would cost Alaric, and he was confident the price would be low.

They would be checking their scanners now, watching the Wolf forces approaching, looking for a weak spot—and finding nothing.

They were not going to escape. They had come at night, making a quick strike on Bravo Trinary and hoping for the quick hit-and-run attack that weak, tactically deficient forces often employ. Though the progress on Gannett was not rapid, Alaric took a certain enjoyment in rooting out these guerilla troops. They had survived too long through their cowardly tactics, and they needed to understand that their constant running and hiding would bring them down just as surely as if they had stood and fought.

"Striker One, what are your scouts telling you?"

"The enemy is edging to the northeast, but the scouts expect that to be a feint, since most of their heavies are toward the front of that formation. I would expect them to make a move to the northeast, then charge southeast."

Alaric shook his head. Pathetic spheroid subterfuge, obvious and ineffectual. "The surats can move in whatever direction they please. Every unit should hold their position until I say otherwise, no matter what the enemy is doing."

"Yes, sir."

The noose was tightening. With each step his *Mad Cat* took forward, Alaric's heart rate seemed to drop a notch. The red and green lines of his HUD were clear and sharp, and the colors of the landscape were equally vivid: the crisp blue green of the leaves on the trees that pushed their way through the sharp-edged, rocky ground. The washed-out blue of the sky. And most of all, the browns and grays and whites of the 'Mechs around him. As he piloted his machine forward, Alaric could almost feel the rocky ground beneath his *Mad Cat*'s feet and hear the brittle stones snapping each time he stepped down. He shaped the planet with each footstep; each meter forward made the planet his own.

"They are making their first feint, Star Colonel," came the report. "The move south will follow right after."

"Alpha and Bravo Trinaries, prepare your long-range weapons. Take a shot in the middle of the militia troops as soon as they shift away from the feint. Striker Trinary, send a few units forward as soon as the long-range volley is complete. Make it fast, though—do not leave any holes in the circle."

The assorted commanders indicated their assent, and soon autocannon and gauss rounds were flying toward the center of the circle. The militia troops would compress a bit as soon as they abandoned their feint—it was inevitable whenever anything bigger than a Star tried to make a rapid shift in direction. And as the militia units bunched together, they would find hot metal raining down on their heads.

Then a fast Star from Striker Trinary made its move, running forward under cover of the cascading shells and blasting at the militia troops before the enemy could form a proper front line. The militia units themselves were still out of Alaric's sight—he had to follow the battle by looking at blips on his scanner. But he knew what was happening, he would know even if he was blind. The militia units were panicking. They were trying to get into formation but stepping over fallen units, trying to hold position while getting fired on from multiple directions. The length of the chaos would depend largely on the skill of the militia unit's commander, but even a brief period of confusion would be enough for Alaric to win the battle. He could send the bulk of Striker Trinary forward, smashing into the disorganized militia units and routing them—if that was all he wanted.

But that would leave a hole in his circle, meaning there was a chance some of the militia troops would escape. That was not going to happen. None of them would get away.

If they were wise, they would surrender now. They should have already realized what the outcome of this battle was going to be, and they should soon understand just how badly Alaric intended to beat them. The militia troops, however, had been quite stubborn, and Alaric was fully prepared for them to fight to the end. Which, if all went appropriately, was not far off.

The Star from Striker was already pulling back. *Good,* Alaric thought. *Let them think they beat back some of our units. Let them believe they have found a weak spot.*

Sure enough, the militia units surged forward after the retreating Wolves. Maybe they thought they could overwhelm the light 'Mechs closest to them, then break through whatever was behind those frontline units. Maybe they were just eager to move forward after being hemmed in by Alaric's slowly tightening circle. In the end, it didn't matter what they thought. They were behaving as Alaric expected, and he was ready.

"Artillery, open fire. Pin them down, keep them from engaging Striker too closely. Alpha, Bravo, take the flanks. I will back up Striker."

Artillery units, which had been waiting patiently behind Striker Trinary's arc, roared to life, and the ground shook. Striker, the fastest Trinary and so the lightest armed, had been assigned the strongest artillery support. Rocks splintered, throwing dust into the air, and many of the blue-green leaves were coated in gray. The fire was damaging, but not so thick that the militia troops were stopped in their tracks. They were slowed, prevented from engaging Striker Trinary in close range but still moving forward. Striker gave ground slowly, its 'Mechs taking careful steps backward while strafing the Gannett militia units.

Then Alpha and Beta arrived. No longer arcs in a circle, they were a backward arrow point. The rearward units, heavies and assaults, kept the militia from retreating while bombarding their rear with long-range weapons. The faster units outflanked the militia on either side, crashing into them even as the Gannett troops were hesitating in the wake of the artillery fire.

The trickiest part of this maneuver was keeping damage from friendly fire to a minimum. As the circle closed, it became far too easy for troops to fire straight through the enemy and hit their allies. The adjusted formation, along with orders to Alpha and Beta to keep their fire to a minimum, should help. The great majority of the fire should land on the head of the trapped militia troops.

Surely they must know what was happening now. They must understand how Alaric intended this to end. He gave them thirty seconds to choose to surrender. When no such offer came over the comm, Alaric pushed the *Mad Cat* into a run and entered the fray.

The rock dust had only gotten thicker, making visibility poor. But that was only a problem for pilots who couldn't see the fight in their head, who hadn't planned every move of the fight before it started. Alaric knew exactly where he was heading.

He did not run. The smoke, the dust, the fast movements of the smaller 'Mechs, the general chaos of the battle—all of that would do more to protect him from his opponents' fire than would speed. And he had enough armor for whatever rounds made it through the fog of war.

He chose his targets carefully, firing the PPCs at a *Phoenix Hawk* that was harassing some of Striker's smaller units, aiming a double blast of his lasers at a *Vulture* trying to rally troops around its position. His shots sowed chaos, preserving the disorder his troops had created.

The battle followed the course Alaric had planned, with the militia troops flailing here and there, desperately hoping for a breakdown that would allow them to exit the circle and escape. The breakdown never came.

We are Clan Wolf, Alaric thought. *You will die waiting for our discipline to fail.*

Verena helped where she could. She made sure people knew she was available, she tried to demonstrate her skills and abilities, but it seemed most of the time she was scrubbing and polishing rather than doing any technical work.

She knew 'Mechs better than she knew practically anything else. But her knowledge was mostly about how to employ them, how to throw them into battle and when to hold them back, how to turn and pivot faster than anyone would expect and how to barrel forward in a straight line and throw everyone out of your way. She knew everything about how to use this tool—but not enough, apparently, to fix it when it was broken.

She could go so far as to say what was wrong—the gyro system was a little off, or the firing system had lost some of its redundancies and was not responding as fast as it should. She could point out on some machines the exact spot where techs should start working. But she couldn't do the work. The technicalities of replacing parts, of putting certain wires in the right places, of making the entire machine like new instead of held together with chewing gum and baling wire—all of that was beyond her. She'd tried pointing, offering helpful advice to the technicians, and the first few times they nodded at her and smiled politely. But before too long they started ignoring her, and now when she made suggestions they shot her resentful looks. The techs, like just about everyone else in the universe, didn't like being told how to do their job.

If she could have been useful, if she could have lent a hand while they worked, that would have been different. But she couldn't, so the techs viewed her as bordering on useless.

So she polished and cleaned. And remembered. When she polished the legs, she thought about how the *Mad Cat* moved, its wide stance and low center of gravity giving it surprising maneuverability for its size. When she polished the arms, she remembered the weaponry, so many more options than she'd had with her old machine, the *Koshi* that Alaric Wolf had destroyed. He had been about to step on her with this very machine when the tide of battle had shifted just enough to move him away.

She reviewed that moment over and over, wondering if that had been a stroke of luck or of extreme misfortune.

Then when she polished the cockpit . . . when she polished the cockpit, she thought of power. And she thought of using that power to blast Anastasia Kerensky out of existence.

She always spent the most time on the cockpit.

"I need a sturdy machine more than I need a shiny one."

The voice startled her. She had been too enthralled by the 'Mech to notice the presence of its owner.

He was slender and not especially tall, with a frame built for slipping quietly in and out of places. He didn't look like a ferocious warrior—unless you looked at his eyes. Those eyes, slightly hooded with a trace of shadow beneath them, had a way of looking down at anyone, even those who stood taller than Alaric. His eyes did not admit the possibility of anyone being his equal.

"The techs do not need me to help make the machine more sturdy," she said, once she had recovered from the surprise of his presence. "I am left to make it shiny."

Alaric looked at his machine from head to toe. "It is not enough. I will find you something more. Something that better contributes to our effort."

Verena knew he was not seeking her opinion on the matter, but she spoke anyway. "Put me in the cockpit of one of these," she said. "I could give you a lot of help that way."

Alaric turned away from his 'Mech to look squarely at her. Was there a smile of amusement creasing a corner of his mouth? Or maybe it was derision.

He reached for her hand, and Verena let herself believe it was a gesture of friendship, maybe even more. There had been that brief moment once. . . .

But then he spoke and chased her illusions away by focusing on her wrist.

"Your bondcord is entirely intact," he said. "Not a single strand snapped. And you have been in my service for less than a year. You have fulfilled your duties well, but not well enough to change your status yet." He let her hand drop. "You do not become a warrior so easily."

"I already am a warrior, *quiaff*?"

Alaric's expression did not change. "*Neg*. You are a fighter. And a skilled one at that. But you are not one of us yet, and so you are not a warrior."

The argument had been lost before she had even started it, so Verena let it go. "You know that I will perform any duty I am assigned."

Alaric ignored the comment, as if it was too obvious to acknowledge. He took another look at the 'Mech, then walked over to the head technician for a few muttered words. Then he walked, taking short, quick strides, out of the hangar.

Just before he disappeared, he made an abrupt gesture with his hand. Verena had been watching for it, and she followed him out.

"Would it be considered impertinent if I asked how folding your clothes contributed to Clan Wolf's triumph on the battlefield?"

Alaric smiled, a real smile this time—though, because it was Alaric, still tinged with a hint of cruelty. "As a matter of a fact, it would. Bondservants do not question their roles."

She was in Alaric's personal quarters. If she was to be his personal valet, it seemed like a simple job, as he had few belongings and all of them were already in perfect order. Uniforms hung in a tight closet, and a small white drawer held the rest of Alaric's clothing. He had a desk, a terminal and a chair, all white. The bed was similarly Spartan.

She looked at the bed, then looked away, then wondered if she had looked away too quickly. Then she stood firmly and wiped all discomfort from her mind. She was not a child. She and Alaric had done what they had done on La Blon, and that had been the end of that. Their relationship had evolved since then, and the past should remain distant.

"From this point on, when I am here, you should be too," Alaric said. "You will prepare my food, clean my quarters and help me in any other way I require. When I am not here, you can continue with your duties in the 'Mech hangar. You should work harder at picking up some of the technicians' knowledge while you are there."

Verena nodded. "May I ask if this is a reward or a punishment?"

The cruelty in Alaric's face deepened. "You have been thinking like Inner Sphere humans for too long. The destiny of the Clan is what is important, not your own individual status. Concern yourself with doing your duty."

"Yes, sir."

She stood in the room and waited. Alaric did the same. She subtly shifted her weight from one foot to another, looking for all the world like she was standing at attention. Alaric did the same.

"Are there any duties I should be attending to right now?" she finally asked.

"Yes. You should get some comfortable clothes for me out of the drawer. And you should listen."

Alaric began removing his uniform as Verena opened his drawer. He only had about four items of clothing that looked at all comfortable, so her decision was easy.

"You have not been on the battlefield for a year, and that is not going to change," Alaric said. "But you should know more about what we have been doing. You have abilities, knowledge. You should be contributing them to our effort."

Verena stood up, holding a dark shirt and slightly lighter-colored pants. It felt like her spine was expanding a little—she felt taller than she had since Alaric had put the bondcord around her wrist.

"You are making me your servant," she said, "so I can be your adviser."

"I have advisers," Alaric said. "I am not going to make a bondservant equal to them. However, if we talk about combat operations while we are in my private quarters, it is possible that it will have a good result."

Alaric was ready for his clothes, and Verena handed them over. She shifted her weight from foot to foot again, this time a little quicker. Visions popped into her head, of 'Mechs on rocky fields, in forests, on plains. She saw formations, troop movements, firing arcs, all of it rushing through her head.

In most places, the move from 'Mech scrubber to chambermaid would generally not be described as a promotion—maybe a lateral move at best. But to Verena, it felt like a gift, the return of a part of her that had gone unused for almost a year. Her body was not returning to the battlefield yet, but her mind was, and she was more than ready.

"Things are going to become more complicated," Alaric said as he got dressed. "We have done well here. We are getting attention from the people who brought us here, and not all of it will be welcome."

Verena listened and tried not to grin.

4

Scripps, Gannett
Marik-Stewart Commonwealth
15 February 3138

It was important to remember that the universe was mostly nothing. After that, it was fiery balls of hydrogen, then clouds of unorganized dust. After those formations, the next most common thing in the universe was godforsaken rock.

An unending supply, it seemed. Trillian Steiner had been on many planets, and occasionally she had the chance to look down at an unfamiliar planet as she landed on it for the first time. She would stare down at the colors and wait for them to coalesce into something recognizable and maybe even interesting. She would see browns that looked like rocks only to find out she was looking at the top of a dying forest. A beautiful patchwork of color from the air became nothing more than parched farmland and swaths of tall, gray grass.

When she was above Gannett, she saw gray, an almost uniform gray, interrupted here and there by dull green. She waited for the bland colors to sharpen or brighten, or for them to resolve into something more visually arresting. But nothing happened. What looked like a plain gray rock from high above showed itself to be a plain gray rock on ground level. A few stubborn trees, gnarled from the effort, had managed to push through the rocky surface, but most of the time the stones had successfully kept all life at bay.

Gannett was not, by any means, the most valuable jewel in the now-shrinking crown of the Marik-Stewart Republic. But it was a border world, and it was in the way. And the journey to glory often required some unpleasant side trips.

Still, she wished she could be somewhere else. She had been picking over the leavings of the former Free Worlds League for long enough. There were other matters that deserved her attention—Fortress Republic was still an opaque mystery in the middle of the Inner Sphere, and the unpredictable leadership of the Combine always needed watching. But the archon wanted her here, so here she would be, above unpleasant, unhospitable ground.

At least there was a DropShip port, and a good thing too—trying to find a decent landing spot on the jagged ground would not be easy.

The good news was that preliminary reports indicated she wouldn't have to be on this planet for long. The Clan Wolf troops were making better progress than Duke Vedet's forces had on this planet, and the Marik-Stewart Commonwealth did not seem inclined to fight a pitched battle for this rock. If the Wolves continued their current pace, Trillian could not imagine the Marik troops holding on for much longer.

This planet would be another victory for the archon. With a new victorious commander at its head. Meaning more work for Trillian to keep everyone in their place— a good reason for her rather than anyone else to be here.

17 February 3138

"Don't get me another appointment," Trillian said. "I don't *want* another appointment. I want to *talk* to the bastard, then I want to get the hell off this planet!"

"I've been told the Star colonel apologizes profusely for not being able to make any of the previous meetings," said Klaus, her aide-de-camp.

Trillian drummed her fingers on the gray plastic desk, annoyed at Klaus' exceptional level of calmness. He was just standing there, looking not irritated in the least. She asked herself if it would help her mood if Klaus put a fist through one of these blank walls, and after consideration she thought yes, it would.

"Would you punch one of these walls for me?" she said.

Klaus barely glanced at the walls. "No, sorry. They're sturdier than they look. My hand would break before they would."

"Then find something that you can slam through the walls, and get in here and do it!"

"I'll get right on that," he said. But he didn't move.

Trillian took a breath. "The apologies you're supposed to convey to me. Did they come from Alaric directly?"

"No. They were conveyed to me through his people."

"Great. Have *they* seen him at least? I mean, is there someone out there who can definitively say that Alaric Wolf is actually on this damn planet somewhere?"

"All evidence suggests that yes, the Star colonel is nearby," Klaus said dryly. "He's just had events come up over the past two days."

"Does he understand that I'm here on behalf of the archon? That I'm effectively here in the role of his commander?" Trillian took another look at the wall. It didn't look that thick. Might just be plaster. She could probably take it.

Then she looked away, stayed in her chair and listened to Klaus.

"I'm fairly certain he wouldn't recognize that fact," Klaus said.

"He's not here for his health! He's here because he made a deal, and I'm representing the person he made the deal with! I'd think he'd want to talk to me!"

"You're free to present that argument to the Star colonel when you see him."

Trillian slapped her desk. The noise was anemic and quite unsatisfying. "Why aren't you more irritated by all this? You've been sitting around on this pissant planet just as long as I have, you've been yanked around by Alaric just like I have. Get angry!"

"You're angry because you're being treated worse than you expected. I, however, am being treated exactly as I expected," Klaus said, his face all even lines, his body still. "I knew the score going in. I'm not thrilled to be here, but I was prepared to have to wait."

"You're right—I should have seen this coming. Never underestimate the arrogance of Clanners is lesson number two of Inner Sphere politics."

Klaus took the bait. "And lesson number one?"

"Peace is an illusion."

Klaus nodded.

"All right, we have to do something," Trillian said. "I've been on this rock for two days and I can feel it making me stupid. There has to be something, some lever I can use to make Alaric put his ass in a chair and talk to me. What is it? What can I use?"

For the first time in the conversation, Klaus sat. His back, though, remained straight.

"Don't try to force him," he said. "There's no threat you can level that he'll take seriously. He's not going to perceive you, or any army you can call upon, as a physical threat. You also can't threaten to back out of whatever deal the archon made with him. He thinks—and he's quite correct—that if the archon was willing to risk bringing him into this war, she's not going to cut ties with him lightly. Trying to pressure him with talk you can't back up isn't going to help."

"Right," Trillian said. "Stick bad, carrot good. What do we have in the way of carrots for a man like Alaric Wolf?"

"Well, if we happened to have Anastasia Kerensky packed away on our DropShip somewhere, that would help," Klaus said. "That would help a lot."

"Now you tell me."

"But that's the question. What can we offer that Alaric wants?"

18 February 3138

He wasn't tall. He wasn't especially broad. From the neck down, he wasn't physically imposing at all.

He was fit, of course, and Trillian had no doubt he was quite strong. But in his brown and gray uniform, he looked trim and rather ordinary.

From the neck up, it was a different story. His eyes, set back a bit in his skull, were steady and imperious. His jaw was angled and firm, his cheeks were hollow and hungry. He looked through Trillian when she walked in, and she did not believe he really looked at her the entire time they spoke. His eyes, and most of his attention, were focused on something beyond her— something, Trillian thought, that was quite large indeed.

"What should I call you so that you will feel you have been treated with a due amount of respect?" Alaric Wolf said by way of introduction.

" 'Lady Steiner' is fine, Star Colonel," Trillian said.

"Fine. Lady Steiner, I realize that you have been waiting to meet with me for three days since your arrival. I am sure you can appreciate that the job of planetary conquest is often complicated, and there have been many demands on my time."

Trillian noticed Alaric did not include an apology for the delay in his remarks, but she didn't expect one. The important thing was that this meeting was happening, and she was one step closer to getting off this planet.

"I understand," she said. "You're doing the job you were brought in to do—and quite well, I might add. You have the archon's thanks for the quick work you are making of this planet."

Trillian might just as well have offered the thanks of

a local butcher for all the impact it had on Alaric. His face did not change a bit.

"I am told you have equipment," he said.

"Almost," Trillian replied. "I have access to equipment. Naturally, I can't just go flying around on a Drop-Ship full of spare 'Mech parts."

Now Alaric's face changed. Creases appeared near the corner of his mouth. Clearly, what Trillian had said differed from what he had believed. She hoped that was the case— Trillian had carefully sculpted her message to Alaric to be both completely truthful and entirely deceptive.

"I need parts, not promises of parts. If you have nothing, we will make do with our own supplies." His eyes fell to the terminal screen on his desk. He seemed to believe the meeting was concluded.

"Ah, but we're closer to my supply lines than we are to yours. I could get you supplies much quicker, if you told me what you needed."

He didn't look up from his screen. "Your supplies are inferior to ours. They may be useful in a pinch, to make field repairs, which is what I thought we would discuss. But we are not yet so hard up for supplies that we need to special-order parts from the Lyran Commonwealth."

"Okay. That's that, then. I suppose I'll be off to Danais—if you don't want the parts I have at my disposal, then I'm sure Duke Vedet would be glad to have them."

Alaric finally looked up. There was something new in his eyes, an expression Trillian couldn't quite read. But at least it was something different. She thought maybe she was doing something right, so she leaned forward and spoke faster.

"You realize that you and the duke will likely be fighting side by side as this campaign continues. Do you really want to go into the field with an army that is comparatively underequipped? How do you think you'll do next to them? How will it look if his forces are outperforming yours?"

Alaric didn't answer right away. He leaned back in his

chair, and then Trillian recognized the expression on his face. Amusement—but not a good kind. It was the amusement of watching a puppy chase its own tail.

"Duke Vedet Brewster," Alaric said, "is a businessman who knows far more about constructing 'Mechs than commanding them. He could have all the supplies you are promising and my army would outperform his—even if we were on foot and armed only with infantry weapons."

"You can't believe that."

"Lady Steiner, I think you will find that it is not worth your while to attempt to tell me what I do or do not believe. Your duke does not understand war. That is why he was struggling here, why his forces were mired by the primitive defense mounted by the Marik forces. Your archon does not need forces with better equipment. She needs more warriors. So we are here."

"You seem to have the whole war figured out."

"As you probably should have before you came to speak with me."

Trillian stood. She had worked carefully on her current expression—anger combined with disappointment. Mostly anger. "Thank you for your time, Star Colonel. I'm sorry that our discussion couldn't be more profitable."

Alaric nodded. Then, as Trillian turned to open the door, his voice stopped her.

"Lady Steiner, I understand you are here in your political capacity. I am sure that means we will be encountering each other again as we proceed through Marik-Stewart territory. You would be well advised not to try to bribe me with supplies or anything else. I am fighting a war, not playing political games."

Trillian gave him a long look, the kind that said "I'm thinking many rude things about you, but diplomatic protocol forbids me to say them aloud." Then she left.

Klaus was sitting at a terminal when Trillian returned to her quarters. The bluish light made his face look spectral.

"Turn a light on," she said. "You'll hurt your eyes."

"Nothing gets hurt by being exercised," he said. "How did it go?"

"Great," she said. "He thinks I'm an idiot with very little understanding of Clan ways."

"So, according to plan, then?"

"Exactly according to plan. I've always said there's nothing wrong with being underestimated."

"And just what do you plan to do with his low regard?"

"I'm banking it. Saving it for a rainy day. He's doing fine here without me meddling. Just make a note for the future—Alaric Wolf thinks I'm an idiot."

"I'm sure that puts you in good company," Klaus said.

"Yep," Trillian said. "With just about everyone in the Inner Sphere. All right, let's get the hell off this planet."

5

There were sausages on the plate. They were mostly gray. Anson didn't like the gray sausages as much as he liked the brown ones. The brown ones had more flavor. Who was buying the sausages here, anyway? Why would they buy gray ones? Didn't they know what he liked? Shouldn't this entire retreat be centered on what he liked? Why else have a mountain retreat, if you couldn't have it the way you wanted it?

He'd have to talk to someone about this, but who? Carol? What did Carol do again? She scheduled appointments. His appointment secretary, that's what she was. She probably wouldn't have anything to do with buying sausages.

So why was he thinking of her? Because he had appointments today. Right after he finished eating his sausages, he was supposed to meet with someone. Who was he supposed to meet with? Wasn't that written down somewhere?

He could just ask his appointment secretary—what was her name again?—but he'd been avoiding people lately, and they seemed to have been avoiding him. It was a good arrangement, worked out for everyone. Kept him from feeling like he needed to break anyone's arms. But it had its limits—for example, if he didn't talk to what's-her-name, he'd have to figure out what he wanted to know on his own.

What did he want to know? Oh, right, the appointment. The appointment he had coming up next. It was—Daggert. It was with Daggert. God in heaven, what a pile-of-shit meeting that was going to be. Daggert was like an undertaker who came around every day to tell Anson someone new had died. That was *exactly* what he was like. So the meeting would be bad, but at least he remembered who it was with. Meaning he wouldn't have to ask Carol (Carol! Of *course* her name was Carol!) about the sausages. No, no, he wasn't going to ask her about the sausages. He was going to ask someone else. Who was he going to ask?

Oh, to hell with it.

Anson stuffed the sausages into his mouth, then sat back in his chair. He had a few minutes before Daggert arrived. He should go for a walk or something. He really needed to clear his head.

Daggert could wait.

There was a back way out of his office, a path through just a few doors that let Anson get onto the mountainside without escorts or security or advisers or anything. This retreat was the only residence Anson had with such an outlet—and if his security chief knew he had it, it would be sealed before sunset.

The mountain was cold. The snow line had long since moved below the retreat, and wind had swept piles of snow against the building. The tree limbs were dark gray, the sky light gray—in this part of the world no colors existed.

Anson took ten steps on a cleared sidewalk outside, then jumped off the path and into the snow. The top layer crunched beneath his feet, and then he sank in to midshin. Walking would be difficult.

"Damn snow with your . . . your *cold* and your *white-*

ness and your bloody . . . *cold*!" he muttered under his breath, and stomped on.

He couldn't walk normally. It felt like he was pulling his knee practically up to his chest with each step, then stomping down through the snow. The stomping was very pleasant.

He kept cursing under his breath, spitting epithets at any object that came into view, at any person that jumped into his head. "Damn tree limbs, bare and empty and *dead* . . . people pretending to be Mariks, pissing on my damned name . . . useless bloody rocks . . . Steiners, Steiners, goddamned bloody bastard filth, thrice-damned scraps of shit . . ." He knew if anyone overheard him, they'd diagnose him as insane within seconds.

The cold was sharp, slicing deep into his skull with each breath. He waited for it to reach into his brain, to freeze the muddled part and shatter it and make his thoughts clear again. The air, plus the stomping, should make him normal.

Thirty minutes later he was back inside, his torso sweating from exertion while his cheekbones felt carved raw by the wind. He shook snow off his head. He shook again. His head had to get clear. He needed it clear!

He walked into his office and saw Cole Daggert sitting in a chair, leaning forward, arms folded across his knees.

"Where the hell have you been?" Daggert said.

"You've gotten a lot bolder in the past few weeks," Anson said.

"Then fire me."

"Shut up. We're not doing this again. You're here because I told you to be here, and you'll wait for me and be patient and hate me for it the whole time but you'll *do* it. Now talk."

Yelling at Daggert felt good, like a small section of the cloud in his mind had parted. That was promising.

Sitting up straight, Daggert began his report. "Gannett is lost," he said.

Anson inhaled. Then, to his surprise, he let the air out. He had nothing to say.

Daggert's eyes widened a touch, but only briefly. Then he continued. "The withdrawal worked generally as planned. We lost a few more troops than I wanted—that Wolf commander is tenacious—but the bulk of the Silver Hawk forces deployed there got off the planet safely." He paused. "Though the planetary militia is almost entirely destroyed."

"Damn . . . damned . . . okay," Anson said, then sat heavily in his chair. He told himself that he was saving up for a better response in the near future.

"Danais has not fallen yet, but Duke Vedet is benefiting from the reinforcements he received from Gannett once Clan Wolf took over the offensive there. The Silver Hawk units there are thinning as well. It seems like this would be a good time to start pulling our units off that planet."

"Give up Danais?"

"Either that or lose just about every unit there."

"Damn it, Daggert, do you have anything to recommend besides retreat?" Anson yelled, and it felt right. Like the kind of thing he should be doing. He went with the feeling. "I did not put the Silver Hawk Irregulars together so they could keep running away! They are there to fight! Do you have any knowledge in that maggot-infested brain of yours about how to *fight* damned battles instead of running from them? Do you have any bloody idea what an army's for?"

Daggert didn't yell back. Daggert almost never yelled, except for that one time. But he argued back—in calm, measured tones.

"I know exactly what an army is for. An army is for our defense. And it can't serve that purpose if we let it be slaughtered, piece by piece, in battles that do us no good. I would advise you not to send our troops to their death needlessly simply because you're angry."

Anson glared at him. "You're pushing your luck."

"I certainly hope so."

Again, Anson felt deflated. "If the troops retreat— where do they go?"

"Intelligence from SAFE has confirmed our expectations of what will happen once Gannett and Danais have both fallen. The Lyran and Wolf forces are going to unite and head to Helm. The Silver Hawks from Gannett are already going there, and if we withdraw the forces from Danais quickly enough, they can arrive well in advance of any offensive efforts. Our chances for a good fight will be better on Helm."

"We'll fight them there, then. I want you to plan." Anson stood. He felt his blood accelerating, and it was good. "I want you to plan a fight on Helm that will *punish* these bastards. I want them to suffer for every damned step they've taken in my realm. I want them *hurt*."

Daggert's response was immediate. "No."

"What?" Anson stomped on the floor. That too was good.

"No. I won't do that."

"Damn it, Daggert, you are sworn to me! I'm your captain-general, and you'll obey my orders, you son of a bitch!"

"Maybe you should just fire me."

"Stop saying that! You're not getting out that easily! Stop trying to goad me, stop disobeying orders and do your bloody job!" Anson's right arm shot up and down, hammering on his desk to punctuate each point.

"My job does not involve getting our soldiers killed because you're pissed off," Daggert said, and Anson heard a trace of fire in his voice. "I want to stop our enemies, thwart our enemies and defeat our enemies but the army is not a tool of vengeance. It is a tool of defense."

"It's a tool of whatever I want it to be!"

"It's a tool of the realm. It will act in the defense of the realm. If you want the army to do something else, fire me."

It had become a very tempting suggestion. He'd put a sledgehammer into Daggert's hands, and Daggert was using it as a paperweight. Anson turned and looked out his window. The wind tossed snow into the air, making his view little more than a white blank. He turned back to Daggert.

"You've become an arrogant bastard recently," he said.

"I've always been an arrogant bastard," Daggert said. "Now I just have the freedom to show it."

"This is what you need to do. Get the damned troops from Gannett and Danais to Helm. I'll want to see detailed reports on troop status, location and plans for when the Wolf and Lyran troops arrive. Your plans better involve a way to beat their asses or I'll do more than fire you—I'll put a bullet in your head for treason."

"You've never needed to threaten me to get me to plan for victory before," Daggert said. "You don't need to start now. Remember what Peter Marik said."

" 'Get off my planet, you scum-sucking Liao bastards'?"

There may have been a trace of a smile somewhere on Daggert's face, but it passed quickly. "No. 'Retreating when you need to doesn't mean you won't fight.' We'll fight. But only when it means something to the Commonwealth. I'm done killing soldiers to satisfy your own personal grudges."

Anson stood slowly. He leaned forward, feeling just how much taller and larger he was than Daggert. He could snap the man in half with a few quick motions.

"I could lock you up for treason just for that," he said.

Daggert stayed in his chair, looking up as Anson hovered above him. "Then do it," he said.

Anson waited, hoping it looked like he was trying to decide, rather than going with the only option he had.

"Get out of here," he finally said. "Keep pushing your luck, though, and it'll run out fast."

Daggert turned and left without a word.

Anson slowly sat back down, his chair squeaking beneath him. This shouldn't be happening. Wolves taking one planet, Lyrans another, and his tactical adviser not intimidated, or scared, or even respectful. There had to be a way to make this all right.

There had to be.

Plans went through his head. Plans for pushing back the Lyrans and Wolves, and for keeping Fontaine and Lester and Jessica at bay. Plans for making a deal with the Sea Foxes, paying them with things he didn't intend to use again just so he could set foot on Stewart. Plans for breaking the kneecaps of individuals who had it coming.

None of the plans coalesced into anything solid. The final shape of his ideas stayed out of reach, distant land beyond the horizon of the ocean of his mind.

He didn't know how long he sat at his desk. It was a while. But it helped—finally, he came up with an answer. Not the entire answer, not something that would address his full range of problems, not by a long shot. But something that would help.

He turned on his intercom. "Find Kabler," he said. "Send him in. Send him in *now*." He didn't wait for a reply.

Kabler came quickly. Kabler always came quickly. His narrow mouth was a straight line, more a hyphen than a dash, and his brown eyes bounced nervously in every direction. The rest of him was composed.

"You summoned me, Captain-General?" Kabler's voice sounded like syrup on sandpaper.

Anson hated his voice, which was good. It made it all the easier to summon the anger he was looking for. "Kabler! How long have you been in charge here?"

"I wouldn't say I'm in charge, sir," Kabler demurred. "I merely direct the hospitality functions—"

"Kabler, damn it, answer the question!"

Kabler looked at the floor, the desk, his own hands, anything but the captain-general's face. "I, um, I have had the honor of serving you for six years."

"Six years! Six years, you thrice-damned scrap of pocket lint! A syphilitic orangutan could have learned how to do your job in that amount of time! So could you explain to me, *please* explain, why the whole damn retreat looks like shit? Did the bloody bastard Lyrans come through and loot this place already when I wasn't paying attention?"

"Captain-General, let me first offer my apologies for any and all deficiencies in your accommodations and—"

"I don't want to hear your apologies, you thrice-damned pustule! It's too late for that! Has anyone done anything to the grounds beyond shovel? Do you think that just because it's winter you and your lazy, ill-bred, brainless staff can stay inside and do nothing?"

"No, of course not, my only desire is to sculpt the grounds to meet your satisfaction—"

Anson was on his feet now, stalking back and forth in front of Kabler, hovering around him like a hawk circling over a mouse. "And the cooking here has been terrible! Sub-Liao, not to mention subhuman! Do you think I can save my Commonwealth on a diet of wood pulp and mashed insects?"

"I will fire the chef immediately," Kabler said, shrinking. "We have a constant stream of applications from the top chefs of the Commonwealth who seek only to please your palate. I am certain one of them will suffice."

"You should be doing this without me having to call you in here to chew off your ass! Do you think your job involves watching your bloody soap operas all day and waiting for me to tell you what you're doing wrong? I need to see this place improve, and improve immediately, or I will pack you in a goddamned snowball myself and roll you down the mountain and right off the edge of a bloody cliff!"

"Captain-General, I understand your anger and it is to my everlasting shame that I must admit it is deserved. I do not wish to waste your time detailing everything I will do to improve the functioning of this house and win back your trust, but suffice it to say . . ."

Kabler carried on this way for a bit, and Anson let him, since every other sentence said something about how wise Anson was to notice Kabler's deficiencies, or how kind he was to give him another chance, or some other such nonsense. Then, when he had heard enough, Anson waved a hand. Kabler cut himself off in midsentence, bowed smartly, and exited with visible relief.

In his self-reflective moments (which Anson tried to keep to a minimum—he was generally too busy for such trivia), Anson might acknowledge that the way he treated Kabler was unfair. In the six years Kabler had been in his service, Anson had gone through this little ritual with him at least a dozen times. Things were not, of course, ever as bad as he made them out to be. Kabler was capable, if not terribly bright or imaginative, and the household usually ran smoothly. But Kabler was so able, so willing to take a verbal beating from Anson, then act like the whole affair had been his fault, that Anson could not resist occasionally calling him in for a very loud, very energetic dressing-down. Somehow, when he was done yelling at Kabler and the man had made his apologies and assurances of improvement, the universe felt like a more sensible place.

And it worked again, almost as good as it always did. Anson's head felt clearer than it had in weeks.

But then he made the mistake of turning to his window and seeing that it was still cold, still snowing, and the landscape outside was unrelievedly stark.

6

Breckenridge Heights
Danais, Lyran Commonwealth
18 March 3138

Knowing when a guerilla war was over was a tricky thing. Duke Vedet was under no illusion that the population of Danais had been entirely quelled, or that every member of the Silver Hawk Irregulars was either dead, captured or off the planet. Some of them were blending with the local populace. Some of them would become terrorist leaders, carrying out acts of reprisal into the foreseeable future. And the situation still was not such that the duke would feel comfortable walking into public without several layers of protection.

But what made the final decision was this: a few weeks ago, Vedet could not have been confident that the planet would remain Lyran territory if he took the bulk of his forces off the world. Now he could. The citizens and guerillas of the planet had not been completely cowed. But they had been cowed enough.

He had reviewed several times the wording of his message announcing his victory to the archon. He had gone through many drafts of grandiose and wordy announcements, efforts that attempted to demonstrate to the archon the importance of his conquest. Despising himself for seeming to beg for her approval, he then went through several drafts that came close to saying, "Today, Danais. Tomorrow, the throne." His better sense prevailed, and all those messages were completely and thoroughly destroyed.

He could be patient. The message could be simple, a declaratory statement of victory. The rest—the triumph, the grandiose gestures—could wait. There would be time. In the end, the message Vedet sent to the archon was simple: "Danais is ours. We will be moving deeper into Marik-Stewart territory." For the time being, that was all the archon needed to know. It might be good for her to worry about why he wasn't providing more details.

He didn't need her input at the moment. He already had too many people offering their opinions, and there was no need to add one more voice to the choir. Besides, before he planned for the future, he needed to bask in the present. The planet was his. He was a conqueror. It was time to enjoy the spoils of war—in a civilized way, of course.

He had arranged for a guide. On any border world, it usually was not too difficult to find someone who had at least a bit of sympathy for their neighboring nation. When conquest came, as it tended to do to worlds like Danais, these people were often employed as liaisons and transition officials, spreading the message to their fellow conquered citizens that what had just happened to them was not all that bad.

Vedet had a certain distaste for these people. True, in his current situation they would prove useful, but in general they were not his sort. They were dissenters, layabouts—political rabble, really, the kind of people who, unable to generate a power base of their own, ease their frustrations by nipping at the heels of those more successful than they. While often happy to see the new government at first, these people often ended up becoming just as discontented with their new government as their old, generating ever-longer lists of complaints and grievances. Some people, Vedet believed, were simply constitutionally unable to be satisfied.

Thankfully, he had an excuse to keep his tour guide at a distance. The way things had gone on this planet, he was quite justified in not letting any native near him, because there was no way of knowing who was an innocent citizen and who was a bomb waiting to go off. Thus it had been explained to the tour guide, a man named Piotr Brunson, that all of his contact with the duke would be through a comm and not in person.

Duke Vedet was in one vehicle, a long hovercraft with a small personal cabin for himself in the rear, and his tour guide was planted in one of the eight or so vehicles that made up the duke's procession. When the duke wanted to know what he was looking at, he could press a button and ask. When he had no desire to listen to the droning of a tour guide who thought his world was more interesting than it truly was, he could turn the comm off. He had the best of both worlds.

At the moment, Vedet didn't think the planet was much to look at. A broad ferrocrete road, a few evergreens pushing through rocks and some admittedly pretty cottages on the outskirts of Breckenridge. But the comm crackled to life as Brunson found something to talk about.

"The road you're currently traveling on is part of a long, snakelike road called Philippa's Highway. Like many other border planets, Danais suffered greatly in the Second Succession War, and not long after the Free Worlds League reclaimed the planet, Philippa Marik embarked on a significant effort to rebuild Danais' industrial base. This road connected several of the crucial industries, including Breckenridge's lumber mills and copper mines."

The road. God almighty, Brunson was talking about the road. Vedet reached for the switch on the comm, but then thought perhaps it was too early to give up on his guide. And though it did not make for the most spectacular view, this road was something he should know about as his forces worked to ramp up Danais' industrial production.

"Two days before his demise, William Marik led his troops past Breckenridge. Not on this exact road, of course, but he traveled near here, crossing the rough terrain in an ultimately successful effort to outflank the Lyran army."

Vedet drummed his fingers. Why did Brunson think he would want to hear anything about a Lyran defeat? He was not a historian—he was here to take advantage of this planet's assets, not study it.

Almost on cue, Brunson suddenly became useful.

"We're now passing the entrance to the Coldcross Copper Mine, the largest copper production facility on the planet," Brunson said. Vedet looked at the road, hoping to catch a glimpse of the facilities, but there was a road, a fence and more road. The mine was a ways off. He was disappointed—seeing the size of the pit might help him guess its production capacity. But Brunson kept talking and made guessing unnecessary.

"This is one of the largest copper mines in the Commonwealth, putting out well over 300,000 tons a year. A fair amount of it is used on-planet, thanks to Philippa Marik's efforts, but plenty flies off-world too."

Vedet leaned back. Just like that, the military façade he'd built up since the archon commissioned him to fight in Free Worlds space melted away, and he was a businessman again. He had conquered this planet, and he was entitled to some of the spoils, and a few thousand tons of copper at below-market prices would be a good start. Danais wasn't that much farther away than some of the other suppliers that brought materials to Hesperus, and he could make sure that receiving copper shipments from here would be well worth his while. It didn't have quite the visceral satisfaction of leaving town carrying chests stuffed with gold and gems, but in the long run he would stand to gain much, much more than a few coins.

He didn't pay attention to much of Brunson's monologue after that, though he caught some bits and pieces. There was plenty of Marik trivia, and Vedet heard the name of that house far more times than he would have liked. He couldn't help noticing that Brunson had a particular affection for the story of William Marik's death. He supposed he could understand that—the man gave his life for the planet, even if he was fighting on the wrong side of things—but Vedet had no real interest in the details of his fate. William had tried to get power and failed, making him part of a very large group of people in Inner Sphere history in whom Vedet had very little interest.

For the most part he tuned out Brunson and instead looked out the window and watched the rocks and the trees and thought of victory.

His good mood lasted until he got back. Two pieces of news were waiting for him; one a minor annoyance, one an ever-growing reminder of the weakness of the archon and her half-witted methods of shoring up her own power while undermining those people in her realm who could truly do something significant if she would only have the grace and common sense to get out of their way.

He dealt with the minor annoyance first.

A Loki report detailed how the Silver Hawk Irregulars—that benighted unit that had been afflicting Danais like a cancer ever since Vedet landed—had a secret supply line that could be traced all the way back to Savannah. *Secret no longer,* Vedet thought, and threw together an order to send some troops to take care of the problem. *I'll cut those Silver Hawks off until they can't do anything but throw rocks at us. Which they'll probably do until they're dead.*

The second item wasn't going to be resolved as quickly. Gannett, it seemed, had fallen before Vedet had managed to secure Danais. Vedet had not been able to take Gannett himself, mainly because his orders from the archon left him spread far too thin for viable action (a claim he had already vowed to stick to until he died). Then, instead of doing the sensible thing and placing more troops under Vedet's command, the blasted archon had brought in Alaric Wolf and his Clanners.

At least the move showed desperation, and where there was desperation there generally was weakness. Allying with Clanners was bound to be unpopular with certain segments back home, segments Vedet might be able to cultivate once he was done tearing through Marik space.

Those, however, were the only good aspects of the situation. In all other respects, bringing in Alaric Wolf was a disaster waiting to happen.

Not that Vedet knew much about this particular Clanner, but how could that matter? Clanners were Clanners. Their sense of superiority, their ridiculous reliance on elaborate combat rituals and their utter failure to understand the delicate diplomatic arts were threads that ran through all of them, as far as Vedet was concerned. They were all cut from the same cloth, and it was a weave for which the duke had little use.

One thing Vedet knew for sure was that the Clanner had ambitions beyond conquering Marik-Stewart planets. He didn't know what sort of deal the archon had cut, but he had to assume that it involved Clan Wolf looking beyond this small collection of planets. The Clanner would be after something more, and there was an awfully good chance that whatever that something was, it would eventually interfere with what Vedet wanted. And that couldn't be allowed.

He had to plan, and the first step would be getting on the move. That much was clear—if the Wolves were already pressing forward, Vedet needed to pick up the pace. His troops needed to move double time until they were off Danais and headed for Helm.

He already had planned to send the bulk of his troops there, gathered from other, nearby planets—it made sense as a waypoint to larger glories—and the news that Clan Wolf was going there as well only increased his resolve. He couldn't let them get ahead of him.

He needed two things: a pretext and a plan. Why should he link up with Alaric when they'd been quite successful going their separate ways to this point?

He walked around his office a few times. He sat down, stood up, then sat down. He glanced at a map, skimmed some intel reports, then stood up again. Then he smiled.

He knew this. He knew how to do this. He had a feeling, and it was familiar from his days on Hesperus. It was planning. It was deal-making. The fighting part of this was important, but now, in his office, with the information spread out in front of him, he was in his element. And it wasn't long before he had his answer.

The pretext was actually quite simple. Loki reports showed the Silver Hawk Irregulars pulling back and consolidating on Helm. He and Alaric could conceivably take a few more planets around Helm while the Silver Hawks got themselves together, but why put off the inevitable? If the Silver Hawks wanted to make a last stand, he intended to let them, and in that situation it only made sense to go at them with everything he had and everything Clan Wolf had. In all truth, he could easily make it seem like it would be a dereliction of duty if he *didn't* go to Helm.

The other part, the strategy once he was there, was where, in his opinion, Vedet the diplomat, Vedet the businessman really came through. If he was going to work with this Clanner, it would be on his terms, not the Clanner's, and those terms didn't say anything about conceding any of the glory of victory to anyone.

It would begin with a simple gesture of magnanimity. He would reply to Alaric Wolf's message of victory with a dignified congratulations and a packet of intel. Vedet would show his team spirit, his willingness to cooperate, by providing Alaric with some hard-earned intelligence about where to land on Helm and why.

At least, he thought, *some of the intel. What kind of fool shows his full hand all at once?*

Then he would see how well this Clanner fought in battles in which he couldn't use his 'Mech.

7

AgroMechs waded through fields of high wheat. It was early—winter takes a long time to end on Helm—but there was always soil preparation that needed to be done once the ground was no longer frozen solid. There were more 'Mechs in the field than might be expected, but many hands, metal or otherwise, make light work.

Zeke Carleton had trouble focusing on his work. Not that it demanded much concentration, as the 'Mech could turn the ground and loosen the soil pretty thoroughly without much input from its pilot. Carleton kept looking up at the sky, mainly because it was blue. Winters on Helm were long and gray, so a day when the sun actually shone and rose high enough in the sky to generate some warmth was something to be appreciated. The moist earth churning under his machine's left arm, sunlight glinting off the other 'Mechs in the field and the lively strains of the Mercy Mountain Pipers playing over his 'Mech's speakers all combined to give Carleton a pleasant sense of well-being.

That made it all the more of a shame, then, that Carleton knew the pleasantness wouldn't last long.

He looked at the sky again. There was nothing in it except the distant sun. Nothing yet.

The temptation had been to land right on top of Helmdown. Alaric had little patience for battlefield theatrics performed simply for the sake of showing off, but he knew the value of intimidation. Few things broke the spirit of a planet like landing right in a capital city and stomping through it, and Helmdown was a perfect candidate for that tactic. There was no real center to the city— it was essentially a collection of adjacent villages. According to the information from the Lyrans, the defenses were similarly spread out, thinly scattered across the city. A hard landing followed by a fierce charge could put those forces back on their heels and never let them recover, making the battle a rout before it began.

But some Silver Hawk units had arrived here before Alaric could make his landing, and Alaric had no doubt they had been active their entire time on the planet, shoring up the defenses and looking for ways to surprise the invaders. There was no reason to walk into whatever traps they had set up. A landing away from the capital might be less impressive, and victory might be slower in coming, but it was a question of priorities. The triumphs to come in the future required a certain amount of caution in the present.

It was almost time. Alaric sat on a black metal stool, staring at nothing. He had no terminals, noteputers or even paper in front of him. Nothing to look at aside from what he carried in his head.

He was watching the battle in his mind. Not every possible move, of course—any veteran of war knows the role of chance and randomness in fighting—but the general sweep of the coming battle, the punches he planned to land and the counterpunches he expected the defenders to throw. He reviewed the land, the fields flanking the city, the mountains enclosing Helmdown and its surrounding farms in a gigantic bowl. He saw the spots he would want to seize first, and the locations he would expect the Silver Hawk Irregulars to have well fortified. He watched the battle, then watched it again and saw how it would be won. No matter what the defenders did, no matter what bad fortune came his way, he saw how he would respond and eventually be victorious.

In his mind, victory took anywhere from three days to six months. He hoped for the former.

Then it was done. All the information about the battle and its various contingencies was stored in his mind, and all that was left was to actually fight it.

He called in Verena to help him with his preparations.

She came in promptly, looking oddly nervous. She put his battle gear on his bed, then helped him put it on.

She wanted to say something. He could see it plainly—her lips kept twitching, and she kept having the small inhalations that generally precede speech, only to let the air out again and say nothing.

Feeling uncharacteristically generous, Alaric showed her mercy. After all, she was a bondservant, and if she was hesitating to speak her mind to him, that only meant she was conscious of her place. Which she should be. He spoke to give her the chance to respond.

"You wish you were fighting," he said.

She pulled his cooling vest over his torso and began fastening it. "Of course," she said dismissively, as if the point was too obvious for discussion.

He looked at her face again. He had misread her. He thought her nervousness was just the blood rush of battle, but there was something else. He did not have time to guess what it was.

"If there is something you want to say, you should say it now."

Verena kept her face impassive—almost. Her cheeks hollowed just a touch in irritation, but that was the only sign she displayed. "Do you know where Vedet is landing?"

"No."

"Have you coordinated your plan of attack with him?"

"No."

"But you are using the information he sent, *quiaff*?"

"*Aff*. To a degree." He was ready. He took the neuro-helmet from her and tucked it under his arm. "You are now out of time."

She followed him as he drifted out of his cabin. "When you land," she said, now speaking quickly, "when you are watching the people in front of you, keep your eye on Vedet and his troops. Watch what he is doing. He should not be trusted."

He grabbed a handrail in the corridor and let his legs swing beneath him as he twisted around. "If all you can tell me is to not trust spheroids, then I clearly overestimated the value of your counsel."

He turned and continued down the corridor. Verena did not follow.

Carleton sniffed. It was a good idea, he always thought, to have your 'Mech pull in air from the outside (provided, of course, that it was safely filtered). Smells could tell you a lot about the quality of the ground, and what was carrying on the breeze. If you were going to work the land, you should never be completely cut off from it.

He smelled damp earth, freshly scrubbed air and . . . something. The something was too distant, too faint, to be recognizable. It might have just been a trace of distant fire from the house of a farmer who already had finished his work. But it was enough to finally take Carleton's concentration off the skies.

He watched the horizon. The distant mountains were dark, and other AgroMechs in the field sometimes were lost in their silhouette. The 'Mechs moved heavily, plodding, as if the soil was a deep swamp. None of them appeared to be conscious of anything other than their work.

Carleton thought about calling to one of them and talking about what he had smelled. But since he didn't know what it was, and certainly couldn't guess what the smell might mean, he stayed silent. He'd just do his work and hope he could go home soon.

*   *   *

There was a large circle of weeds, those around the perimeter leaning toward their neighbors and away from the charred ground behind them. The burnt plants were a dark brown on the outskirts of the circle, transforming to pure black and then to ash closer to the center. Some of those ashes had been crushed into the ground by the ship that had just settled on top of them.

There were several other circles like this spread across the empty field. The Clan Wolf landing had gone without a hitch.

The trinaries were already forming up while infantry troops prepared to follow. Alaric had brought few aero units, mostly scout craft, and they were already out looking for Marik troops. They had found some farmers but no hostiles yet.

The ground was wet, the weeds thick in places—'Mechs would be slow in these conditions. Not slow enough to truly matter, though.

"All units, follow Battle Plan Alpha," Alaric said. "Move out."

Helmdown was 120 kilometers to the west. Battle Plan Alpha called for a more or less direct approach to the city, with a quick stop to destroy an electric plant on the outskirts of town. Striker Trinary should be in range of the plant in ninety minutes, if all went smoothly.

"Aero One, have you seen where the Lyran units landed?"

"Yes, sir. They have put down in the mountains north of the city."

"How deep into the mountains?"

"Approximately five kilometers."

He saw it. He saw it immediately. "All units halt! Stay exactly where you are. Except minesweepers—minesweepers, move out front and proceed in active scanning mode."

There were few good landing points in the mountains, and most of them were within range of Marik artillery. Alaric had chosen to land in the fields, preferring to deal with 'Mechs after he landed to artillery before. Vedet, though, had chosen the more difficult landing, and Alaric had a good guess about why.

The confirmation of his theory was not long in coming.

"We have found mines and begun neutralizing them," reported one of the sweepers after only a few minutes of searching. "There are not a lot of them, but they are irregularly placed. Progress will be slow."

Alaric nodded to himself. There had been nothing in the information he received from the Lyrans about a minefield here, yet Duke Vedet had landed in the mountains—as if he had known of its existence all along. The duke's lack of honor was neither disappointing nor surprising. Alaric had come to expect nothing less from the leaders of the Inner Sphere.

"Focus on clearing a kilometer-wide path. All units, prepare to follow directly behind the sweepers, with Striker Trinary in the lead. Move out."

Ahead of him there was a muted rumble. The first mine had been harmlessly detonated. Clan Wolf's march on the capital would continue.

"There's smoke on the horizon."

The music in Carleton's 'Mech shut off as soon as the comm came to life.

"How many plumes?" he asked.

"Two—no, now there's a third."

"Okay," Carleton said. "They've chosen their path and they're on the move. You all know what to do. Just don't be obvious about it."

There were various grunts and noises of assent, and then many of the AgroMechs made a subtle shift. It would not be immediately obvious, but they were all slowly coming around to face the distant columns of smoke.

Carleton pushed his left joystick back and down, planting the tilling attachment on his left arm into the soil behind him, then took slow, plodding steps forward. He hoped, soon, someone would be able to benefit from all the work he had been doing out here.

He took a few more steps. The tilling attachment stayed buried behind the jury-rigged 'Mech, in the dirt.

"Aero One, all those units are AgroMechs, *quiaff*?"

"Aff."

"All units, cut speed by half. Everyone except the sweepers."

That meant they were going from plodding to near-motionless. As long as they did not stop moving entirely, though, Alaric's purposes would be served.

He kept his eyes glued to his scanner, carefully watching the movements of the AgroMechs. They were slow, but still significantly faster than Alaric's troops at their new speed. Their movement appeared random, uncoordinated. They drifted across the fields, never getting within a quarter of a kilometer of each other, but never losing sight of each other either. Alaric doubted that was a coincidence—their meandering appearance was likely just for show.

It took almost half an hour before he finally could be certain that he was seeing what he thought. He could draw a line on his scanner, an invisible border that the AgroMechs never crossed. They knew exactly what they were doing—or, to be specific, what they were avoiding. And they had told Alaric what he needed to know.

"Sweepers, the mines end two kilometers in front of you. Once you reach that point, move aside and get out of our way."

His units knew better than to ask him how he knew this. They simply complied.

Alaric switched to a broad channel on the comm. "Helm farmers, this is Star Colonel Alaric Wolf. You have ten minutes to abandon the field or you will be treated as enemy troops. That is all."

He switched back to his unit's channel. "These 'Mechs will attack us within five minutes. Be ready."

"Are we leaving?" Carleton asked over the comm.

The chorus came back quickly. "No!"

"Even though we're all going to die?"

They were louder this time. "No!"

"All right. No more planting, then. Let's reap."

Just like that, the AgroMechs went from being randomly scattered across fields to marching in a staggered formation toward the Clan Wolf forces. The ones closest to the minefield walked the slowest. The first line of defense against the Clanners was gradually abandoning its camouflage, and Carleton hoped their subterfuge would make up for the barely-off-the-scrap-heap equipment fate had forced them to use.

"Don't get into a slugfest if you can avoid it," Carleton said. "We're here to slow 'em, not beat 'em. Start shooting before they get out of the minefield."

He was near the back of the pack, wishing he was in firing range but reminding himself he was supposed to be in charge. His job in the battle was to die late.

The first shots were fired, LRMs and autocannon rounds flying toward the advancing brown 'Mechs. And his blood was up.

He wasn't fast, he couldn't be fast, but he was smooth. He knew how to work the pedals, how to ease off just before the 'Mech's feet hit the ground, to keep it running clean over the damp dirt. Except when he was turning or changing direction—then it was a hard stomp, planting the foot into the ground and letting the gyroscopes figure out what kind of shift he intended. Damp farmland was his element.

He had no real plan. He never did. You could figure out how many troops you would send into battle, he always thought, and where they would meet the enemy, but once it started . . . once it started, you let it take you. You get into the current of the battle, the flow, and let it push you. The battle itself tells you how to win it, if you know how to pay attention.

Or, in this case, the battle would hopefully tell Carleton how not to get wiped out too quickly.

The Wolves were firing back. Their lasers, those damn Clan lasers, were firing, and the slow, modified Agro-

Mechs couldn't avoid the fire. Armor on the frontline 'Mechs was melting away quickly, and some of them had started to fall.

Earth was flying through the field, flecks of dirt spattering Carleton's cockpit window. He could feel the pressure in front of him, like the heat from a furnace, burning his face the longer he looked at it. He moved right, plodding over the ground, calling on his troops to come with him, to rally in the face of the Clan Wolf pressure. The mud was everywhere: all the 'Mechs were becoming a uniform brown.

Carleton was relying on his autocannons, filling the air in front of him with metal, hoping to slow the Clan advance. He looked at his scanner, then looked again. There were too few green lights. What had happened to all his troops? It was happening too fast, they were losing too fast. Missiles were coming at him from two different directions, and there wasn't much he could do but watch them come. He blasted his autocannon, hoping at least to make the machines that had fired at him pay for stopping long enough to take a shot.

Then he felt it. He felt the flow, and the current pushed him forward, and he ordered his units to come with him.

He hoped he would live long enough to find out where his instincts were taking him and why.

They came like Alaric thought they would. They tried to bottle up his troops near the edge of the minefield. They obviously hoped their ruse of using modified Agro-Mechs and trying to look harmless would buy them some time, but it did not. Alaric was ready for them, and the AgroMechs did not get a single shot off in surprise.

That charge on the left side of his lines, however, was somewhat unexpected. The AgroMechs were badly outnumbered, and a charge into his lines seemed like it would gain them nothing but a quick death.

Then Alaric saw it. It was not a large advantage they would be gaining but, if their commander executed the maneuver properly, he would be able to isolate a cluster of 'Mechs while handcuffing a large part of Alaric's forces, who would have to shift to avoid catching other Wolf units in friendly cross fire. It was, Alaric had to admit, a cunning and brave move.

It was also a move he could counter.

"Striker Trinary, divide and pull apart. Give them space as they are coming through. Alpha and Beta, swinging gate."

The frontline units of Alpha and Beta would remain essentially in place, keeping the AgroMechs engaged, while the rearward units would swing around into a new position that would set up a charge to push back the enemy—or destroy them outright.

He was farther back than he wanted to be, so he swung around with the maneuvering forces. It was quiet back here, so quiet that it barely felt like a battle. He needed to move forward fast. Or as fast as he could make the *Mad Cat* go.

The 'Mech's feet felt heavy and slow beneath him, even slower than normal. His fingers kept reaching for his triggers, but he was not approaching the front fast enough. When he got there—once he was there, he could picture it, his lasers and PPCs cutting through everything, beaming blue into the heart of the defending 'Mechs. He could destroy them as soon as he was in position.

Then he was there. He had made his way around. He was moving forward, into the battle, and he pulled the PPC trigger. It was a wild shot, poorly aimed, and did not hit anything. But it was a shot, and Alaric felt much better for it.

The AgroMechs saw what was happening. Alpha and Beta were closing on them, and they had no choice. Their short-lived charge was over, and they started falling back.

"Keep a solid line," Alaric ordered. "We want to keep them moving backward for the time being."

He had position now, he had the correct facing, he could fire at will, and he did. The AgroMechs were falling faster now—Alaric saw one stop in its tracks when his laser caught it up high. The enemy was retreating faster, almost running. The victory would soon be a rout.

Then his comm sprang to life.

"Artillery fire incoming! At least ten emplacements are firing!"

Alaric frowned. "Where are the guns?"

"Two groups, one west, one northwest. They just came up from underground."

"Bomb them. Shut them down."

"Yes, sir. The emplacements are defended, though. It will take some time."

He checked his scanner. The AgroMechs had been reduced to a mere handful, but they had slowed. They obviously knew about the artillery emplacements, but that would not be enough to save them. If they were slowing, that likely meant . . .

"All units, slow the advance. Regroup, form up, prepare for enemy reinforcements."

The report from Striker Trinary came only moments later.

"Star Colonel, new units are approaching. Mostly 'Mechs, with some ground support."

"Numbers?"

"Somewhat less than our own."

Alaric only took a moment to decide. "Move back, beyond artillery range. Then we hold our ground."

He could still see the battle in front of him, but now he was taking slow steps backward. The artillery rounds had started landing, peppering the ground and making the sky a threat. Alaric did not spare an upward glance, though; he only had a few moments left to fire at the defenders in front of him. He knew that once he started back, the defenders would hold their ground, content to hold him to a stalemate for now. The battle would end too quickly.

He fired a few more times and was rewarded by the collapse of another AgroMech. He consoled himself that there would be more soon.

8

Like Gannett, Helm was pretty much a rat hole, but it was at least a rat hole that many powerful people had worked hard to turn into something it was not. In some small areas, Helm was palatable, even pleasant.

Unfortunately, Duke Vedet's troops hadn't managed to secure any of those spots. They had landed on rocky ground, moved quickly over more rocky ground, then ground to a halt on rocky ground that had the benefit of almost being in eyeshot of the outskirts of Helmdown but had no other positive qualities.

At least Trillian's quarters were nicer than they'd been on Gannett. That was one benefit of traveling with a Lyran duke instead of a Clanner—Lyran royalty had a much better understanding of the importance of creature comforts.

She had a small room, but it had a soft bed, a reasonably spacious desk and a table where she ate some of the best military cuisine she had ever sampled. She worried that if the capital city didn't fall soon, the Lyran chefs would run out of their more specialized ingredients and she'd be reduced to regular military chow. For that admittedly petty reason alone, she hoped victory would be swift.

She was at her desk, studying troop positions one more time before she met with Duke Vedet. No matter how many times she looked at the map, it made little sense to her. The map showed two armies, who appeared to have nothing in common beyond the fact that they were on the same planet, invading Helmdown at the same time. Their positions, and the movements that had led them there, showed no coordination. The armies were like two independent arms without a controlling head.

Alaric and Vedet would have been better off staying separate, carving their own paths through the Marik-Stewart Commonwealth. But, Trillian supposed, convergence was inevitable when both were after the same prize. Armies could only inflict flesh wounds for so long before they aimed a blow straight at their enemy's heart.

The armies were getting deeper into the Marik-Stewart Commonwealth. The question was, which leader would lead the charge that would shatter the nation once and for all?

The answer wasn't in front of her, so she closed the map. She switched to her incoming messages, hoping there would be interesting news from other parts of the Inner Sphere—maybe something about how the Liaos were proceeding in their attempted friendship with Jessica Marik, or any news about what was happening on the other side of the Marik-Stewart Commonwealth, but all she read was dry diplomacy. Official announcements, bureaucratic requests and the other items that helped governments tick.

She turned off her terminal. She didn't have the information she needed—and she wasn't sure that Duke Vedet would be any more forthcoming.

The meeting with Vedet started on the wrong foot and then went downhill. The duke's uniform was spotless and smooth, and his face clenched. He didn't wait for Trillian to sit down before he started speaking.

"I'm sure you have an agenda for this meeting. I don't care. You are going to listen to what I have to say and then you are going to leave."

Trillian sat down slowly and managed what she hoped was a friendly smile. "Duke Vedet, I understand there have been difficulties here, but please remember to whom—"

"I know *exactly* who I'm talking to!" he snarled. "The cousin of the damned archon who created this pile of shit! You need to hear this and then help your cousin pull her head out of her ass!"

"You're walking on dangerous ground, Duke."

"I'm walking on ground that has two enemies instead of one! Do you know what that Clanner is doing out there?"

"Please, tell me."

Vedet picked up a stack of handwritten notes. The pen he had used had left deep impressions, almost tearing through the paper at some points.

"He has not responded to a single communication from me!" He flipped to the next paper. "He has refused to exchange supplies in any way, shape or form!" Flip. "He identifies himself only as a part of Clan Wolf, not as a part of the archon's forces!" Flip—followed by a crumple as Vedet wadded the paper into a small ball with one hand. "He has refused to conform to protocols for attack schedules that I established shortly after landing!" Flip, crumple and a toss to a small trash can by the desk. The paper landed inside with a light clink.

Trillian held up her hand. "Okay, okay. I don't suppose I could ask you to just give me the papers and not read them all out loud?"

Vedet slammed the papers onto his desk. "I will not be ignored or trivialized!" he growled. "You *will* face up to how the archon has bungled this invasion!"

"You were stalled on Gannett before the Clanners

came in. You are advancing now. Forgive me if I can't see how anything has been bungled."

Vedet pushed the papers toward Trillian. "If you can't see it, you are blind."

Trillian took a deep breath. An angry, out-of-control Vedet would serve no one but himself. "Look, I understand the situation is difficult—"

"Oh, for God's sake, don't start with your empathy and understanding and all that shit! It won't work—I'm not a woman! You can't talk your way out of this. If you want the problem resolved, march over to Alaric Wolf and tell him to submit to my command!"

Trillian surprised herself by laughing. Not surprisingly, this did nothing to calm Vedet.

"This is amusing?" he said. He was lightly rocking in his chair, his torso completely stiff. "This is funny? Clan Wolf is making a mockery of the archon's army, of the archon's authority, and all the archon's goddamned emissary can do is sit and chuckle? Is *this* how your cousin intends to rule?"

"The archon will rule in her own way, which will not be influenced in the least by my behavior. But if you think there is anything I, or the archon, or any power in the universe can do to make Alaric Wolf submit to non-Clan authority, then you are more deluded than anyone in the Inner Sphere who is not part of the Liao family. He will never see himself as part of your forces, and he was never intended to *be* part of your forces. Don't ever count on having him under your command."

"Why was he brought here if he wasn't going to be a part of the archon's army?"

"He is a tool," Trillian said, then mentally added *Just like you.* "He is in the Commonwealth to occupy a portion of the Marik-Stewart forces so you don't have to deal with them. A function he's performed quite well so far, I should point out."

"Tools need to be controlled," Vedet said. "It doesn't have to be by me. The less I have to do with this Alaric, the better, in my opinion. But someone needs to know what he's doing if we're not going to flail through this invasion like blind idiots."

Blind idiots keep their composure far better than you, Trillian thought, but again she managed to keep the comment silent.

"I agree with you that the lack of communication is a problem," she said aloud. "I don't know how much coordination you can expect, but the two of you should at least be able to talk to each other."

Vedet nodded curtly and seemed about to speak, but Trillian cut him off.

"But if it's going to work, you need to treat him like an equal. Not a subordinate."

Vedet frowned. "I assume you will be talking to the Wolf commander soon?"

"As soon as I can get to his camp."

Vedet smiled, though the effect was like a hyena baring its fangs. "Try to give him that same message," he said. "Try to convince him that I should be his equal." He made a short barking sound that might have been a laugh. "Good luck. Now get out."

Trillian decided now was not the time to enter into a discussion about the duke's lack of courtesy or respect for protocol. She walked out without a bow or salute.

It didn't feel like the meeting had accomplished much, but at least she had managed to leave without having the duke vow rebellion or utter disloyalty. That had to be worth something.

There was a road through the mountains that was secure, for two reasons: first, it was not so much a road as a stretch of ground through the mountains north of Helmdown that was slightly smoother than the surrounding rocks; second, due to its poor quality, the road was seldom used and was essentially secure even before any hostile forces landed on Helm.

Trillian was in the middle of a small convoy, three vehicles with large tires that were bumping over loose rocks and potholes. None of the vehicles were very well armed, and should an ambush erupt the enemies would overwhelm the entire convoy. But if any Marik-Stewart troops wanted to wait on these cold, inhospitable rocks for whatever troops trickled along, Trillian figured they had earned their prize, and she would not be too disappointed to fall to them. Plus, a little firefight would break up the monotony of the scenery.

No ambush emerged, however, so Trillian occupied herself with business.

"Did you make any friends while we were in camp?" she asked Klaus.

" 'Friends' might be too strong a word," he said. " 'Acquaintances' is probably more accurate."

"And they talked to you?"

"Plenty. Once word got out that a Steiner had landed and I knew her, I became rather in demand."

"By admirers and well-wishers?"

"By complainers and malcontents. There may be some admirers in camp, but they weren't the ones who talked to me."

Trillian looked up at the dark blue sky. "And what was the gist of their complaints?"

"It went something like this." He took a deep breath, puffed out his cheeks and bugged his eyes in imitation outrage. "How the *hell* could you bring Clanners into this? Since when aren't Lyran soldiers good enough? The Mariks will just be a speed bump on the Clanners' road to invade Lyran space!" Then his face relaxed.

Trillian blinked.

"That's what I can recall. After hearing the same basic speech a dozen times or so."

"Wasn't there anyone grateful to be moving forward after being stalled?"

"Not that I heard. They would rather have been stalled on their own than moving with Clan Wolf assistance."

Trillian sank deeper into her seat, but all that meant was she felt the bumps in the road a little more.

"People just keep missing the big picture," she said,

and spent the rest of the trip trying to stay convinced that Melissa's choice of ally had been wise.

A tall, lean woman with short blond hair stared at Trillian when she climbed out of her jeep. Her fists were planted on her hips, and her face was long and weary.

"Trillian Steiner," the woman said. Trillian nodded. "The Star colonel wishes to see you."

"Really?"

"Yes."

"Right now?"

"Yes."

"Wow," Trillian said. "He wasn't that eager to talk to me the last time we were on the same planet."

"He is now," the woman said simply.

"Okay," Trillian said. "Let's go."

The room the woman led her to was familiar in its lack of color. Alaric was carrying the same quarters with him as he traveled, though Trillian had trouble seeing the attraction. But the simplicity of the surroundings allowed her to focus on emptying her mind and preparing to continue her stupid act for the Wolf commander.

Alaric looked very self-possessed when Trillian entered his office, leaning back in his chair and wearing an expression that was not too distant from a smile. "Thank you, Verena," he said to the woman who had escorted Trillian. "Wait for me in my quarters." The woman nodded and left.

"Trillian Steiner," Alaric said. "I will not waste time by asking what you are doing here."

"Okay," she said. She remained standing, since she had not been invited to sit.

"I assume you visited Duke Vedet before you came here."

"That's true."

"I assume he had numerous complaints about me."

"That's also true."

"And now you are here thinking you can change something about the situation."

"I'm just here to help," Trillian said.

"Then my message to you and to your duke is the same—I have no need of your help. Either of you."

"I don't doubt that," she said.

"Then we do not have anything to discuss."

Trillian put on her best confused expression. "Okay," she said. "Then why did you want to see me as soon as I got here?"

Alaric remained still, but he looked poised and taut. Like he could pounce in a moment, if he had a mind to. "To tell you that there was nothing for you to do here. To send you on your way."

"That's very considerate of you. But I can't leave yet."

She saw tension increase in Alaric's jaw, but otherwise his face was unchanged. "Why is that?" he asked.

"Well, my job's not done. I can't leave without doing my job. I figured you'd understand that."

"I understand commitment to duty," he said, "though the commitment may not be as strong when the duty is less meaningful."

"I suppose, but that kind of discussion is a little abstract for me." Since she was still standing, Trillian started pacing in the small room, waving her hands loosely as she spoke. "Look, there's no reason for me to beat around the bush here. The archon wanted me to come here to make sure there was decent coordination between the forces, and I talked to Duke Vedet and he said you weren't responding to anything he said. So, no communication, no coordination. I have to do something about that. That's my job."

"Go back to Vedet Brewster," Alaric said. "If you want to know why there is no coordination between our forces, I believe he can enlighten you."

"That's a long way to travel. Why don't you just tell me?"

Now his expression was changing, but not in a good way. His eyebrows were becoming a V, and his cheeks became hollow. "Vedet is not interested in coordination."

"Then why does he keep sending you messages?"

"For his own purposes, I am sure. Like most of your politicians, he has his various games that he needs to play, and he is trying to drag me into them. I have no desire to play, though."

Trillian stopped walking. "Have you ever met the duke?"

"No."

"Can I ask how you know so much about him, then?"

"Through his actions. The same way I know anything about anyone."

"What did he do?"

Alaric leaned forward, then moved back so quickly Trillian wondered if she had imagined it. "He pretended to share information about Helm with me, but what he passed along was incomplete. He wanted me to land in the wrong place, to slow my advance."

"Oh. Well, that's no good. Must've made you angry."

"It would only have made me angry if it was unexpected. I took the information at face value in order to put Vedet's character to the test. He failed. I have no reason to deal with him further."

"But wouldn't it do you some good to know what he's doing? So you two aren't running into each other?" There was a chair near Trillian, but she didn't look at it or touch it. She did not want to appear to be thinking about sitting down.

"The affairs of people without honor are of very little interest to me," Alaric said. "If you are worried about our armies running into each other, tell him to stay out of the way of my forces when we advance." He stood. "I believe our conversation is over."

"Okay," Trillian said. "But I can't leave camp here until my job is done."

"You are free to stay with my forces as long as you want," he said. "But do not count on me to make myself available to you."

"Heard and understood," she said. Then she left.

*   *   *

Trillian had given Klaus the fun of walking around the duke's camp and talking to his forces, but she wasn't cruel enough to make him mingle with Clanners. He stayed in their quarters while Trillian went to walk among the troops.

She wasn't sure what she expected to see, but she was pretty sure it wasn't this. It was so—familiar. There were times when she could shut her eyes and everything would sound like a Lyran army camp. Well, there were a few exceptions, and they went beyond the lack of contractions. There was occasional flirting among a few soldiers, just like there was in almost any group of soldiers not currently fighting, but among the Wolves it was much more direct. She heard a few direct requests for sexual congress, and the back-and-forth dance of Inner Sphere romance was rare. In fact, that seemed to be the biggest difference overall—the directness of everyone. People said what they wanted, expressed what they meant clearly and expected others to understand (and, if they were subordinates, carry out whatever was said).

But mixed with all this was the normal talk of war—some bragging and boasting, some comparisons of wounds taken and kills registered, even some laughter over stories of the battlefield.

She wasn't sure why, but she had always had trouble remembering that Clanners occasionally laughed.

No one addressed her. She saw several people look at her, but their glances never lasted long. They would see her coming and give her a quick evaluation, which she inevitably seemed to fail. Before long they would turn away and let her pass in peace. None of them said a word to her.

She decided to take the initiative, walking up to soldiers and addressing them directly. But they either quickened their pace to pass her before she could talk, or looked her in the eye and told her to talk to their commanding officer. The one thing they never did was look away from her.

Her job, though, was not to be dissuaded, so she pressed on, walking up to people, talking to people, trying to get them to talk while the artillery constantly rumbled in the distance.

Her progress was halting, barely moving faster than the stalemate with the Silver Hawk Irregulars near Helmdown. But finally, finally, Trillian found herself in the presence of Star Captain Xeno of Alpha Trinary.

He was tall—what Clan MechWarrior wasn't?—with the face of a poet and the body of a mountain ape. His eyes were wide, brown and even a little watery, and his mouth lacked the severe lines that were prevalent in the Clan forces. Any ideas Trillian might have about this face indicating overall gentleness, however, were erased by the sheer power of the man's body. Her instincts told her to stay out of reach of his arms, because it looked like anything he grabbed could easily be snapped.

He spoke before Trillian could.

"You have been interrupting my troops," he said.

And this was where half of diplomacy took place, in the small moments before saying the first words to someone new. Trillian had fractions of a second to take her read of Xeno, guess what he thought of her and decide on an approach that would use his impressions and instincts to her advantage. There wasn't time to reason it all out, it was a function of instinct, and as she spoke, she hoped, like she always did, that she had made a good choice.

"And your troops have been wasting my time," she said. "So I guess we come out about even."

He did not immediately flare to anger. That much had worked.

"I am more concerned with my troops than your time," he said, the amusement she heard in his voice strong for a Clanner. "What is it you are after?"

"Some acknowledgment by your forces of the reason you are here. Of what brought you here."

A cold wind blew down from the mountains and the plastic walls of some of the portable shelters rattled. Xeno frowned, but not at the wind. "You wish us to act like we are indebted to you."

Trillian shook her head. She had left all her flighty gestures behind at Alaric's office, and spoke directly and firmly. "No. You are putting your lives on the line for the archon's purposes."

"For our own purposes," Xeno said.

"That too. The point is, we're the ones who are indebted to you. I'm not here to give orders to you. I'm here to help. You want to conquer Helm and move on, and I want that too—as soon as possible. Neither of our goals will be served by your commander treating Lyran forces like an enemy."

Xeno squinted at the mountains to the northwest that hid Vedet's troops. "If we truly thought of them as an enemy, they would know it by now."

"Then talk to them. *Communicate*. Coordinate with each other."

Xeno folded his arms. Trillian thought she heard a faint creak. "Communication will do little good when we cannot trust what the Lyran commander says."

"That's it, then? It's a personality issue?"

"It is an issue of honor. And of people who have none."

That was it, then. The solution was simple—while also being quite complicated and liable to cause severe difficulties down the road. The first step, though, was plain. If honor was what this fight needed, honor was what it would get.

"Thank you for your time and forthrightness, Star Captain," Trillian said. "I will leave your troops to your preparation."

The Clanner nodded and turned away.

Trillian walked quickly. She could leave now, go back over the rough road and sleep in the Lyran camp and eat whatever good food was left before she had to resort to military rations. But before she ate or slept, she would send the summons that would bring Roderick Steiner and his Broken Swords—the unit now known as the First Steiner Strikers—to Helm.

9

New Edinburgh, Stewart
Marik-Stewart Commonwealth
5 April 3138

The solution to Anson Marik's problems were, it turned out, quite simple. He had been isolated for too long. Alone in his mountain retreat, with no one around him but servants and his bloody advisers, he had been cut off from what really mattered. He needed to take the fight forward, to be where the invaders would be. And to be on a planet that mattered.

The negotiations to get him to Stewart had been excruciating, and would not have worked with any other group than Clan Sea Fox. The mercantile Clan had used their previous victory over Anson's forces as leverage to extract every last concession they could from him. Mining proceeds from Helm, agriculture proceeds from Stewart along with an enclave to call their own, and a list that went on and on. If any members of Parliament knew the entire series of concessions Anson had made, they would have had a conniption. Which is why it was good that they both didn't know and didn't have the power to do anything if they did.

He'd brought about twenty members with him to Stewart, the ones who still jumped at any order he gave even after he had neutered them. He had a plan, and for once Parliament could play a helpful role. His return to Stewart would be a triumph, and Parliament would help him rally the people around him. The price he paid to Clan Sea Fox would be worth it—especially considering that most of the concessions Anson made were for planets that were on the verge of being conquered anyway.

And now he was on the ground, surrounded by people. His people! How could he not be energized when he felt the crackle in the air, the compressed tension of millions of people around him? He breathed their air and heard their rumbling voices, and he slowly started to feel like himself again.

He was in a long limousine, winding slowly through the city streets, and he did not feel a particular need to get anywhere quickly. The people were out doing their business, buying, selling, talking, arguing, and he could almost hear them through the thick windows of his vehicle. He thought about jumping out and buying a pelo fruit, a native delicacy that was not exported, but then decided it was not worth the frenzy he would cause in his security forces. He'd just order some fruit brought to the Stewart palace that would now bear the Marik name. Then he would feel reasonably content.

The car made a right. They were, by his estimate, only three kilometers away from the palace, and a right turn was taking them in exactly the wrong direction. He heard a faint sound of static and chatter—his driver was talking to someone.

He pressed the button on the car intercom. "What's going on?"

"We have to take a slight detour, sir," said Lydia Brigham, a security officer sitting with the driver. "Center Street is jammed, best for us to go around it."

No matter, Anson thought. *Just more time to watch the city.*

The world outside was vivid but dim—Anson couldn't see clearly out since no one was supposed to be able to see in. He could see enough, though, and watching people go about their ordinary business continued to have its calming effect.

He could not help but notice, though, that the path his vehicle was taking was a roundabout route to the palace. If all they needed to do was avoid Center Street, they were going a long distance out of their way.

He turned the intercom on again. "Just how big is this traffic jam?"

"Rather sizeable," Brigham said. "Some of the advance vehicles are finding the best path. They will hold the streets open for us."

This was nonsense. "What do you mean, finding the best path?" he barked. "I am the captain-general, and this is my motorcade! Clear a path and take us through it!"

"Yes, sir."

The limousine continued to crawl through the streets. Anson pulled out a bottle of native Stewart scotch from a small cabinet in front of him and poured himself a shot. Two fingers—well, three, maybe four. The way things were going, he'd have plenty of time to collect himself before he reached the palace. And four fingers of scotch was well below his normal limit.

The scotch was smooth, warm—and did not go down right. The good feeling that had been building in him since his departure from the DropShip port faded some, and anger built. Anson had always been a belligerent drinker, which was not, of course, a surprise to him or anyone who knew him. For some reason, though, the anger building in him now was not as comfortable as it should be.

The limo had stopped. Cars were moving in front of it, but the limo was making no effort to close the gap. Other cars were backing up behind and alongside it, but since most of them were part of his motorcade, none of them were honking.

He looked forward, backward, forward, but didn't see

anything that made him feel any better. He bounced his right leg, which made the entire limo shake. Since when did traffic hold up a head of state?

"Brigham, damn it, why are we sitting on the side of the road? Have the lead cars shove the damn cars out of the road and get us to the palace!"

"They're trying, sir."

"Trying? *Trying?* What kind of *trying* do they need to do? Turn on a few sirens, yell through a few bullhorns and tell anyone who isn't me to *get the hell out of the way*. I'm not asking them to reinvent the fusion engine, for God's sake!"

"Yes, sir, but this is not a normal traffic jam."

"Then what in the hell kind of traffic jam is it?"

There was a pause, like Brigham was measuring her words. Though Anson had no idea why anyone would have to be careful when speaking about traffic.

"It's not a traffic jam *per se*," Brigham said. "It's more of a . . . disturbance."

"What *kind* of disturbance?" Anson bellowed. "And if you use the words *per se* again, I will rip out your vocal cords with my bare hands."

Through the tinted glass in front of him, Anson saw Brigham look at the driver, then at the other security officer riding in the front of the car. Then she spoke.

"It's a demonstration, sir," she said. "A mass demonstration. It looks like there's more than a hundred thousand people on foot, blocking the roads. They're not moving."

"They're on *foot*," Anson said. "We're in *vehicles*! Run into them fast enough, and they goddamned sure will *move*!"

There was a pause again before Brigham answered.

"That . . . that was already attempted, sir," she said. "There have been some injuries. The crowd . . . did not react well once the people were hurt."

"Goddamned bloody hell in a shit basket!" Anson yelled. He didn't turn on the intercom, but he had no doubt he made himself heard. "What is *wrong* with these people? Why won't they move?" He paused briefly. "What are they demonstrating about, anyway?"

"It's . . ." Again Brigham hesitated, choosing her words carefully. "It's an antiwar protest."

"Well then, what's the problem? I'm just as against this war as anyone else! I'm going to have Archon Steiner's head on a platter for starting it, but I can't do anything about it if these people won't let me through!"

"It's not so much the archon they're mad at as . . . as you, sir. I'm afraid the brunt of the protestors' anger is directed at you. Your arrival has left them . . . displeased."

Anson sat quietly. Could he hear it? There was a distant sound, trickling in through the insulated walls of the limousine, and it might have been the roar of a hundred thousand voices. Or it might just be traffic.

His heart was racing. He was breathing faster and faster, like a man running uphill, even though he was sitting completely still. There was not a coherent thought in his mind, just a dark cloud. He strained to hear the distant roar, and as he listened, he thought he could even make out individual voices, and what they were saying was quite unflattering.

His hand reached for the car door before he knew what he was doing. His legs were moving before he knew where he was going. He was out of the car without a thought of whether it was a good idea to be leaving.

"Captain-General!" Brigham's voice came from behind him, sharp and alarmed. "Sir, get back in the car!"

He didn't turn. He strode ahead, taking firm, heavy steps. There were no cars on the street besides his motorcade. Everyone in the city had gone some place else.

He heard footsteps behind him, so he started jogging. Now that he was out in the clear air—and it was quite pleasant, warm air, a distant part of his brain noted—he could hear the roar more clearly, and he knew it was voices. Angry voices, a sound he knew very well.

"Sir, you must return to your vehicle! This is not safe!"

He didn't know how far away they were, and he didn't

know what he would do when he saw them, but he was going to make them *listen*, damn it, and he was going to make them *pay*. This was not the welcome he deserved! This was not the way to greet the man that would defend them!

Suddenly Brigham was in front of him. She was quick, he had to give her that.

"Sir, you have to get back in the car. We can't allow you to get any closer to the demonstration."

"You are not captain-general!" Anson yelled, and he brought his left arm around in a heavy, looping swing.

Brigham blocked it with ease. She made a solid impact on her arms, but it didn't seem to affect her.

"Sir, we are on your side," she said. "That's why I will do whatever it takes to keep you from going farther."

Anson let his hands fall. He glared at Brigham for a few moments, then turned to walk back to the car.

Then he turned again, shoulder lowered, and charged into Brigham.

She couldn't do anything to deflect him now. She bumped off him like a Ping-Pong ball off a bullet train.

He was running at a good clip now. Maybe he'd run all the way through the crowd, knocking over protestors like bowling pins. That would shut up at least a few of them.

Afterward, he was never able to recall the sensation of the two electrodes hitting his back, or the five hundred thousand volts of current that froze his legs and brought him twitching to the ferrocrete. When he was told about it, though, he briefly hoped the security people had had to struggle to get his bulk back into the limo.

He was not in a good mood when he came to. He was in the back of his limousine, which was finally moving, albeit slowly. He reached for the door handle but his arm didn't feel right. Come to think of it, his legs didn't exactly feel right either.

Brigham's voice came from the front. "Captain-General, I apologize for the action I had to take, but you have to understand I could not let you run into a crowd of hostile demonstrators."

"You can let me do anything I damn well please."

"Sir, with all due respect, my job is to protect you, and I can't very well do that when you are running into a crowd that is burning you in effigy."

Anson's head fell a little bit to his right. "Burning me in effigy?"

"I'm afraid so, sir."

"I didn't start this damned war. What the hell is wrong with these people? Tell them to burn goddamned Melissa Steiner in effigy!"

"Yes, sir."

Anson opened his mouth, then closed it, then looked out the window. City blocks were passing slowly.

Burning him in effigy. Idiots. Blaming the wrong person. Angry because life's gotten hard, so they get mad at the leader who happens to be closest to them. Stupid bloody ignorant sheep.

They didn't understand war. Citizens never did. All they could do was count the dead—the bigger picture, the elements of power, the maneuvering kept escaping them.

He'd had this conversation before. With Daniella Briggs. Some members of Parliament had been pissing and moaning, right before he defanged that whole damned body, and Anson told Daniella about it. She'd said something. Something about how people count the lives because they're the ones paying them, and how wars can't be won if you throw too many people into the meat grinder, because they'll eventually turn on you.

"But I'm not the one throwing them into the grinder, Daniella!" he said, before he remembered she wasn't really there. *Damn stun gun,* he thought.

He'd waged war before, of course. Power demanded it. But this war, the one that was making people mad right now, wasn't his war. It was someone else's grab for power, not his!

If Daniella was here, he'd explain it right. But she wasn't, so instead she just kept taunting him in his head.

The limousine accelerated, not much but a bit. Then some more; then it was almost going a normal speed.

"We have a path, sir," Brigham said. "We'll be in soon."

Good, Anson thought. *Get me out of the damned city.*

Daggert was waiting for him outside the executive office, standing like a stalagmite that had grown from the floor of the reception area. Anson walked past him without a word, sat at his massive desk and buried his head in his hands. He'd felt pretty good when he landed, but now his head was a complete swamp. The stun gun had probably messed him up.

A buzzer sounded near his head. It was followed by a voice.

"Cole Daggert is here for your briefing," Carol, his appointment secretary, said.

"Really?" Anson said. "I didn't see him when I came in."

Carol offered no reply.

"Okay, send him in," Anson said. The day he let a pushy security guard with a few electrodes shape his life was the day he'd step down and hand all his planets over to a Steiner.

"Daggert," Anson said as his adviser walked in. "I'm sure you have news. Do you want to go from bad to worse or the other way around?"

"Our forces have achieved a stalemate on Helm," Daggert said.

Anson sat up a little straighter. "Get the hell out of here."

"It's mostly due to the inexplicable tactics employed by the invaders," Daggert said. "If they were better coordinated, they would be in Helmdown already. I expect they'll be making a more significant push soon."

"And how do we deal with their next offensive move?"

"I recommend moving as many of our troops off Helm as possible before it happens."

Anson wanted to lie down. Instead, he pushed himself back and put his feet on his desk, where they landed with two heavy thuds. "Imagine my surprise."

"They are not well positioned on Helm. If the Silver Hawk Irregulars are to make a stand, it should be somewhere with a better planetary militia, with more built-in defenses, with terrain we have mapped thoroughly and on which many of our troops have trained."

Anson had the plan figured out halfway through Daggert's speech. "Here. You want to take them on here."

"Yes, sir. If we are going to make a firm stand against the invaders, I believe Stewart is the place for it. We will have some time before it happens—not much, but enough to bring in more troops to stand against the invaders." He paused. "And if word gets out that you are here—and it will—that will make Stewart an attractive target."

"Those people standing around the palace right now aren't going to be happy that the war is coming to their front door."

Daggert shrugged. "I think their approval is already out of your reach."

"Just like yours, right?"

Daggert didn't say anything, but his eyes had a cold spark.

Anson shoved aside some papers and a keyboard with his feet so he'd have enough room for his large boots. "All right. Get the planet ready. Make sure the militia's in as good repair as they can be. Get as much ammunition here as you can. Get us ready."

"Of course. And the people?"

"What about them?"

"Perhaps you'd like to start moving some of them off-world. Establishing an evacuation plan."

"I'm not running a cruise line!" Anson barked. "They want to leave, they can leave, but I'm not making their damned plans! I've got more to worry about!"

"Sir, the planet is going to be *invaded*."

Anson waved his hands, and he suddenly realized how

tired he was. It had been a long trip—and that damn stun gun didn't help. "I know, I know, I know. Bloody protestors . . . anyway, we have plans in place. We'll get some people off before the Elsies get here."

Daggert nodded, then turned to leave.

"Just . . ." Anson started, and Daggert looked at him over his shoulder. "Make sure none of them bloody pus-brained protestors get off the planet. You can relocate them to the Elsies' landing site for all I care."

Daggert didn't even nod this time. He just left.

Damn Daggert. The lack of respect was getting to Anson, even though he was the one who'd talked him into staying. Insolent underlings were one of the great annoyances of power.

As if summoned, Daggert walked back in.

"Damn it, what now?"

"I just received some news that . . . news I thought you'd want to hear."

"What?"

"They've found Daniella Briggs," he said.

Anson felt a brief moment of elation before he understood what Daggert was saying. "So she's gone from MIA to KIA," he said.

"Yes. Her remains will be sent to Atreus."

"Fine. You're dismissed." This time he managed to say it before Daggert started to leave.

Anson leaned back in his chair after Daggert left. Another weapon in his arsenal was lost. She was a fighter. Irritating as hell, but a fighter.

She would certainly have something to say about this mess—the protestors, the losses so far, the inevitable invasion. It wouldn't be flattering, it wouldn't be optimistic, but it would be direct and most likely accurate.

He tried to imagine what she would say. He tried to hear her voice in his head. But he couldn't.

10

Klaus Wehner walked carefully. He was in uniform, since at this point in time it was better for people to know who you were than be forced to guess. The uniform was an aid and a hindrance—it clearly showed his rank of colonel, which immediately set him apart from the enlisted men, who often lowered their heads when he passed to hide a sneer. But the diplomatic markings on the uniform showed who he was, and most people knew he was there as an aide and liaison to Trillian Steiner. He wasn't a decision maker, which garnered him the sympathy with the vast numbers of other soldiers who weren't decision makers either. These middle officers, the soldiers not quite on the top but well elevated from the bottom, were drawn to Klaus, seeing a sympathetic soul. And Klaus was practiced enough to let them come.

It was from these officers that he first heard the rumblings that became more and more common as the days went along.

A lot of these conversations took place in makeshift officers' clubs, which were often little more than stripped-down field kitchens with appliances removed and foldable tables and chairs brought in. The lights were kept dim so no one saw much besides their glass and the end of their own nose. The accommodations were sparse but they were *theirs*, and in the field every part of the army relishes having a space of its own.

It had gotten late one night, and most of the officers had let the pressures of responsibility take them to other places. Klaus had glanced at his watch a few times and thought about the possibilities of a good night's sleep, but there were still a few officers in the club, and they were talking. Klaus stayed and listened.

"Wait, wait, wait," said Leutnant Porter Mann, a veteran artillerist. "You won't believe this. We've been moved."

"Again?" asked Leutnant-Colonel Maria Schellendorf. "Where to now?"

"Same place we were last week! Back to that same damn ledge! What do you think of that?"

"Maybe the spotters saw something," ventured Leutnant Andrew Cjell.

"The spotters didn't see anything," Mann said with a dismissive wave. "I mean, they didn't see anything *different*. The Silver Hawks are right where they want to be, they're not moving. We're just shifting from position to position so we have something to do."

"That seems pointless," Cjell said.

Klaus smiled to himself. Cjell was the youngest in the group and hadn't yet become accustomed to the pointlessness that was at the heart of so much military downtime.

"Tactically, yes, it's pointless," Schellendorf said. "But it keeps people busy. The more troops just sit around, the more lax they become. Better to be futile than lazy."

"I've never had a problem with a little laziness," Mann said.

"That's why you're only a leutnant," Schellendorf said.

"That's where I want to be," Mann replied. "The right balance of high pension and low authority."

Schellendorf smiled. She had a face that might have been kind in her youth, but years had made her cheeks hollow, her eyes wrinkled and her brow creased, making her seem more severe than she really was. She had been in the Lyran military for thirty years and wore her experience like a skin.

"Didn't one of your people almost fall off that ledge last time?" Klaus asked. He took a sip of the beer everyone was drinking. It was dark and bitter, which suited Klaus' tastes just fine.

"I think *all* of them almost fell off it at one time or another," Mann said. "Once we have the guns set up, there are a few spots where we've got less than a meter between the equipment and the edge. When the wind kicks up, walking's not easy."

"At least you already have your distances measured," Cjell said. "You can get the angles reestablished right away."

"Yeah, but they'd be better if I could actually lob a few shots down on them," Mann said, light coming into his blue eyes. "Nothing gives you the right measurements like a few live rounds."

"Then shoot a few," Schellendorf said. "Who's going to complain about a few shots being taken at the enemy?"

"Duke Vedet Brewster, that's who," Mann said. "Every single order we get comes with the same line— *You are not to discharge weapons fire at enemy troops.* Hell, I'm practically required to tell the troops that every time they go to take a piss. Because as any soldier knows, the last thing you want to do in a war is fire at the enemy."

"The duke probably doesn't want to provoke a counterattack," Klaus said.

Mann snorted and thumped his glass on the table. "You're right, but not in the way you think. No one's worried about a Silver Hawk counterattack—they've got two armies pinning them down, and they'll be hard-pressed to defend the territory they've got, let alone move against us. No, the army the duke's really worried about is the one on the other side of the city."

"The Clanners?" Cjell said. "But they're on our side!"

Even Cjell laughed at his words. The youngster might be naïve, but not naïve enough to believe Clanners were ever on any side but their own.

"The question right now isn't whether the Silver Hawks can hold on to Marik," Mann said. "They can't. I've even heard rumors that they've been drawing down their lines, shuttling troops off-planet so they can fight another day."

"You're planted up in the damned mountains!" Schellendorf said. "How are you hearing rumors?"

"None of your business. But the thing is, if we weaken the Silver Hawks too much, then the battle for Helmdown, when it comes, will be too easy. The duke doesn't want the Clan forces to get to the capital clean. Because if they're feeling healthy enough when they're done with the Silver Hawks, the smart money says they'll go right on to fight with us."

"Why would they do that?" Cjell asked.

"Because they *can*," Mann said. "They're Clanners!"

"That might not be enough to make them risk a war," Schellendorf said dryly.

"Then how about the fact that their commander hates the duke? The duke screwed him over, you know. Told him to land in the wrong place. You don't think he wants the duke's head for that?"

"Not enough to start a war with us, no."

Mann leaned forward. "I'll tell you what. When we get back to our ledge, since we don't have to take new measurements to the Silver Hawks, I'm going to take some time to see what it would take to get a few shots into the Clan Wolf troops. Because when it comes down to it, I think we'd be well advised to take them on before we rub out the Silver Hawks."

Klaus had heard enough. He stayed a while longer and finished his drink for decorum's sake, then left, hoping that Leutnant Mann's sentiments were unique to him.

They weren't. Days went on, Klaus had more conversations, and the idea kept coming up. The Silver Hawk Irregulars were retreating and would not pose a real threat. The true danger came from the lurking forces of Clan Wolf. That was who should be attacked first.

He brought word to Trillian, who spoke to Duke Vedet. As soon as that conversation was over, Trillian emerged from the duke's quarters, walking briskly, face tight.

"We're going back to talk to Alaric," she told Klaus.

He didn't say anything, just followed her into a jeep and back over the rocky road to the other side of Helmdown. And back into the presence of Alaric Wolf.

Klaus wasn't sure, through the entire journey to the Wolf Camp, if Alaric would see them or not, and what leverage they might use to get his attention. When they arrived in Alaric's quarters, both Alaric and Star Commander Xeno were waiting for them. Trillian had been doing some work, playing the two off each other. Whatever she had done had worked.

Klaus guessed the addition of Xeno to the meeting accounted for his presence inside the room, instead of being forced to wait outside. When you were dealing with Clanners, it was never a good idea to be outnumbered.

Alaric sat at his desk, tense and poised as always, his hands clasped in front of him. "Trillian Steiner," he said. "The fact that I am here talking with you more often than I am in my *Mad Cat* is one of the larger frustrations of the current situation. What do you want?"

"I want to break the stalemate. I want you to move forward."

Alaric spread his hands. "Then we want the same thing. However, it has become more difficult to advance on my main front when I need to keep watching my right flank."

"Do you honestly think the duke wants to start a war with you while he is in the middle of Marik territory?"

Klaus watched Alaric's face carefully. Any change in

the Clanner's expression was minuscule; his emotions were all written in small print. But if he knew anything, it was how to watch faces. He saw the slight raise of Alaric's eyebrows, the brief widening of the eyes. Something about what Trillian was doing was surprising Alaric.

"The duke honestly believes I may attack him here. It would make sense, if he truly believes me to be a threat, to preemptively strike, to fight us before we fight him. I have to defend myself."

Trillian, to Klaus' surprise, strode forward until she was practically leaning over Alaric. "You two are guarding against phantom threats instead of dealing with the one in front of you! This is war! Attack the damn enemy!"

Alaric paused before responding. Klaus thought he saw one eyebrow arc slightly.

"You are unusually direct today," he finally said. "I find it refreshing."

"I'm absolutely *delighted* to hear that," Trillian said. "Can you move your troops forward now?"

Alaric smiled. Klaus almost drew back. It was not a friendly expression.

"If the threat from the Lyrans—and my threat to them— is really an illusion, then we should be rid of it." He stood. "I will give a message to your duke. Record me. I will promise not to attack his forces on this campaign. That should set his mind at ease. Then we can move forward."

Trillian nodded. Klaus saw an exchange, a fraction of a second where Alaric looked at Xeno. It was a strong glance he gave his subordinate, and it was not a look that sought approval. Rather than asking "Is that enough?" it was a look that said, firmly "This *will* be enough." And Klaus then understood the relationship between the Clan commander and his officers.

The recording was made quickly, and as soon as it was done Alaric dismissed Trillian and Klaus with a wave. They hurried back to the Lyran camp to deliver the message to Duke Vedet, hopefully to convince him it was time for Helmdown to fall.

New Edinburgh, Stewart
Marik-Stewart Commonwealth

It was a hell of a thing when a leader could not go out among the people. Anson was under no illusion that he was beloved, or even liked, but he didn't care. He ruled his way, and some people would like it and other people wouldn't, which was the same for every leader throughout the history of all humanity. It wasn't important to be liked; it was important to be respected. And, barring that, feared. That had always been enough so that he could speak and be listened to, so that he could walk among them and watch them give way.

Not that he ever walked the streets as an ordinary man, but now he could not even show his face. The populace was that angry.

Well, they should be angry. They just shouldn't be angry at *him*. That could work to his advantage, since as he well knew, it was much easier to redirect anger than to calm it.

He was going to talk directly to the people, even though every adviser was against the idea. There was no way to guarantee his safety, they said, over and over. Then they proposed he just deliver a broadcast message from his office.

But that would not be enough. He could not be isolated when he said what he wanted to say. He needed a crowd to play off of, so he could feel their rage and mold it with his words.

This was why he'd brought the members of Parliament to Stewart with him, along with their staffs and other hangers-on. They might not like him, but they'd be obedient and listen when he spoke. They would be the core of his audience. The rest would be local politicos—as

long as they promised to behave themselves—along with
security personnel and members of Anson's staff, people
who would give him what he wanted.

Plans for the address came together quickly. Two
weeks after he landed on Stewart, Anson stood to address his entire realm, which seemed to be shrinking
daily.

Stewart had its own parliamentary hall, which was used
by the local government. It reminded Anson of a football
stadium, with its U-shaped rows of plush seats being
capped by the lines of chairs holding the members of the
current administration. When a solo speaker addressed
the entire body, he stood about where one of the goal-
posts would be, right at the level of the playing field.

Anson was in a back room, watching a closed-circuit
television that showed him the crowd arriving. Their
faces, for the most part, were calm and comfortable.
Those already sitting in the comfortable bleachers looked
like they were about to nod off.

He would change that. He'd give them a speech that
would put a charge into the room, and those damn MPs
would leave thinking they actually had some sort of
power. That they could play a useful role in this fight.

It was time to go. Anson walked from his back room
with long strides, taking heavy steps that he imagined
could be heard inside the hall. The sergeant-at-arms
started his introduction as Anson approached, and he
entered the hall at the bottom of the U. The audience
stood, a slow, wavering motion rather than the crisp military jump that Anson would have preferred. There was
a smattering of dutiful applause, but Anson didn't care.
By the end, the applause would be genuine.

He walked up to the podium, a brushed metal stand
that was cold to the touch. His speech was displayed on
a small screen set into the podium, as well as on prompt-
ers placed at strategic locations. He wouldn't need them.
For the first time in ages, he had written the entire
speech himself, the words storming out of his head. He

knew exactly what he wanted to say, and he could have given the speech perfectly in a blackout.

"Ladies and gentlemen. Fellow citizens," he said, in a loud voice that echoed off the wood-paneled walls. He let the echoes die down, let the MPs understand just how forceful he intended to be throughout the speech. Let them wake up a bit.

"We have returned to Stewart, a magnificent accomplishment in the midst of our present difficulties. We bask in the warmth and good graces of its native citizens." *That's complete bullshit,* Anson thought. *But useful bullshit.*

He continued. "Though our arrival on Stewart is positive news, we are still faced with the worst crisis in the history of the Marik-Stewart Commonwealth. The Lyrans, whose thirst for power and gain cannot be quenched, are driving into our realm. Their desperation, their thirst for victory is such that they have even turned to the enemies of the Inner Sphere, the Clans, for aid. Their combined forces are strong and have scored many victories. Their troops show no sign of slowing their advance, and I believe they will press the issue until they cut out the heart of our Commonwealth."

A few mutters ran through the crowd. They knew all this already and weren't thrilled to hear it again. But Anson was just laying the groundwork.

"In crises like these we ask ourselves, what will we be? How will we respond? How will we fight?

"Fear is natural. Their armies are strong, their reinforcements keep coming. But do we give in to fear? Do we shake in the face of enemies who time and time again have tried to conquer us, and time and time again have failed? Or do we stand again, confront them head on, and tell them they will go no further into Marik territory?"

He thought there would be a response to that line, possibly a muted roar of some sort. But he only heard muttering.

Damn them, he thought. *They're more castrated than I thought.*

"Our people have been battered. They have lost homes, family—and too many have lost their lives. They are angry. I have heard the people speak. They are angry about this war, and damn it, so am I!"

His advisers always warned him against profanity in public addresses, but this was *his* speech, and he would put in the words he wanted to say.

"We are the defenders here. The Lyrans, the Wolves, the Falcons, even our former Free Worlds League neighbors, are the aggressors. Everything we have suffered can be laid at their feet. So let's turn it back on them! Let's make them pay! Every drop of blood shed by our people should be paid twice over by the Lyrans! I will wring the last drops of the payment out of the archon with my bare hands if I need to!

"I need your passion. I need your anger. I need you to never forget what the archon is doing to us, and to never rest until her debt is paid. This may be our darkest moment, but it's not our last. We will continue forward, and the road ahead will take us over the bodies of the entire Lyran army!"

He paused. There should be a roar. Or applause. Or something. But there was silence. He looked out at the faces of the crowd and saw frown after frown after frown. Heads shaking and heads bowed. What was wrong with them? Where was their fight?

Then one of them stood. Edward Murlock of Lancaster. One of the biggest toadies in Parliament and a principle reason Anson had been so happy to strip away as many of their powers as he could. Well, screw him. He didn't say anything about taking questions. Murlock could stand as long as he wanted, but he wasn't going to talk.

Anson had to ad-lib. He had planned to have everyone in his corner by now, but they weren't. Rather than launching into a description of his next actions, he'd have to do a little more work to win them over.

"The reasons for the Lyran attack are clear—they are cowards. They have seen how we have been beset, seen how those who pretend to carry the Marik name have attacked us. They know we are under pressure, so they come after us like a pack of weak hyenas after a wounded lion. Or vultures waiting for the fall of an injured eagle.

"We cannot yield. We will not yield! The archon will feel our vengeance, and then we will turn to the pretender of Oriente and teach her what the Marik name really means!"

Then Murlock said something. Anson didn't hear what it was—Murlock's voice couldn't compete with the amplified echo of Anson's—but he heard the traces of words floating through the air. It didn't matter. Murlock could talk all he wanted. Anson would finish his speech.

"We are the true heirs of the Free Worlds legacy! If the League is to be reestablished, it will be through us! Our first step to reclaiming that legacy is to grind the archon's army under our feet!"

Murlock's mouth was still moving, and Anson was hearing other sounds. Other people were speaking. It sounded like the hum of passing electricity.

"Rally the people! Tell them to fight! Tell them to stand with me as we prepare to deliver *pain* to the archon!"

It was louder now. It was voices, voices throughout the hall, talking simultaneously, some of them yelling. He had the microphone, but they had the numbers. He spoke a few more words, but they were lost in the growing din.

It was a roar now, shapeless and coarse, rumbling around the hall in waves. More people were on their feet, and a few of them were throwing wads of paper across the hall. Some security personnel were attempting to control the crowd, but it was too large. There was too much anger. Anson's grand assembly had turned into a disorderly fourth-grade classroom.

Anson waited. He yelled a few calls for order into his

microphone, but nothing happened. The shouting continued, and the supposedly powerless MPs and the leaders
of Stewart looked at the captain-general with faces con-
torted in anger and hate.

Anson remained at the podium for twenty more minutes, waiting for the crowd to come to its collective
senses. Then, abruptly, he walked away, out a back door
of the hall, with the wordless shouts ringing in his ears.

11

Helmdown, Helm
Marik-Stewart Commonwealth
24 April 3138

"**D**id I apologize yet for bringing you to a rat hole?"
Trillian asked.

Roderick Steiner smiled. "A couple of times, yeah."

"Good. Because in the time I have been here, I have
come to truly detest this planet, and I can only believe
it will also infect you with its soul-crushing properties."

"Don't worry about it. I'm not here for sightseeing.
The countryside doesn't matter."

Trillian pointed at the surrounding mountains as she
drove toward the Lyran camp. "Even if you *were* here
for sightseeing, the countryside wouldn't matter. It's just
that drab."

"Honestly, I'm surprised you're still here," Roderick
said. "There's plenty of other things going on, especially
near the Republic and Combine borders. The reports I
got while I was on the way down didn't make the defenders seem too tough."

"Well, their numbers aren't great, but their position
will cause us some problems. We've given them plenty
of time to dig in while we settled a few things amongst

ourselves, so it won't be easy getting off the mountain and down into the fields."

"Couldn't the Clanners put some pressure on the defenders from the other side? Make the way down a little easier?"

Trillian's mouth somehow twisted itself into an S shape. "If the armies were able to work together, yes. But only after some delicate negotiations did I manage to convince each of our armies not to attack the other on sight. That's the best we can hope for at the moment."

"Uh-huh."

"I thought I had them ready to move forward a few days back, but then word spread that reinforcements were on the way. Duke Vedet and Alaric Wolf wanted a chance to size you up before they moved."

Roderick looked at the gray rocks climbing into the similarly gray sky. "Am I supposed to be a bridge or something?"

"No. More like a cushion. Give them some space to operate without coming into contact with each other."

"Easy enough," Roderick said.

"I hope," Trillian replied. "The more time we spend here, the stronger Anson Marik can make his defenses on Stewart. This planet needs to fall so that we can get the hell out of here."

"Who do we talk to first?"

"The duke."

"Duke Vedet." Roderick spoke slowly. "Face-to-face."

"Is that going to be a problem?"

"For me and my fist? No. For the duke's face? I imagine so."

"Roderick . . ."

"Relax," Roderick said. "I'm not as dumb as that. We both have our personal feelings about the duke, but punching nobles generally hasn't proven to be a good way to get ahead in the world."

"Then you'll control yourself."

"As much as he does."

"Could you go for more than him?" Trillian asked.

"We'll see," Roderick said.

Duke Vedet was quite shiny, from the gleaming dark skin on top of his head to the medals on his chest to the light glinting off his watch. He looked brand-new, as if he had just rolled off the Defiance Industries assembly line. It was a pretty surface.

Roderick felt his right hand twitch, but he was able to keep from squeezing it into a fist.

The duke took a step forward, right hand extended. "Colonel Steiner. I'm honored to finally meet you in person."

Roderick took his hand and made the handshake as brief as possible without jerking his hand away. "Duke Vedet. I'm glad to meet you as well." Roderick had thought through a thousand possible greetings, and that one sounded the most honest to him. He was, in fact, glad to meet Vedet Brewster—but because it was always a good idea to size up potential obstacles, rather than because he took any actual pleasure in being in the duke's presence.

"Please, sit," the duke said. The room was as comfortable as quarters in a battle camp got, right down to the red velvet padded armrests on the chairs and the black fountain pen adorning the oak desk. It was likely a step down from what Duke Vedet was used to, but it was far nicer than anyone serving beneath him had seen in months.

"I was pleased to hear the archon had ordered you here," the duke said. "Our campaign has been going quite well as of late, and we have an outstanding opportunity to push the Marik forces off Stewart and beyond. The gains from this war will be substantial. Having your troops with us will make the offensive even smoother."

Roderick nodded, already fairly certain what the duke really wanted to say.

"I should point out, however," the duke continued, "that not everything here is as rosy as it might seem.

Your cous—ah, the archon has put us into a tricky situation. When we were on a parallel track with the Clan forces, things worked out easier. Once we arrived on the same planet, there were complications."

"So I've heard," Roderick said.

Vedet leaned back in his chair, his shine making him look like a thoughtful mannequin. "I have not, as you know, been a field commander for very long. There are still things about the experience that are new to me. One thing I've noticed recently is there is a tendency among soldiers of all ranks, once they have been in the field for long enough, to start to lose sight of their overall goal. They get caught up in petty feuds and squabbles, and conflicts they might be able to ignore at home become bigger and deeper until great schisms develop within what should be a unified force."

Roderick smiled crookedly. Duke Vedet likely didn't know the whole story of Roderick's time on Algorab, where Roderick had violated orders of a superior officer, a move that saved dozens of lives. It was a move that could have cost Roderick his career. No one had to tell him about the divisions that sometimes appear between soldiers.

"Maybe it would help," Roderick said, "if you told me what you think the overall objective is."

The duke's answer was rapid, almost rehearsed. "The safety and security of the Lyran Commonwealth. That should be the goal of any soldier of our army, wherever they may serve."

Even soldiers multiple jumps from the Lyran border, fighting an army that can barely muster a threat against a single city, let alone a Lyran planet, Roderick thought. The threat posed by Anson Marik's troops seemed distant, perhaps nonexistent, to Roderick, but he kept that notion to himself. This was the war the archon chose to fight, which meant he had to fight it.

"Are you saying there are some soldiers who have forgotten that goal?" Roderick said aloud.

"We landed here with soldiers for whom the safety

and security of the Lyran Commonwealth is meaningless, if not an outright obstacle to their larger purposes. Naturally, they have been a complication. Forgive the obvious metaphor, but many of my soldiers find it difficult to concentrate on the Mariks with a Wolf at their door. His presence is a distraction, to put it mildly, and it is the sort of distraction that can make people forget what they are supposed to be doing."

"It was my understanding that Alaric Wolf had pledged not to attack any Lyran forces."

"Yes, yes, and believe me, we are grateful for that assurance," Vedet said with an empty smile. "But another thing I have learned in my short time at the head of an army is this—there is more to war than the physical battles."

Trillian had once explained to Roderick the value she found in acting stupid. You didn't want to overdo it, of course, but sometimes acting like you didn't understand someone forced them to explain themselves more than they wanted to. It was then, as your targets danced around on the border of circumspection, that they made mistakes, saying more than they meant, revealing more than they intended. Roderick thought this might be a good time to use that tactic.

"I thought that was the very definition of war," Roderick said. "A campaign of battles."

Vedet rubbed a hand smoothly over his scalp. "That's the soldier's view. But tell me, what do people think of when they think of the Fourth Succession War? Do they think of any particular battle? No, they think of Hanse Davion, and a wedding, and a man who had the balls and the arrogance to give his nation one of its greatest victories ever. That's why they love him over in the Suns, because of how he waged that war—even more, for the way he started it. For his flair. That war was, and still is, about more than fighting for Capellan territory. It was about Hanse Davion reclaiming his nation's soul."

"So war is about throwing away the lives of soldiers to fulfill the ambition of politicians."

Surprisingly, Vedet smiled instead of scowled, and the expression even looked genuine. "Of course! I would never put it so bluntly, but what else could it be? That's why a nation has leaders, to guide it. To make sure it does not waste its strength fighting an unending series of border skirmishes, but instead to fight in broad and bold strokes that show all people, within and without a nation, the true nature of that nation's soul! To use those soldiers for worthy ends!"

"This is getting a little abstract for me," Roderick said. "I'm here to take Helm."

"You are a colonel now, Roderick. You need a broader vision. I don't need to tell you how much power a victorious military commander can have."

"I haven't given it much thought." Roderick felt himself sinking farther and farther into his chair, as Vedet's words and very presence repelled him.

"Then you are the only Steiner never to have done so. We are going to conquer this planet, Roderick. The real question is what happens afterward. You would be well advised to start thinking of that now, and start planning for it immediately. The real outcome of this battle won't be our armies beating the Silver Hawks. It will be in how we position ourselves."

"I'm afraid I haven't had time to get skilled in the art of using war for personal gain." Roderick allowed more scorn to color his voice than he intended.

His tone didn't faze Vedet, though. "Then it's time you learned. You are a commander. The only leaders who do not take time to think about how to maintain their position are the ones about to be deposed." He stood. "It's good to have you on Helm. My door is always open, if you would like to come by and discuss any of these matters further."

Roderick stood. "Thank you," he said, but what he thought was: *This is the last person I would ever talk to about the larger purposes of war.*

*   *   *

Roderick scratched his temple. He had never seen Trillian so put out by landscape.

"I mean, it's just so much *nothing*!" she said as they drove over the road to the Wolf encampment—a road that, thanks to the number of trips that had been made over it in the past month, had grown increasingly smooth. "There aren't even weeds trying to poke their way through the rocks! The weeds just take one look around, see the dim light, no water, and rocks like ferrocrete and they say 'No, thanks' and hop on the next DropShip out of here along with anyone with sense. Except for me, since I have the privilege of staying here and watching two perfectly adequate armies refuse to move."

"Three perfectly adequate armies," Roderick said.

"Shut up." She looked out the window. "Just *look* at this place! Were settlers so desperate for planets that they'd live on *anything*?"

"Yes," Roderick said.

"Well, they should have skipped this one."

"Alaric and Vedet have thrown you for a loop, haven't they?"

"What? No! Well, kind of. But that's not why I hate this planet! I hate it because it's ugly."

The gray rocks outside didn't give Roderick anything to rebut her claim. "Mm-hmmm."

"Fine," Trillian said. "Act all wise and nonchalant. You'll see soon enough."

"Oh, I've already seen. Duke Vedet was as bad as I thought he would be. He thinks war is about career advancement."

Trillian's eyes closed and her shoulders sagged. Roderick felt like he'd just told Trillian she had tested positive for cancer.

"What?" he said. "What did I say? You already knew he was bad. I don't think that's news to you."

"No, no. I mean, yeah, I already knew that. But that's not the problem."

"What is?"

"The problem is that Vedet's right. About this war, at least. There was no threat here. Not right now. This isn't a defensive war, or even a war of revenge. It's a war because we could. Anson Marik has taken a beating lately, and Melissa knew he wouldn't be able to defend his territory too well. She invaded because he was weak. That's it."

Roderick didn't say anything for a minute. He looked out the window, but the rocks provided absolutely no distraction. He suddenly understood why Trillian hated this planet.

"Anson Marik's not a good man," he finally said. "Don't waste your pity on him. He might not have the means to invade, but left alone, he would have. He would have attacked eventually."

"That's what Melissa said. But is that enough? We're killing people and losing our own. Should we really do it on an 'if'? Should we wage a preemptive war based on a vague 'maybe'?"

Roderick cocked his head. "Self-doubt is kind of a new thing for you, isn't it?"

She opened her mouth. Then she closed it. Roderick could see the decision slide over her face. There was something she had thought for a moment about revealing; then she decided not to. "Yes. I guess it is," was all she said.

"Okay," Roderick said. He knew better than to press her when she wasn't ready to talk. "Maybe talking to Alaric Wolf will help both of us feel better about the justness of our cause."

Trillian laughed almost all of the rest of the way to the Wolf encampment.

Roderick was a good third of a meter taller than Trillian, but he was struggling to match her pace. He kept glancing at her to see if she had slipped into a jog.

"Where are we supposed to find him?" he asked.

"Who knows?" Trillian said. "I guess he's grown tired

of sitting in his office and talking, so we just have to find him in the middle of whatever he's doing."

"He's an accommodating sort, isn't he?"

Trillian rolled her eyes. "He's a Clanner."

Roderick couldn't help but be impressed by the order in the Wolf army camp. Their temporary buildings were laid out on a perfect grid, and all the soldiers and support crew he saw walked in quick, straight lines. The soldiers appeared focused and intense. In this camp, discipline wasn't something the soldiers put on or took off according to circumstance.

Alaric turned out to be easy to find: usually, if you can't find a 'Mech commander in his office, you look in the 'Mech hangar. Sure enough, Alaric was walking around his *Mad Cat* inspecting every inch of it and listening to a tech giving him a rundown of the work that had been done on it. Roderick wasn't sure why, but he felt a predisposition to like the Clanner as soon as he saw him. His eyes held the familiar arrogance Roderick always associated with Clanners, but Alaric carried himself with the straightforward, efficient movements of a fighter. Whatever faults he might have, it was unlikely that Alaric Wolf was in this fight solely for personal gain.

Alaric waved off Trillian before she could speak, allowing him to focus on what the technician was saying. He pointed to a woman standing near the 'Mech with her hands on her hips and made a gesture toward Trillian and Roderick. Clearly, they were the woman's problem for the time being.

The woman walked over to Trillian and Roderick. She was an attractive blond—or might have been if she could soften the ferocity of her face. She had deep lines around her mouth, as if she had practiced scowling for so long that it had become her only natural expression.

"The Star colonel is occupied right now," the woman said. "But he expected you. If you wait here, he will speak with you."

"That's fine," Trillian said.

Roderick watched Alaric inspect his machine. The Clanner had a good eye and he knew what was important. There were dings and scratches that he ignored, minor flaws in the armor that would not make a bit of difference when the fighting started. But then he'd pause at the knee, or inspect the foot to make sure it would be as stable as possible. Appearance didn't matter—functionality did.

Roderick waited quietly. A military background provided exceptional preparation for those times in life when you have to stand still and say nothing.

Finally, the Clanner was ready to talk. He glanced at Trillian, took a longer look at Roderick, then focused on Trillian again.

"I had hoped not to have to talk to you again before this planet fell," he said.

"War brings about all sorts of unpleasantness," she replied.

"I assume this is Colonel Roderick Steiner?"

"It is."

Alaric nodded his head at Roderick. Roderick nodded back. He assumed that was all there would be as far as pleasantries went.

He was right. "This is your latest attempt to move the battle forward?"

"It's a little more than that," Trillian said. "Roderick is going to move forward within the week, with or without the rest of you."

This was news to Roderick, but he knew better than to say anything, or even react to what Trillian was saying. He'd let her play whatever hand she thought she was holding.

Alaric look a long look at his *Mad Cat*. "Forward movement would be refreshing," he said.

"It's coming. It's time to get your troops ready. The only choice you have to make in the next few days is if you're going to lead the charge against the Silver Hawks or follow once the fight starts."

Alaric was silent for an uncomfortably long time.

"Trillian Steiner," he finally said. "I believe it is possible that I underestimated you after our first meeting."

Trillian waved her right hand vaguely. "Okay. That doesn't matter much now, does it? We're going forward. I assume you'll be coming along."

Alaric turned his gaze to Roderick. His eyes, Roderick noticed, were cold and steady. Marksman's eyes.

"We will be ready," he said. "We are always ready."

"Fine." The interview was over then, with as few formalities as with which it had begun. They had spent far more time looking for Alaric than they had talking to him.

"Did I really need to come all the way out here for this?" Roderick said as they walked away.

"Do you mean to the Wolf camp, or to Helm altogether?"

"Either. Both."

"Yes. To both. You're going to get the battle moving here. And that's only the first thing you'll be doing for me during this campaign."

"That sounds ominous."

"It just means it will be nice to have someone I can trust commanding an army here."

"I guess that's okay. But you haven't told me the point of coming out here to the Wolf camp."

"To show you off," Trillian said. "To let Alaric size you up."

"How could he do that? I didn't say anything. What could he find out by just looking at me?"

Trillian smiled. "That you're not Duke Vedet. For the time being, that's plenty."

"This is quite a war we've got going here," Roderick said. He tried to keep his voice light.

12

It was a long run, but it was the only approach that made sense to Roderick. It wasn't efficient spending the time to make his way through the mountains, he wouldn't pick his way through Vedet's troops and climbing over the rocky ridge above the Helmdown fields would be suicidal—the Silver Hawk Irregulars had had plenty of time to line up shots on the ridge, and Roderick knew that any troops that crossed onto the wrong side of the mountain would be met by a barrage of fire. He could have wheeled to the west, but the mountains got worse in that direction before they got better, and that slow climb would be a waste of time. So he opted for the eastern approach, running behind the Clan Wolf troops, then curling into the city and hitting the Silver Hawks on their vulnerable southeastern flank.

They had started moving in the early morning, when the bright stars in the sky presented a decent semblance of scenery. He watched them as his *Rifleman* trundled forward, occasionally checking his scanner out of habit. He didn't see anything—the Silver Hawks were not likely to be hiding out on the wrong side of the Clan Wolf troops.

The lights of the 'Mechs gleamed in the night, assorted blinks and beams of his army and the Wolves to the west making it look like he was close to actual civilization instead of wandering around a mutated farming town. Spotlights swept the ground here and there, apparently keeping a close eye on various assorted rocks.

Then there was more light. Not just blinks or beams. Flashes. Bright flashes, like lightning coming from the ground.

Roderick knew what it was before the spotters reported in. "Sword One, we have weapons fire to the west, and it's not just practice. The Wolves are advancing. Repeat, the Wolves are advancing."

That's the other advantage of moving behind the Wolves, he thought, as he kicked his *Rifleman* into a quicker pace. *There's always the chance we could inspire them to go in ahead of us.*

The flashes and distant laser beams started appearing more and more frequently. The Battle of Helm had finally restarted.

"Guard One, the engagement has started. Clan Wolf forces have advanced and have engaged the Silver Hawks."

As tall as he was in his *Atlas,* Duke Vedet could not quite see above the final mountain ridge separating him from Helmdown. If he had been high enough, he would easily have seen the lights of battle flashing below him. Hopefully, he'd also see the damn Silver Hawk Irregulars moving backward, finally making it safe for him to move over the ridge and down into Helmdown.

But if Alaric had started the engagement, Vedet was damn sure not just going to sit back and let him finish it alone.

"Artillery units, this is Guard One. Time to show me how good your measuring has been. Fire at will."

The orange trails behind the artillery shells darted into the sky, tracing long arcs over the mountain ridge and down into the Silver Hawk Irregulars. Vedet watched a couple of rounds go overhead and then decided it was enough.

"All units, this is Guard One. Let's get down the mountain and push them back. Move according to the Point Thrust Battle Plan. Go!"

He walked forward, keeping his pace slow. The top of the ridge drew closer, flashes on the other side growing brighter and brighter until he reached the top and looked down and saw the lights and the beams and the battle, finally the battle. The slope made him speed up as he moved down toward it, but he resisted the temptation to run and instead busied himself making sure he didn't fall over.

"Stalker One, what can you tell me about the Silver Hawks position?"

"They're on the move, sir. Hitting and running."

Vedet rolled his eyes. Of course they were running. After all this time, why would the Silver Hawk Irregulars choose now to engage in a toe-to-toe fight?

"Bottle them up on the west side of the city," Vedet said. "Don't give them an escape route. I'm not about to let this become another Danais."

"Yes, sir."

"Command company, with me," Vedet said. "We're pulling west."

He took his command unit diagonally across the rocky slope. The explosions below and the information from his scanner helped him piece together where the front was, and it looked like it was already disintegrating. Alaric and his troops were pushing hard and would be breaking through the Silver Hawk lines soon, if they hadn't already.

But geometry was on the duke's side.

The Point Thrust plan was fairly straightforward, with Tiger Company at the center of it, driving toward the heart of Helmdown while the other units provided support and, as Stalker company was supposed to be doing, keeping any stray Silver Hawks from getting away. He had hoped to be able to make a claim on Helmdown before Alaric Wolf, but the way the Silver Hawks were fleeing it looked like it could be a dead heat.

Artillery shells streaked orange through the sky, arcing high over Vedet as he continued down. More and more smaller rocks covered the ground the farther downhill he got, and the fight for balance became even more difficult.

Then the comm came to life. "Guard One, this is Stalker One. The Silver Hawks have changed direction and are moving back toward the center of the city."

Tiger Company had done its work. The Silver Hawks weren't ready to fight through them to get out of the city, and now Vedet would be able to close on them in force and finish them.

"Keep a steady pace," he ordered his units. "Be patient. They've got nowhere to go."

Right about now, Zeke Carleton thought, *would be a good time to be off the planet.*

At least he didn't have to pilot an AgroMech. That little charade was over, and he could ride a machine he felt more comfortable in. His *Ocelot* wasn't going to blow anybody off the battlefield, but he could stay ahead of almost anyone. When you pilot a light 'Mech, you never underestimate the value of wearing down the enemy.

But he was running out of places to run. He didn't know what the signal had been that told the invaders to attack, but clearly it had been given. The Clanners and Elsies were both coming in and coming hard, and their first attempt to get outside the Elsies running down the mountains to the north had failed. More than ever, he envied the Silver Hawk troops that had been ordered off-planet while the Wolves and Steiners waited for . . . well, to be honest, Carleton had no idea just what the hell it was they had waited for.

The force left was small, but it was fast, and it had a few tricks up its sleeve. At least, Carleton hoped it did, or else they'd be nothing more than bugs for the big armies to the north and east to stomp underfoot.

He didn't have to tell the troops around him where to

go. They'd planned the battle at least this far. If they had managed to get around the advancing troops coming from the north, that would have been great, but not too many of them believed that would happen. So they'd prepared a contingency plan, and everyone in Carleton's company knew what it was.

He passed by the small stores and homes of Helmdown's outskirts, putting new cracks into the old roads with every step. From a distance, his 'Mech looked like a human jogger, legs churning and arms bobbing. His cockpit, the *Ocelot*'s head, looked unwaveringly ahead.

"Hades Three, are they keeping up with us?" he asked as he jogged.

"Not really," Sam Brooks replied. "They're being pretty deliberate."

"Great," Carleton said. "All right, Hades units, let's slow down and give them some incentive to stay with us. Hel One, you wanna provide some backup?" The Silver Hawk companies that had been left behind had decided to take up new names for their defense of Helmdown— names they believed to be a fair reflection of their prospects in this battle.

"You got it. Right behind you."

The streets on the outskirts of Helmdown were haphazard, as this was a part of the city that sort of just *happened* without being planned. One wrong turn and Carleton could be sent off course and forced to endure the humiliation of stomping on buildings in the city he was supposed to be defending. He settled for slowing down his machine and making a U-turn. Then he put himself into a jog and headed for the lagging Elsies.

Even though he was in the outskirts of a planetary capital, this fight would likely play out more like rural combat. The buildings were too sparse, too low and too fragile to be a real obstacle or to provide any cover. He wasn't going to be able to hide around a corner and jump out to surprise the Elsies. He'd have to catch them off guard some other way.

The Steiner forces out in front had edged to the west,

making sure they would be able to cut off Carleton and his troops if they tried to get away again. So Carleton took his troops northeast, heading for an apparent gap between the advancing Steiner and Clan armies.

He leaned into his machine, pressing the pedals down, feeling the legs beneath him driving hard into the ground. He needed speed now, lots of it, to make this look right. Roads ahead of him wavered, edging to the left, then the right, then the left again, refusing to be straight, so he wavered with them, making the small moves that would let him run their crooked lines. His company was with him, except for Brooks in her *Spider*, who was running ahead mainly because she could. That was okay—with her jump jets and the winglike protrusions on her 'Mech's back, Brooks was practically a jet fighter with legs.

"All right, everyone, let's not all turn at once," Carleton said. "But it's time to start—edge around to ten o'clock when you get the chance."

One by one, the 'Mechs of Hades and Hel companies turned, now running toward the Lyrans' left flank.

"Hades Three, are they waiting for us?" Carleton said.

"Probably," Brooks said. "But they're trying to act like they're not. They just keep ambling forward, like they're on a Sunday stroll."

"Okay. I want everyone to be ready to turn. If Brooks is right, they're going to pounce pretty quickly."

Carleton angled his 'Mech slightly. It would still look like he was charging the flank, but he'd started heading slightly to the right. It would make the "run" part of this hit-and-run a little easier.

The first rounds were being fired, and most of them were coming from the Lyrans. They had the bigger machines in this fight, so they had a little better range. Autocannon rounds and gauss slugs flew through the air, ripping through the flimsy Helmdown buildings. Ahead of Carleton, one house shook under the impact of a volley and its walls collapsed, the roof falling with a puff of dust.

Carleton searched for a target. If this was going to work, he couldn't just fire wildly into a crowd. He had to draw blood.

Then he saw it—a *Jaguar*, loping toward him smoothly, the gun mounted on its back sending rounds in his direction, rounds that so far fell short. He twisted his torso a touch to bring the *Jaguar* in line, staring at his heads-up display until the bounding machine was right in his crosshairs. Both machines were fast and both were running. There wasn't much time.

He pulled the trigger once, twice. Heat immediately washed through the cockpit as the red beams shot out. The first one passed over the *Jaguar*, but the second one caught it square in the back, melting away plenty of armor, maybe even breaking that big gun.

Carleton wished he could stay to watch, especially since he would stand a pretty good chance against the *Jaguar* now, but that wasn't the plan. He turned another degree or two, his angle sharper now, edging farther and farther away from the Lyrans. He had his *Ocelot* running hard, leaving waves of heat behind him. He watched his scanner, saw the other troops taking a similar path, hitting and running. Getting away pretty clean.

Too clean.

"Slow down, everyone, slow down," Carleton said. "If they don't think they can catch us, they won't chase us."

He pulled his 'Mech back to a jog, watching carefully to see how the Lyrans would react. There had been a lot of metal and energy flying in the sky when Carleton charged—hopefully the Elsies would think he caught some of it. Hopefully they wouldn't figure out that he was just bait.

They bit. They were coming. Even the *Jaguar* Carleton had clipped was running ahead, its four legs making the machine look lighter than several tons of metal should.

"We've got them. Watch your six, now. Don't let them get too close. Or too far."

If this was going to work, Carleton had to make sure the Lyrans kept thinking they were in range. The moment the Silver Hawks got out of range, the Elsies that had dashed after them might return to the ranks, and this whole ruse would come up empty.

That meant he had to endure a constant stream of fire from behind. A laser caught him in the torso, right behind his large laser. Sensors showed that most of his armor was gone in that spot. He couldn't take too many more like that.

The street ahead was pockmarked with embedded shells, and more fell each second. Carleton wished he could order his troops to turn around, to stand and fight, but that would finish the battle too fast. He couldn't stand against them—he wasn't supposed to. He was here to run.

The twisting streets provided a small degree of shelter, but not much. Most buildings came barely past his knees, leaving his torso open for anyone in range to target. His whole company was taking fire now, catching hell from the Lyrans they had let stay with them. A *Cougar*, a slightly slower machine than the others that had been left behind, was caught by a *Wasp* and a *Blade* who danced around behind it while pouring laser fire into the *Cougar*'s back. That was Eddie Carson back there, and he was going down. The order to help Eddie rose to Carleton's lips, and then he swallowed it. Trying to save Eddie would make a lot of other troops fall. He had no choice but to continue what he was already doing.

The *Cougar* went down and didn't move again, but the other Silver Hawks kept running. It wasn't far now. Hades and Hel companies drew together, allowing the Lyrans to concentrate their fire, setting a stretch of a few blocks ablaze as the lasers and shells burst into the small wooden buildings. The air behind Carleton grew orange and black, as if the sun had set directly into the ground instead of gracefully settling behind the horizon. They were taking heavy damage now, and the Lyrans were practically howling as they gave chase.

It was exactly as it should be.

It took a dash of five hundred more meters before it

happened. Behind Carleton, the street exploded, erupting beneath the feet of the Lyrans, hurling ferrocrete through their underbellies. After the first explosion, a second, then a third. Smoke billowed through the streets, and in the confusion the Silver Hawks got out of range. Then the artillery in the center of town, which had made precise calculations during the weeks of waiting, unloaded on the Lyrans who were stumbling through the fiery streets.

The retreat didn't take long. The Lyrans knew enough about the Silver Hawks to understand that a renewed charge was likely to follow a sprung trap. The Elsie breakaway force dashed back to the comfort of their larger army.

They were wrong, though. Carleton, or any other defender for that matter, had no intention of charging the Lyrans. That was the behavior of an army that intended to win. All Carleton was supposed to do was hold on as long as possible. And do damage where he could.

Duke Vedet Brewster towered over a small store. Its sign flashed the daily specials to no one—the streets were empty, the doors of the store locked and gated. The sign was lively, every word written in flashing colors in order to make words like "milk" and "chicken" seem exciting.

He found the sign quite irritating, so he made the *Atlas* kick it and was rewarded with a shower of sparks as the display shattered. He kicked it again, then brought his left arm down on the store's roof. The building looked barely able to withstand the winds that blew down from the mountains to the north; the designers had not anticipated a pummeling by a one-hundred-ton 'Mech. His fist slammed a crater into the roof, and he heard a very satisfying crack.

He kicked in a few windows, tore away the cheap siding on the wall and turned a support beam into an L. He battered the roof a few more times until it ripped away from the walls in several places.

He pushed his *Atlas* back a few steps so he could see

his handiwork. He was breathing heavily, even though the 'Mech, not him, had been doing the real work.

He felt better, though. His mind was a little clearer than it had been when he heard about the Silver Hawks' trap.

His scouts had gathered enough information to tell him that a significant portion of the Silver Hawk Irregulars that had been on Helm were now gone. He wouldn't be able to wipe them out entirely here, sad to say. But he would make them pay.

The Silver Hawks were moving south. It was an obvious choice—no other path was open to them. Vedet was going to catch them, and he fervently hoped he would get the chance to beat them just like he had battered the grocery store.

13

On the whole, Alaric Wolf would rather have been fighting in the mud. Movement had been slow in the fields around Helmdown, but nothing compared to this slow plod through the streets of the city. He could not imagine how the inhabitants ever traveled across this city in peacetime—wandering through its maze of rough, pothole-filled roads was almost like pushing through an overgrown forest where the vegetation rarely parted to form a path.

The Silver Hawk Irregulars were squeezing every bit of strategic value they could out of the urban jungle, hitting and running, harassing instead of fighting, just like they had done on Gannett. Their latest move had them pulling back, trying to move south, likely hoping to escape to the mountains on the other side of the broad valley.

If they got out of the city they would revert to their guerilla ways, and Alaric had no desire to hunt down the Silver Hawks 'Mech by vehicle again. It was time for him to dictate the flow of battle.

"Aero One, bring your units in on Pattern Gamma. Bring them in *now*."

The units were already in the air and arrived quickly. Alaric heard the roar overhead and watched the bombs fall ahead of him. They fell thick, the aerospace fighters dropping line after line onto the city. Dozens of explosions flared up, throwing debris along a kilometer-wide path. Then the first line of bombers pulled up, and the second line came in.

The ground shook, and Alaric stood in place and watched the aeros work. Smoke and dust filled the city, billowing toward Alaric's position. The bombers could not see what they were hitting, but that did not matter. They were not supposed to be hitting any particular buildings; they were supposed to be clearing a path.

Travel to the heart of the city still would not be easy through the smoldering buildings and scattered debris, but Alaric would not have to follow the wandering roads, allowing him to make a more coherent advance. The wind was blowing from the mountains, and smoke was already moving away from the bombing path. Where there had been dozens of buildings, there was now a swath of bricks and smoldering wood.

"The city is ours," he said over the comm. "Now finish off its defenders."

His *Mad Cat* stomped ahead into the ruin he had created.

He hadn't seen much actual fighting yet, but the battle had still been interesting for Roderick. It was like watching a really good war documentary holovid, one that got into the ins and outs of troop movements, of who went where and why. Between his own scanner and the reports from his spotters, Roderick was able to keep tabs on what was happening as he made his way around the back of the Clan Wolf army, and once he had a clear path to Helmdown ahead of him, he knew what he needed to do.

"All units, we're going to move west and move fast. Saber Company, lead the way. We get to be the ones to break the Silver Hawks' back."

His *Rifleman* was moving now, running to get across

the city as fast as he could. With its broad feet, heavy legs and stubby cannon arms, the *Rifleman* would never be graceful, but it was moving fast enough to suit Roderick. He'd get to where he needed to be.

Then, to the northwest, the city erupted. He heard the explosions first, coming rapidly, like a long string of firecrackers going off but louder. He swiveled his torso a touch to look and saw aero units—were they orange and brown?—flying low over the center of Helmdown, dropping bomb after bomb.

Roderick almost stopped in his tracks. The firepower Alaric was unleashing was devastating, and it didn't look like the Wolf pilots were carefully choosing their targets. The bombs just fell, one after another, setting an entire swath of the city on fire. Alaric seemed to be taking out the frustrations of the past month's wait on the citizens of Helmdown.

Roderick hoped the natives had been smart enough to get out of the city, hoped the buildings Alaric was leveling were empty. He hoped the civilian death toll wouldn't turn this battle into a massacre.

When he turned his eyes forward again to watch the streets he was running over, his legs felt heavier. Much of his enthusiasm for the fight stayed behind him as he advanced.

The Wolf forces had gathered together, most of them concentrated in the line of destruction opened up by the bombers. Many of the fires that had flared were already barely more than embers—there had been so many bombs in one place that the blazing heat had consumed in short order most of what could be burned. The wind raced from the mountains and carried the smoke into a sky already clogged with charcoal-gray clouds.

The Silver Hawks had changed their tactics. There was no more hitting and running—just running. They did not dare approach the Wolf forces when their enemy's firepower was so consolidated. Alaric's sensors said they were pulling together a little and moving south, trying to find time to regroup. Alaric would have been happy to cut them off, but that would mean abandoning the path he had just cleared. He chose to stick to his plan.

Striker Trinary had entered the heart of the city, where the buildings were taller and the streets somewhat better maintained. There would be opportunities for ambush by the defenders here—or at least, there would have been had not Alaric forced the Silver Hawks to go on the run.

He stepped over the rubble of buildings and furniture and whatever else had been here, grinding it into even finer dust with each stride. He had time before he engaged the Silver Hawks, so he decided to check on the status of some of the variables beyond his control.

"Stalker One, what is the duke up to?"

"His units were slowed by a Silver Hawks' trap," the scout leader reported. "They are through it now, though, and they seem to have picked up their pace. The duke seems eager to catch up to the defenders."

I do not blame him, Alaric thought, but kept the idea to himself. He would not have anyone hear him agreeing with Duke Vedet.

"How far away is he from the nearest Silver Hawk units?"

"Not much farther than we are, Star Colonel. It is possible our forces will converge as we are giving chase."

It was not exactly what he wanted to have happen, but it would do. As long as the defenders were routed and overwhelmed, Alaric would be content.

"Have any of your units spotted the First Steiner Strikers' location?"

"Not precisely, Star Colonel. We know they are in the south part of the city, but not their heading."

"Keep your eyes open. We do not want to catch cross fire from them."

"Yes, Star Colonel."

Alaric flicked a few switches on his scanner. All of the units it was displaying disappeared, and he was left looking at a blank map of Helmdown. He stared at it as his *Mad Cat* moved ahead, his mind calling up images of the units of the four different forces in this fight. He envisioned where they would move, how others would react and how the battle would flow.

But he did not know Roderick Steiner well enough. His acquaintance with Vedet Brewster was almost as brief, but the duke was a much simpler man—blunt, direct, easily possessed by anger. He was not sure, though, what drove Roderick, and how that would determine what choices he made. So the battle models he tried to design had a cloud at the south end, a question that had too many possible answers.

But Alaric had been in many battles before, including plenty where he could not predict what was going to happen. He could fight the unknown almost as well as he could fight the known.

Saber Company was running, spread out so the Silver Hawk Irregulars wouldn't be able to concentrate their fire. Once the First Steiner Strikers were south-southwest of downtown, they had turned and headed almost due north. Their visibility was hampered by the blowing smoke from the Clan Wolf bombing, but the Silver Hawks would have the same problem. Roderick updated his companies on the battle plan, then moved them deeper into the heart of Helmdown.

The smoke passed in waves, hiding and revealing the city as he moved. This section, far from the camp of the invaders, looked untouched and empty. A few lights were on here and there, but they were likely on automatic switches—Roderick had not seen a single nonmilitary person in town. Helmdown was no longer a city; it was a collection of man-made obstacles strewn on a battlefield. Roderick couldn't guess how long it would take before it was a city again. If it ever was.

He split his attention between watching the street and monitoring the scanner, watching the faster Saber units drawing closer to the Silver Hawks. Both were moving fast, charging toward each other as the Silver Hawks fled from the two armies giving chase. Roderick knew that, given a choice, the Marik defenders would rather run through his forces than turn to face the larger forces at their rear.

His job was to make them regret that decision.

The comm crackled to life, and he listened as Saber Company got within range and his forces finally joined the fight.

"Saber Three, this is Saber One." Trace Decker's voice was steady and confident. "You're going to draw the brunt of their fire. I'm sending a few units in your direction. Drop back and let them give you cover."

"Thanks, Saber One. They're moving hard. They don't want to slow down just because we're here."

"Don't stand still, Saber Three. Get your cover, then move according to the plan."

The smoke cleared for a moment and Roderick saw the flashes of explosions ahead. He wasn't far off, only five kilometers from the front line. Things would happen quickly now.

Decker spoke again. "All Saber units, we're done. Keep moving and veer west. It's Savage Company's job now."

Roderick watched his scanner to see the Saber units start to move away from the Silver Hawks' fire. He saw a little movement by the Silver Hawk units, some of them tracking the Saber units, hoping to get a few more shots off. But they didn't have much time.

"Into them, Savage units!" Jamie Kroff's voice was intense, crackling and popping since Kroff was talking too loud into her mic. "Go right into them!"

Now the area ahead of Roderick lit up like a fireworks display, flashes popping up everywhere. He saw a few laser shots carry up into the night sky, shots likely fired by a 'Mech as it toppled to the ground.

"Don't worry about the units we just passed!" Kroff yelled. "Get on the second-line units! Don't let any of them set up a position."

The scanner was becoming more difficult to read, with Steiner and Marik units mixed together. Kroff and Savage Company had broken through. Now Roderick's job was to make sure the frontline Silver Hawks didn't turn and pin Savage down.

He stomped through the streets, pivoting his torso, looking for targets. A Silver Hawk *Stinger* poked its head over a jet-black, blocky building, its antenna appearing first and catching Roderick's attention. He pointed his left arm toward it and unleashed a torrent of autocannon rounds, most of which flattened themselves against the metal walls of the black building. A few flew over the edge, and the *Stinger* ducked out of sight.

Roderick didn't pursue it. The Silver Hawks were being squeezed and were looking for a way out; most likely they'd come to him without him having to look too hard.

The clouds above were low, bunched together against the mountains to the south. They put a ceiling on the battle, glowing with the distant explosive lightning from the ground. It looked like it could rain at any moment, or like the heavy sky could just collapse on them.

Roderick moved smoothly forward, watching the movement of the Silver Hawk troops. Savage Company had disoriented them, shattering their order, and they weren't sure where to go from here.

It was time to move a little faster. The longer the Marik troops were confused, the better.

Roderick pushed down his pedals and the *Rifleman* lumbered ahead. Now that he was getting closer to the Silver Hawk lines, he could see smaller vehicles darting back and forth, looking for a way out while trying to stay hidden from the barrage of fire. Roderick added to it, peppering intersections with autocannon rounds and ripping into the sides of the Marik craft.

Then he saw the 'Mechs.

There were two of them. Roderick couldn't make out their models in the smoke, but they looked shorter and spindlier than him. Meaning they were probably faster.

After a few pounding steps he fired both autocannons, moving his arms so he could strafe the entire street around the two 'Mechs. They reacted instantly, going in different directions so he couldn't concentrate his fire. The diagonal streets of Helmdown forced one of the 'Mechs to edge a little closer to Roderick, and he rewarded it by blasting it with pulse lasers. Waves of green throbbed into the squat head of the machine. Roderick recognized it now—a *Blade*. A lightning-fast machine, but one without anywhere to go.

Roderick turned his legs to the right while keeping his torso pointed at the *Blade*. He moved ahead, letting his left autocannon keep the Silver Hawk 'Mech pinned down. The *Blade* had nowhere to go but forward, so it went into a run, the narrow thighs of the machine punching the thick lower legs into the ground as fast as they could. But forward movement only brought it closer to Roderick, who slowed down to get a better shot. He brought both autocannons into play again, and he saw the sparks as the rounds clattered into the *Blade*. The *Blade* finally got off a few shots of its own, firing autocannon rounds from its right arm. But he hadn't seen Roderick slow his pace, and most of the rounds passed harmlessly in front of the *Rifleman*. The *Blade* then sprinted, running for its life to get away from Roderick.

Roderick's pulse laser was waiting for it. The beam shot right into the middle of the *Blade*'s torso, and something inside it went wrong. The legs wobbled, then stiffened, and the momentum of the thirty-five-ton machine made it topple on its face.

Roderick turned away from it and advanced toward the Silver Hawk line, hoping to find the other 'Mech that had been with the *Blade*. But the scanner showed that the Silver Hawks were in retreat. Saber Company had returned—after angling away from the Silver Hawks, they had come around in a circle and smashed into the Mariks' right side. The pressure was too much, and the Silver Hawks had given up trying to make a breakthrough to the south.

"All units, form up," Roderick said. "They've decided they can't go through us, so let's herd them to the middle."

Then, he continued silently, *the remaining Silver Hawks can choose which army they want to wipe them out.*

"What did he do then?" Alaric Wolf asked one of his scouts.

"He appeared to be playing more of a mop-up role, staying toward the rear to make sure no one got through. The first two companies in did the real damage—the commander made sure their effort paid off."

"And the scout company started making its turn back toward the battle as soon as they were out of firing range, *quiaff?*"

"*Aff.* They moved well as a unit—I would say they were following a preplanned route the whole time, and following it well."

"The commander—how aggressive was he in engaging enemy units that came into his range?"

"With all due respect, Star Colonel, there are many units in this battle and most of what I saw was on my scanner. You are asking about a level of detail I cannot provide."

Alaric had known that as soon as he asked the question, but pressing too hard for information in battle was not something he considered to be a flaw. Battles were won first by the brave, and then by the knowledgeable. Those who were both did not often face defeat.

But he had occupied his scouts with the Steiner commander long enough. The Silver Hawks seemed to be caught in a vise. It was time to close it swiftly and firmly.

"Bring your units back east. And give me your evaluation of where the Silver Hawks are going."

"They are in disarray. Their numbers are fewer than we expected, and the pressure has routed them. I expect the rest of the battle to be a rout."

Alaric nodded, but he did not agree. One thing he had learned about the Silver Hawks is that their appearance was almost always deceptive. They likely had another trick up their sleeve.

This one, though, would be their last.

14

The next move of the Silver Hawk Irregulars, retreating away from the attackers coming from the south, was clear. Everything after that was chaos.

An argument had taken place over the comm while they ran from the pressure of the First Steiner Strikers. An argument! Practically every line of authority had broken down. A lot of soldiers had been following unfamiliar commanders from the beginning of the fight, and half of those commanders had fallen on the battlefield, so now no one was listening to anyone. Carleton had issued a number of orders that first had been ignored and then met with streams of curses and invective. Most of the units were going where they were supposed to be, but that was out of habit—and because, with enemies all around, they didn't have many other options.

"We should broadcast a surrender offer *now*," said Fred Parsons, whose commander had been overrun in the Steiner breakthrough. "We're outnumbered by at least four to one. We don't have a chance!"

"We *never* had a chance," Carleton snapped. "We weren't *supposed* to have a chance! That wasn't our job here. We're not saving our own skin, we're holding them off as long as possible and taking as many of them with us as we can. None of that involves surrender!"

"You can get yourself killed if you want, but we don't have to," Parsons said. "I'm making the offer."

"You don't have the authority to surrender!"

"Not for you. But I can damn sure surrender myself."

A low, dry voice broke into the conversation. "To whom?"

"What?" Parsons said.

The new speaker was Mitch Coos, who was taking a 'Mech into battle for the first time—the Silver Hawks that had been left on Helm really were a skeleton crew.

"Which army are you going to surrender to?" Coos asked. "There's three to choose from."

"Not the damned Clanners. I don't want anything to do with them." Parsons paused. "The Lyran noble. He should have some sense of honor."

Carleton rolled his eyes. "He's a Lyran! A Skye noble! Since when have we been able to count on their honor?"

"There's no time to argue!" Parsons said, an edge of hysteria on his voice. "They're coming!"

"Then follow the plan!" Carleton said.

"I'm not . . . I'm not dying here!" Parsons said.

Anyone watching on a scanner might have seen a pattern to what looked like random movement as the last Silver Hawks on Helm pulled together to make a stand. Carleton could only hope that the stand would involve firing their weapons instead of laying them down.

"Sir, we've confirmed that the message is from one of the Silver Hawk Irregulars."

Duke Vedet frowned. "Anyone with any sort of authority?"

There was a slight pause. "At the moment, it's difficult to tell who has what authority over there."

Vedet had to stop his *Atlas* in his tracks. He'd been thinking like a military commander, filling his mind with troop movements and lines of fire and the like. Now he had to think like a politician.

The transition didn't take long.

"Set up a coded channel," he said. "Me and him."

"Yes, sir."

The channel was ready in seconds. Vedet tuned his comm to the settings his people provided and spoke.

"Who am I talking to?"

"Lieutenant Fred Parsons, Your Honor. Your . . . Your Grace."

" 'Sir' will do for now," he said. "I understand you want to surrender."

"That is what I am offering, yes, sir."

"Good," Vedet said. "Here are the terms."

"Alpha Trinary, head north. Beta, Striker stay in the middle. Command, with me to the south." Alaric looked at his scanner. "Be ready. They will be making their move soon."

It might be an explosive move, sending the Silver Hawk troops out in all directions, but he did not think they had the numbers or firepower for that. They were more likely planning to make one last charge, a concentrated effort to break through the enemy lines and make it to the mountains. He did not think they even had the firepower for that, but it seemed the more likely option. So that was what he focused on stopping.

Since he had the longest path to the Silver Hawks, his unit was moving the fastest of any Clan Wolf troops, curving around so he could cut off the southeast escape route and slam hard into the Silver Hawks when they made their move—or, if they delayed too long, before then.

Somewhere behind the clouds, the sun was getting lower in the sky. From where Alaric was sitting, though, it made no difference. The light had been the same all day and would be the same until it was dark. Nightfall would bring only a slight change.

"Star Colonel, this is Alpha One. The Silver Hawks are in position and firing. They are relatively stationary and launching heavy fire."

"In what direction?"

"All of them. But they are directing their heaviest fire toward the northeast."

It was as Alaric suspected. The Silver Hawks hoped the invaders had swung too far south to cut off their first line of escape, leaving troops thin behind them. Alpha Trinary would take care of that.

Alaric thought briefly about sending this information to Duke Vedet in case he wanted to shift some Lyran troops to the east to keep any Silver Hawks from getting away, but he rejected the idea. Vedet had access to the same information as Alaric, and Alaric was not going to do the Lyrans' intelligence work for them. Besides, he did not need their help. Alpha Trinary would prevent the breakthrough on its own.

"Alpha Trinary, be ready. The charge is going to come to you. You will repel them."

"Yes, Star Colonel," was the only reply.

"You will have my support," Alaric added, then moved his *Mad Cat* north to help finish off the battle.

"The Wolves are shifting north," Carleton said. "If we're going to go, we've got to go now!"

"We're not leaving," Parsons said. "We've worked out the terms."

"I don't care! We can't surrender—that's against the orders. We are moving north!"

"You can move north if you want," Parsons said. "And you can be the first one killed."

"We have *orders*!"

"Our orders said to hold them off as long as we could. We've done that—we've already lost. There's nothing more to do here."

"As long as we're alive, there's something to do!" Carleton said.

"There's no point in dying for nothing," Parsons said.

Carleton took a deep breath, mainly to keep himself from letting loose a stream of expletives over the comm. "I am making my advance to the northeast now. Those of you who are not giving up can come with me."

He moved. He didn't care about formations now, since he didn't know how many troops would be with him. He was only concerned with inflicting as much pain on the Wolves as possible before he fell.

He checked his sensor as he moved. About half of the surviving Silver Hawk troops were coming with him. Some of the units staying behind didn't have a choice, since they'd been too damaged to advance. The others—Carleton could only hope they would not be remembered as traitors. Or maybe he hoped they would.

He couldn't look at what was behind him now. Ahead there were Wolves, already shifting over to cut off what little space might have been there. He could see a few of them in the fading light, turning to face him, beams shooting out to his position.

He let loose with his laser, stabbing his beam ahead, and he started running. Anyone who was going to take him down would pay.

Roderick looked up when the ground ahead of him stopped spitting up dirt. He looked to his left, to his right. He didn't see any incoming fire. It had stopped.

He checked his sensor. The Silver Hawks had divided into two groups, one moving to the northeast, one stationary in front of him. The stationary group wasn't firing.

What was going on? Was this another Silver Hawk trap? If so, it was a foolish one—the Silver Hawks could hardly benefit from dividing their small, lightly armed force. He didn't see the strategic sense of it at all.

But he didn't have to understand, he only had to react. "Saber One, how's your company?"

"A little battered, but mostly functional," Kroff said. "I have a feeling that's a loaded question."

"Damn straight. There's a small breakaway group

northeast. Run around east, then north and help the Wolves contain them."

"And you'll take care of the rest of the Silver Hawks?"

"Since it looks like all they're doing is sitting around? Yeah, we'll handle it."

Duke Vedet switched to a common channel, one that would hopefully reach every unit in the field. Or at least every functioning unit.

"Attention, all military units on Helm. This is Duke Vedet Brewster, commanding officer of the First Hesperus Guards. The remaining Silver Hawk Irregulars on the planet have surrendered to me, and I have accepted. We are moving forward to disarm them."

"This is Star Colonel Alaric Wolf," said a measured, slightly raspy voice. "You should wait for the battle to be over before dealing with the formalities of surrender."

"The battle *is* over," Vedet insisted. "I have accepted their surrender!"

"Then it seems some of their troops did not get the message," Alaric said with dry scorn. "They are attacking my right."

Damn them to hell! Vedet thought. *Another Silver Hawk trick!*

He switched to the channel he had used to negotiate the surrender.

"Parsons!" he yelled. "Explain this."

"I'm sorry, sir, but some of us thought the surrender wasn't . . . appropriate. They refused to stop fighting."

"Then *order* them to stop fighting!" Vedet said. Some people desperately needed to be schooled in the art of leadership.

"It's not . . . it wouldn't work that way," Parsons said. "I'm not exactly their commanding officer."

"Not *exactly*?"

"The chain of command is not intact. There is some question about who is in charge, and at the moment troops are taking order from more than one commander."

Vedet swore to himself. "All right. You and whoever

is with you should stand down until your other units are brought under control. Any sign of hostilities from any of you and we'll wipe all of you off the planet."

"Yes, sir. We've fired our last shot." Parsons' voice was heavy with fatigue.

"Good." He checked the position of units on his scanner. "Tiger Company! Move east and help finish with the cleanup."

These damn Silver Hawks, Vedet thought, *are far too skilled at delaying the inevitable.*

There was a *Phoenix Hawk* running ahead of Alaric. One of the most humanoid 'Mechs, the *Phoenix Hawk* could easily outrun Alaric's *Mad Cat* if given a chance. But it would not have a chance.

The *Phoenix Hawk* had edged south to avoid heavy fire from the core of Alpha Trinary only to stumble into Alaric's path. The pilot had turned quickly, knowing it had more speed, hoping to get away or at least find cover.

Alaric was outside of the path his bombers had cleared, but the buildings were sparse and low. He would not be able to run over them, but they would not interfere with his shots.

He started with the PPC, sending a blast deliberately in front of the *Phoenix Hawk*. The Silver Hawk 'Mech was forced to slow down and was rewarded by twin lasers melting off a good portion of its rear armor. The *Phoenix Hawk* ran forward again, and when Alaric fired his PPC again, it was ready. It did not slow down; instead, it angled right to avoid the beam, then turned forward again at top speed.

And it ran right into cross fire from a 'Mech that had been directed into position by Alaric.

The *Phoenix Hawk* powered its way through the intersection where it had been ambushed, smoke drifting out of the holes made by autocannon rounds. It would not be able to keep its top speed for long—heat or mechanical failure would catch up to it soon. Alaric sent out another PPC beam aimed right at the torso of the *Phoenix Hawk*. The distance threw him off a little, and he only caught its arm. The Silver Hawk 'Mech kept running, starting to slip out of Alaric's grasp.

That was when his LRMs caught up to it. Explosions riddled the *Phoenix Hawk*'s left side, and something broke inside the machine. It looked like a giant with a numb leg—the left was dragging behind. Alaric ran a few steps, then slowed to line up one more PPC shot.

He held the trigger for a moment, waiting. Then he saw what he was waiting for. The top of the cockpit flew off, and the pilot ejected—he knew staying in that disabled machine meant a fairly rapid death.

Alaric turned away, leaving the disabled 'Mech and its grounded pilot where they stood. There were a few more Silver Hawks to whittle away.

There was no strategy to what Carleton was doing. Sweat ran into his eyes, down his sides and back, into his socks—any place that could perspire on his body was doing it. The cockpit was unbearably hot, but he couldn't stop doing anything he was doing. Run, fire, run, fire, run. Those were his only thoughts. He had no shortage of targets. Turn this way, or that, Lyrans. Run ahead, Wolves. The crosshairs on his heads-up display turned green constantly, and Carleton tried to pull one trigger or another every time they did.

He didn't know if he hit anything, and he was fairly certain some of his weapons were no longer working. Internal sensors flashed across the display, some yellow, some red. His displays were a riot of color on top of the gray that was Helmdown, and he squinted into the dark trying to find likely targets.

His machine shook and rounds poured into it. Where was this fire coming from? He wavered again before he came up with the answer—it was from two units, one behind, one to the right. He wanted to run away from them, but there was nowhere he could go. There was no safe place.

He turned, blasting his lasers, hoping to hit something. But he saw lasers coming the wrong direction, at him instead of from, and then the orange glow of flying hot metal raced toward him and battered his *Ocelot* one last time.

It felt like he fell forever. There was no direction but down, no choice but to fall. Down, down, down. He could see the sky now, the uneven gray soaking up all the noise and light from below and turning it into rain, rain that fell down, down, down, splattering on his cockpit as the back of his *Ocelot* hit the ground. The impact was hard, taking Carleton's breath away, but he kept his eyes open so he could watch the rain.

"How many more of them are there?" Vedet asked.

"Not many," Hans Lanz, leader of Stalker Company, reported back. "A handful."

"A 'handful' is not a number!" the duke retorted. "How long before this is over?"

"Not long," said Lanz. "We're down to isolated skirmishes."

"'Not many'?" Vedet said with heavy scorn. "'Not long'? Are you gathering information out there or are you just guessing?"

"I'm giving you estimates since war is imprecise, sir," Lanz said. "I will be more precise as soon as I am able."

Vedet did not bother to respond. The Stalker One position had caused him nothing but trouble. True, nothing Lanz had done had risen to the level of Nordhoff's betrayal, but the man had already worn out his patience. He would have to find a smooth way to replace him when he had the chance.

He needed someone he could trust in this army—someone like Nordhoff had been before he finally showed his true colors. He needed advice he could trust, but he was having trouble finding someone who would tell him what he wanted to hear.

"Guard Company, this is Guard One. No more sense in waiting around. Let's start taking surrenders."

"With all due respect, sir, do you think that's wise?" asked Mercy Billings, Vedet's current Guard Two. "There is still fighting going on. This still could be a trap."

"If it's a trap, it's a damn poor one," Vedet said. "They've waited too long."

"Still, there's no need to rush. What do we lose if we officially take their surrender once everything's calmed down?"

Damn soldiers, Vedet thought. *They have trouble thinking of anything beyond the battlefield.* Accepting the surrender meant he could declare victory, and being the one to declare victory would look great on the screamsheets back home.

But the argument likely was not worth his effort. "All right. We'll wait for the mop-up to finish."

He shifted uncomfortably in his *Atlas.* He was not in the mood to sit and wait.

"Jamie, is it as confusing as it looks over there?" Roderick asked. He had found a position on a small rise that let him get some visual contact to go along with what he was seeing on his scanner.

"More," Jamie Kroff said. "The few of them that are left are running like crazy, and neither us nor the Wolves have any sort of formation. I've seen more friendly shots come near me in the past half hour than hostile ones."

"If you're just adding to the confusion there, you might as well pull back. Let Alaric and his people finish it up."

"Roger," said Kroff, and Roderick could hear the gratitude in her voice. "I've had enough running around in circles after these people."

"Drop back, then. Take a break," Roderick said. "It's over."

"Command units, there is a *Vulture* standing next to a *Stinger* to the southwest," Alaric said. "Make them the next target. I will support your advance."

"Star Colonel, those are units that are surrendering, *quiaff?*"

"Neg," Alaric said. "They were firing on us. They need to be decommissioned."

There was a pause. Alaric could tell some in his unit were pondering asking him if he was sure. When none of them actually posed the question, he took it as a good sign. Unquestioned faith in a commander was a desirable trait.

"As long as they are content to imitate surrendering units, approach them slowly," Alaric said. "The closer we get to them before opening fire, the less we have to chase them."

"Yes, Star Colonel."

Alaric's *Mad Cat* stomped forward.

"All firing to the east has stopped, sir," Billings reported. "The situation seems calm."

For the first time in a month, a smile tugged at Vedet's mouth. "Good. Let's finish this. Guard units, form up behind me." The surrender of Helm should be done with a sense of occasion.

"Parsons, we are advancing to accept your surrender. All your MechWarriors should exit your vehicles."

"Yes, si—fire! Someone is firing!"

"What are you talking about?"

"We're getting fired on from the east! Some of your troops—shit! Your troops just took out two 'Mechs! What the hell is going on?"

Vedet looked around. The sky was dark now. He could see distant flashes, but they told him nothing. "Hold on," he said. "I'll find out. Do not return fire." Parsons didn't respond. "Do you hear me? Do not return fire!"

"Your people are killing my troops!"

"It's not my people! Hold your fire!"

Again, Parsons did not say anything.

"Looks like we got out just in time," Kroff said. Roderick had fallen back with her, pulling his units together southwest of Helmdown's center.

"What's going on over there?" Roderick asked.

"I'm not sure. Looked like everything had calmed down, then someone unleashed a whole torrent of fire. Pretty sure it was the Wolves."

"Why did they do that?"

"Do Clanners need a reason?"

"Good point. All right, this is their fight. Let them finish it."

The two 'Mechs wilted under the barrage from Alaric's units. They did not even have time to return fire, and Alaric did not see them eject. The machines were neutralized.

"All units to me," he said. "There are more Silver Hawks ahead."

This time, no one in his command mentioned that these troops might be surrendering. They simply obeyed.

The Clan Wolf forces were gathering closer together, and the next volley was blinding when it came. The targets made a few surprised, hesitant steps, but then stopped moving forever.

The voice of Duke Vedet, insistent to the point of panic, came over the comm. "Wolf units, stop firing! For God's sake, stop firing! These are surrendering units! You are destroying units that are surrendering! Cease fire!"

"We do not take orders from Lyrans," Alaric said over the Wolf-only channel. "Continue forward."

His troops kept marching, pushing fire ahead.

"I won't just stand here while he butchers us!" Parsons screamed.

"He'll stop! Give me more time!" Vedet replied.

"We're dying! We have no time!"

"If you return fire, you will give me no choice but to restart our attack."

When Parsons' reply came, his voice was torn and ragged. "Bloody Lyrans! Bloody piece-of-shit Lyrans! Couldn't trust . . . you *shits*!"

That was the last Vedet heard from Parsons. A few

feeble lasers sprang from the Silver Hawk survivors, only to be met with a screaming volley of shells from Duke Vedet's troops. The Silver Hawks tried to run, but most of them didn't have a chance to take more than ten steps.

Roderick made his 'Mech take a step forward, then stopped it. The battle had seemed over, and then downtown Helmdown had erupted into a firestorm.

He knew what was happening, but it was too late to do anything. He couldn't stop the Wolves, and now the Silver Hawks had returned fire. Nothing in the universe could save them now.

The only thing he could do was keep his troops from participating. So he held them back and stood by as the last defenders of Helm were massacred.

The voices kept creeping into Carleton's head. They sometimes got lost in the patter of the rain, but then they would get louder. He swatted at them absently, but he couldn't control his hands well, and they just bumped into his nose and ears and didn't do anything to keep the voices away.

None of the voices made any sense. What they were talking about seemed foreign, distant. The rain on the canopy seemed much more pressing, much more deserving of his attention.

But then there was a voice that seemed familiar to him. It didn't sound happy. Something was wrong. Carleton wished he knew what it was.

Then he felt pain. He'd been in pain for a while, in all parts of his body, but this was new. Stabbing pain in his head. Like something was screaming. But not the voices. They seemed to have stopped.

He closed his eyes to ward off the pain, but he still saw stars. So he opened them again and watched the rain and didn't feel any better.

15

Helmdown, Helm
Marik-Stewart Commonwealth
29 April 3138

There would be time for rest. To sleep, to forget, or to just think of something else. Not much, but some. A few troops would stay behind; the others would prepare to move on and continue the campaign. Moving on was a process that took time and mostly did not involve the fighting men and women, so they could take some well-deserved time off while the support personnel did what they were supposed to.

There were officers who wanted to rest as well, but a flurry of messages and demands were flying back and forth between the highest ranks. The negotiations to get two people in the same place sometimes seemed more complicated than interplanetary trade agreements, especially when those people were deliberately avoiding each other.

Vedet felt he had the advantage in this particular game. Part of good business leadership involved finding people who didn't want to be found, and that was experience Alaric Wolf did not have. Vedet would pin him down, and pin him down soon.

He had brought support with him on his campaign to

confront the Wolf leader—multiple witnesses were always good for the type of confrontation he was planning. Along with a beefed-up security detail, he had brought along Mercy Billings, who was not the boldest fighter in his unit but had a great memory and a sharp eye. Two guards walked ahead of Vedet, two on each side, four behind. They walked firmly through the rain, which had fallen throughout the night and threatened to cover everything with mud. They were a good-sized group, and Vedet thought the tramp of their feet made an impressive noise, though there was a bit of a slosh to it thanks to the muddy ground.

Two massive guards, each holding an Imperator SMG, stood in front of a door leading to a Wolf 'Mech hangar. Between the two of them they had the door well blocked.

"Stand aside," Vedet barked.

"No entry for non-Wolf personnel," one of the guards said.

"I am the ranking officer on this planet! You will stand aside!"

The guards were unimpressed. "Lyran rank means little in Wolf space," one of them said.

"This is not Wolf space! Helm has fallen to the Lyran Commonwealth. It is our planet, and I am the ranking commander on it. I have authority here."

The guard's eyes looked quickly at Vedet, like the brief flick of a snake's tongue. "Where our Clan is, Wolf space is," the guard said. "You do not hold authority over us. Your archon will tell you the same thing."

Because my archon is a fool, Vedet thought.

"I wouldn't worry about a distant Steiner," Vedet said aloud. "I'd be more concerned with the Lyran standing in front of you right now." He leaned toward the guard as he spoke.

The guard took no notice. "Entry into this hangar will do you no good. Star Colonel Alaric is no longer here."

"And where is he now?"

"He did not tell us where he was going."

Vedet turned away, unwilling to waste another moment with the guards. This pattern had repeated itself several times throughout the morning. It wasn't, Vedet believed, that Alaric was avoiding him—he did not think the Wolf commander backed down from many confrontations—but simply that he was quite busy after the end of the battle and was making no effort to wait for Vedet to catch up to him or to make it easy for Vedet to find him. That is to say, avoiding Vedet might not be his primary purpose, but it was a happy side effect.

He would have to slow down eventually, though. Like Vedet, Alaric had likely been up for more than an entire day, much of it spent in battle. They were both weary, Vedet imagined, but Alaric lacked one thing Vedet possessed—the adrenaline of outrage. That would carry Vedet forward when Alaric was starting to settle down.

For the next hour and a half, though, Alaric showed no signs of slowing. Vedet and his entourage pursued him across the Wolf camp, consistently arriving at every location just after Alaric left. But finally Alaric became involved in a task that made him stay in one unsecured point long enough, and Vedet caught up to him.

Alaric was standing in the rain at a makeshift airstrip, reviewing the supply of munitions and arranging to replace the bombs he had unleashed on Helmdown. He was soaked, his hair dark brown with moisture, but he did not seem to notice the rain. He had no slicker or umbrella or anything else—he still wore his 'Mech uniform, every centimeter of which was soaked.

Vedet spoke loudly as he walked up to Alaric. He had already planned what he was going to say, choosing his words carefully for maximum impact.

"Star Colonel Alaric!" he yelled, making sure he could be heard above the patter of the rain. "You fought without honor!"

It worked. Alaric turned immediately to Vedet. The duke could not make out his expression through the rain and darkness, but he had a guess what it looked like—Alaric did not have the most expressive face, and it was likely on the angry end of its limited range.

"I am impressed, Duke Vedet, that you believe you are in any position to lecture anyone about honor." Alaric's voice was resonant, carrying through the rain though he did not yell.

"They were surrendering! I had accepted their surrender, and you massacred them!"

"I neither received nor accepted an offer of surrender," Alaric said. "There were enemy troops on the field, and I dispatched them as I would any other enemy. It was war."

"It was bloody *murder*!" Vedet said. "Cold-blooded murder! The Silver Hawk units were not even returning your fire!"

"I am not responsible for their poor tactics," he said. "I also do not feel an obligation to explain what they did. My job was to win the battle. Which I did."

"You did nothing! It was my victory! I had convinced them to surrender, and you couldn't accept that, so you massacred them!"

"You may be surprised to learn this, Duke Vedet, but all the circumstances of battle do not revolve around you. You did not convince them to surrender—you merely responded to their desperation. And my actions had nothing to do with you. Perhaps it will comfort you to know that I gave no thought to you throughout the battle." Alaric paused. "Or perhaps it will not. Narcissism does not like to be ignored."

Vedet's fingers opened and closed. He would have liked to reach for his sidearm, but knew he would die if he did. "You should watch your words," he growled.

"I believe you started the conversation by questioning my honor," Alaric said. "I was merely matching your rhetoric."

This was getting off-track. "This isn't about me," Vedet said. "This is about you massacring the Silver Hawks."

"I killed the enemy, which is the point of war," Alaric said. "And this is entirely about you. You care nothing for the lives of the Silver Hawks—you hate them more than I do. You are only upset because you thought to crown yourself the conqueror of Helm, and now that opportunity is gone."

"My motives are not the point! You were reckless and bloodthirsty. Do you know what will happen if the story of what you did gets out to the general public?"

Alaric leaned forward, and rain streamed off the top of his head and ran in rivulets off his brow. "I am fighting a war. I am not conducting a public relations campaign."

Vedet threw up his hands. "You're nothing more than a barbarian."

"And you are a craven politician, but why waste our time on name calling?"

"This is hopeless." Vedet turned to Billings. "This is what the archon gets for enlisting the help of people who have no understanding of political realities." Then he waved to his security officers. "Let's go."

He took a dozen steps through the muck before Alaric's voice stopped him. The voice carried perfectly through the rain, though it did not seem like Alaric was speaking any louder.

"How do you suppose Anson Marik will react to this battle?"

Vedet stopped. He wasn't anxious to continue the conversation, but the question interested him. What was Alaric implying?

The duke turned. "What do you mean, how will he react? He'll hate it!"

"And if news of the loss of his troops—and the way they were lost—reaches his ears?"

"He'll be furious," Vedet snorted. "He's a pool of anger on his best days. Your massacre will drive him insane with rage."

"And if he knows I intend to move deeper into his realm?"

Then Vedet saw it. He blinked a few times, then hated himself for showing any sort of reaction to the Clanner's stratagem.

"He will want you dead," Vedet said grudgingly.

"He'll throw extra troops at you to slow you down. They'll fight instead of running."

Alaric nodded. "He and his army will make their stand. He will not be able to retreat in front of us again. We will not have to chase the Silver Hawks all over the Marik-Stewart Commonwealth—he will bring them all to me so he can have a chance to defeat me."

"The Silver Hawk Irregulars will not be an easy foe, no matter how badly we've hurt them. You're bringing a large force down on yourself—and me, if I stay anywhere near you."

"I am not concerned about fighting them head-on instead of piece-by-piece," Alaric said. "Are you?"

Vedet fumed silently. He was supposed to be exposing Alaric's tactics for their cruelty, not admiring them. But he wasn't about to let Alaric see any of that. "This is a big risk you're taking. One you took without consulting any of your fellow commanders."

Alaric's face was completely hidden by the dim light and thick rain. "This is war," he said. "I assumed everyone was here to fight."

There was nothing more to be said. Vedet glared at Alaric for a time, hoping he conveyed anger at the Clanner's tactics instead of frustration; then he turned away so he could get the hell out of the Clan Wolf camp.

It probably is best to finish this campaign as soon as possible, Vedet thought. *So I can take my army away and never fight on the same side as a Clanner again.*

Perhaps he could have moved northwest. Then he could have brought his forces east and approached the Silver Hawk forces from the opposite side of the Wolves. Then he could have . . . he could have . . .

Roderick shook his head. There was nothing he could have done from that position. The problem was not a matter of location. He'd have to try again.

He could have said something over the comm, when Clan Wolf started firing on the stationary troops. He could have talked to Alaric, asked him what he was doing, made sure he understood that the troops he was firing on had surrendered.

No, no, that wasn't any good, either. First, Alaric wasn't about to explain what he was doing to anyone. Second, he had no doubt that Alaric knew perfectly well what he was doing. Explaining it to him would not have changed a thing.

Then perhaps he should have become involved in the situation earlier. As soon as the Silver Hawks broadcast their willingness to surrender, maybe he should have been involved instead of Vedet. Alaric's execution of the troops may have had something to do with his personal grudge against Vedet, though Alaric seemed to fight from a purely tactical standpoint. There was usually much more at stake in Alaric's moves than personal grudges—though Roderick was certain the Clanner wouldn't mind settling a few of those if the opportunity happened to arise.

Maybe if Roderick had intervened and negotiated the surrender properly . . .

"Either that map is the most beautiful piece of paper you've ever seen, or you've fallen asleep with your eyes open."

Roderick blinked several times. His eyelids felt like sandpaper. He raised his head while trying to rub some soreness out of his neck and looked for whoever had just spoken.

The room was dark except for a light on his desk. The map was well illuminated; everything else in the room were shadows in the dim morning light. He had to squint to see Trillian Steiner standing in front of him, her lips wearing a slight smirk. Her eyes, though, were worried.

"What are you . . . when did you get here?"

"A few minutes ago. At about the time I said 'Hi, Roderick.' "

"You said hi?"

"Yeah."

"Oh." Roderick twisted his head to one side, then the other. He heard light snaps and pops from his neck. "I didn't hear that."

"Yeah, I noticed." She sat down. Roderick thought she looked a little rumpled—a wrinkled brown shirt and blue pants, and heavy, mud-stained boots. Her hair looked like it had been pulled back a long time ago and then ignored—loose strands fell everywhere.

"What have you been doing?"

"Waiting. Watching. Gathering info. The things I generally do."

"Have you been up all night?"

"Of course."

"You didn't need to be."

"There's fighting going on," she said. "If there's anything to do to be useful, I should be doing it. Not sleeping."

Roderick looked ahead and watched as his vision blurred. Trillian was barely more than a smear in space. "All right," he said absently.

She leaned forward a bit. "If anyone's going to sleep, it should be you. You look wrung out."

"I'll get some rest soon. There's just . . . just something I was working on."

She looked at the paper he had been staring at. "A map of Helmdown?"

"Yeah."

"Why are you looking at that?" She leaned over farther, twisting her head to get a better look at it. The light shone beneath her chin and made her look ghoulish. "It's not exactly accurate anymore. Not after what Alaric's aero units did."

"It's accurate enough. For what I'm doing."

"What are you doing?"

He looked down at the map again and rubbed his forehead with both hands. The map blurred in front of him. His eyes, at least, were ready for sleep. "It's . . . it's nothing. Just reviewing some tactics."

"Maybe you'd do that a little better with a clear head," she said. "After some rest."

"I don't feel like resting just yet."

"Bullshit. You almost look like you're asleep right

now." Her eyes narrowed. "Something's wrong with you. What's going on?"

"Nothing. I just like to do my review when the battle's fresh in my mind."

"Fresh? Roderick, you almost fell asleep in the middle of that sentence! *Nothing* is fresh in your mind at the moment."

"It's just what I like to do, Trill," he said. He tongue felt thick in his mouth, so he spoke slowly.

She stared at him silently for a minute. "No," she said. "Something's wrong. You're not just following routine. Something's bothering you. What is it?"

Something in Roderick collapsed. It was like there was a platform in his mind holding all the blackness that had built up in him at the end of this battle, and when Trillian spoke the thin twig holding the platform up snapped in two and the blackness ran free. It poured through his mind and out his mouth, and when it did it washed away the weariness and pain and left only anger. He jumped to his feet and planted his hands on his desk so he could lean forward and bark at her.

"You have to ask?" he said. "You say you've been watching the battle, you act like you know what's going on, and you ask me what's wrong? Good hell, Trillian, how can you not know? How? Are you that far gone?"

Trillian absorbed his words calmly. "Okay. I thought that's what it was."

"Did you? Did you, now? How *clever* you are, Trillian. How goddamned *insightful*."

Trillian fanned the fingertips of both hands on her chest. "Me?" she said. "You're mad at me?"

"You brought me here, didn't you? You put me in the middle of these two idiots."

"Do you think I knew this was going to happen?" she shouted back, matching his anger. "Do you think I *wanted* it to happen?"

"Who the hell knows? Do you even want anything anymore, or do you just do what your damned cousin tells you to?"

"She's the archon! Of course I do what she tells me to do! Don't you?"

"Don't question my loyalty, Trillian. Don't take a single step in that direction. I let myself be called a Steiner and went wherever I've been ordered to. You know I follow orders."

"Right. We all do. That's why we're here. Because we're trying to follow orders, all of us."

The anger had already faded. The blackness inside Roderick had spent itself in a short burst. It drained away, and the weariness returned.

"It was a massacre, Trill," Roderick said, easing himself back down into his chair. "They might as well have just lined them up and executed those troops. They mowed them down before anyone really knew what they were doing."

As soon as Roderick said those words, he knew it was a lie. He had known what Alaric was doing, Vedet had known and the Silver Hawks for damn sure had known. The problem wasn't that they didn't know what was happening—it was that no one could come up with a way to stop Alaric Wolf from doing it.

"I'm controlling it, Roderick. I started controlling it as soon as it happened. To the Inner Sphere, this will just be a battle, one where the Silver Hawk Irregulars were badly outnumbered and paid the price."

"But that's not the truth."

"It will be."

Roderick shook his head. "What are we doing here, Trillian? Damn it, what in hell are we doing?"

"Pro—" Trillian started.

"And if you say 'promoting the good of the Commonwealth,' I swear I'll shoot myself in the head."

Trillian didn't say anything for a time. He could hear her exhaling, trying to force herself to breathe slowly.

"We're going to win this war," Roderick said. He leaned back, away from the light, into the shadow. "And in the end, the Commonwealth will have some more territory, and we'll have to deal with conquered people who don't particularly like us. Plus, instead of having Marik-Stewart neighbors who hate us, we'll have a whole new set of neighbors who hate us beyond the former Marik-Stewart borders. And that's why we're fighting here, and that's why Alaric Wolf had to massacre a bunch of Silver Hawk troops. So we could get a victory that makes the archon feel good about herself and lets her get a few new asskissing headlines for her clip file. *Dulce et decorum est.*"

"What?"

"Nothing. An old phrase."

"I think you're overthinking this. It's a war and, like you said, we're going to win it. That's not a bad thing."

"People are dying—our people, their people, and some people who never had anything to do with any of this. Me thinking is not the problem—the problem is that Melissa hasn't thought about this enough."

"You're not being fair," Trillian said sharply. "Melissa has thought through this plenty, and she feels each death. This is agony for her. Don't ever assume she takes this lightly."

"I'm sure it's tough for her," Roderick said. "But ask any of the dead soldiers how willing they'd be to trade their agony for hers. And ask her the same thing."

Trillian stood, her face almost entirely out of the range of the light. "All right. I came to check on you. Looks like you're fine—nothing's more fun than staying up all night playing the martyr. I'll leave you to it."

Roderick nodded. He was too tired to goad her anymore.

"The good news is, you don't have to like this war," Trillian said. "You just have to fight it."

She left quickly.

Roderick thought about following her out, maybe talking to her about something besides the battle. Or maybe he should just leave and get some sleep.

But the map of Helmdown was still in front of him. He looked down at it, and it would not let him go. *Somehow,* he thought as he looked at it, *there had to have been a way. There had to be a way to make it different.*

16

Marik Palace
New Edinburgh, Stewart
Marik-Stewart Commonwealth
12 May 3138

Cole Daggert only appeared to walk slowly.

He was taller than most of the people he passed in the halls of the palace, and most of his height was in his legs. His motions were smooth but his strides were long, and he covered a lot of ground while looking unhurried.

People talked about it all the time, making the kind of small talk people make when all they know about a person is his appearance. They wondered how he could deal with Anson Marik in the middle of a losing war, suffering setback after setback, and remain calm and unhurried.

His reply was always the same. "What you see is my way of hurrying." People would laugh as if it were a joke, but it was nothing more or less than the direct truth.

He was now hurrying to a briefing with the captain-general and most of the ranking military officers on the planet. He was going to be late to the meeting, delayed by a conversation with someone who had just arrived on-planet. The assembled commanders, especially the captain-general, would not be happy at his late arrival, but they would understand once he told them what he was doing. Then they would be even unhappier.

The palace on Stewart was an architectural mishmash, an uninspired appropriation of the major design movements of the Stewart Commonality and the early days of the Free Worlds League. This particular hallway mimicked the New Braddockism of the late twenty-third century, with its emphasis on nontraditional geometric forms. Designed as a black hexagon with ridges along its top three sides, its walls bowed outward, which, as far as Daggert was concerned, did nothing but waste space and make it difficult to design the adjacent rooms. The fact that those rooms tended to ape styles like Diaspora Revivalism and Crooked Classicism made the whole building look thrown together, a Frankenstein ensemble with no attempt to stitch the parts together.

He hadn't worried about the appearance of the building much, of course, since he had arrived on Stewart. One possible benefit of the current situation was that Daggert had too much on his mind to worry about niceties like architecture.

The black floor of the hallway was dark and shiny, and he could see his dim reflection moving underneath him. That was when he realized he had been walking with his head down.

He lifted it just in time to pass the first security checkpoint. Then the second. Then he went through the third and was in the situation room.

It didn't seem to matter what building they were in; situation rooms throughout the Inner Sphere—at least the ones Daggert had been in—all looked about the same. A large, austere table, chairs you could never quite get comfortable in, and displays. Lots and lots of displays, on the walls, set into the table, occasionally suspended from the ceiling. Troop statistics, news feeds and maps, maps, maps. Daggert found it a little sad that walking into a room like this felt more like coming home than walking into his own quarters or even his house.

Anson was already there, and he was sitting. That was strange. Anson did not have a lot of patience for discussion or deliberation. He preferred to arrive at meetings like this late, then storm in, bully the cabinet into making decisions and stomp out. It was part of his . . . well, Daggert supposed the best word for it would be "aura." It was what the captain-general did, how he took control of a situation. So to see him at a meeting on time, already seated—it was unnerving.

"Siddown, Daggert," Anson growled. "The sooner this is done, the better."

At least his greetings are normal, Daggert thought, and sat down in his chair.

Director of Planetary Defense Callie Ferguson walked in practically on Daggert's heels, and the table was full.

"Let's make this brief," said Pavel Krist, Anson's chief of staff. "The captain-general has a very full schedule. Force Commander Cameran-Witherspoon, you can go first."

Force Commander Ian Cameran-Witherspoon, commander of the Silver Hawk Irregulars, leaned forward like he was about to pounce across the table. "We've almost doubled the number of Silver Hawk units on-planet in the past week. That means we've left most of the Lyran front bare, but that doesn't matter, since all the Lyrans will likely be coming here." He paused. "We also have what will probably be the last DropShip with troops from Helm. There won't be . . . I don't think any of them will be in a condition to fight when the Lyrans arrive." Cameran-Witherspoon glanced at Daggert. "I believe your tactical adviser has debriefed some of those troops."

Daggert nodded but didn't speak. Anson's meetings did not invite anyone to speak out of turn.

"Fine," Anson said. "What do the numbers look like?"

"With the functional units that just landed, we now have a total of—"

Anson cut him off with a wave of his hand. "Never mind. Tell it to Daggert, he likes that sort of thing. You two and Ferguson plan the details."

"Yes, sir," Cameran-Witherspoon said.

"General Ferguson, how is the militia training and recruiting going?" Krist asked.

The pattern continued. Ferguson gave a bare-bones report, Anson asked for more details, then changed his mind and cut Ferguson off, deciding he wasn't interested. They went through the air force, infantry and 'Mech commanders as well, and then it was Daggert's turn.

"Mr. Daggert, anything to add at this point?"

He did, in fact, have plenty to say, but nothing that Anson would be interested in hearing. "There are some matters of troop movement and deployment that I'd like to discuss with the various commanders, but I'm sure we can do that in a separate meeting."

"Good. Fine. Do it." Then Anson asked the question Daggert had been dreading. "You've been debriefing the stragglers from Helm. What the hell happened there? We knew we were going to lose, but what we lost compared to what they lost is a goddamned joke. Was this your screwup or someone's in the field?"

Daggert knew better than to try to dance around the question. "It was a breakdown in command, sir," he said. "Their initial path out of the city was cut off, and they lost several ranking officers early on. Once enough officers were lost, discipline failed. It appears that some officers made an offer of surrender."

Anson slammed a fist on the table. "Surrender? Since when was that any part of their orders?" He glared at Cameran-Witherspoon. "They shouldn't have even *thought* the word 'surrender'! The Silver Hawk Irregulars do not surrender! What the hell happened?"

"Sir, permit me to point out that the majority of units did not surrender," Cameran-Witherspoon said. "Many of them fell before the surrender offer was made, while others attempted a late breakthrough even when some of the other soldiers were surrendering. For the most part, discipline held."

"I don't care that some of your people fought the battle right!" Anson said. "I asked why some of them failed! What happened out there?"

Cameran-Witherspoon leaned even farther forward, until he was almost leaning over the table. "Sir, stalemates tend to have a negative effect on morale. I can't, from this distance, be sure exactly what happened, but it seems probable that the stress of the prolonged standoff combined with overwhelming odds and the loss of their COs broke the troops' spirits. It was a unique set of conditions—I don't think we'll see another breakdown from the Irregulars."

"You 'don't think'?" Anson bellowed. "What kind of shit is that? You need to do better. You should damned well *know* that it won't be repeated, or it's your ass. Do you understand? I'll bring the next failure all the way up to you."

"Yes, sir."

Anson held on to the table, looking like he could easily snap a piece off the end. "So now the Lyrans have some of our people. We should get them back. What do we have to offer them in exchange?"

"I'm afraid it won't work like that," Daggert said, his voice low.

"Get the hell out of here. You mean we don't have a single damned thing we can trade them? Good hell, can't some of these troops get the upper hand at least once and capture something for us that would be useful?"

"I'm afraid you're misunderstanding the problem," Daggert said. "From the information we've gathered, the Lyrans did not take any of our people captive."

"They didn't? Then what happened to them? Where in hell are they?"

"They are dead," Daggert said flatly. "I can't say exactly what happened or why at the moment, but the surrendering forces were massacred."

Once he was done talking, Daggert sat and waited. He knew when to expect torrents of fury from Anson Marik, and he was prepared to sit through a long burst right now. He almost looked forward to it—the news of the massacre of some of the Silver Hawks left behind on Helm had left a hollow feeling in his gut. Since Daggert was generally not given to emotional displays, he could use Anson's anger as a suitable replacement and live vicariously through the inevitable diatribe.

Everyone else in the situation room was waiting for it as well. Anson's face was red, his hands and arms looked ready to push on the table and launch him to his feet and he was inhaling long and slow, getting the air he would need for the invective he was about to spew.

Then the air came out, without much of a sound. Anson remained seated, arms still, eyes focused on some spot near the middle of the long table. He didn't say a word.

Krist looked around at everyone else in the room, then at Anson, then back at everyone else. He made a small, helpless shrug. It was as if the tantrum had been planned into the meeting's agenda and no one knew what to do when it didn't happen.

Finally, Krist spoke.

"I, ah . . . I imagine there are more details you have learned about what happened on Helm."

"Yes," Daggert said. "If the captain-general would like, I can give him a more detailed account of what I know later in the day."

Krist looked at Anson. The captain-general had not moved a muscle, and his eyes still glared at the table.

"Yes," Krist said, looking back at Daggert. "That, um, that would be good. I'm sure the captain-general would be happy to talk with you shortly."

Again, Krist paused, giving Anson a chance to talk. Anson remained silent.

"I . . . I suppose that's it," Krist said. "Thank you all for your work on behalf of the Commonwealth, and may your efforts turn aside those who assail us."

Anson was on his feet before Krist finished speaking. The others in the room, believing this was the outburst come at last, leaned forward in their chairs. But Anson still did not speak. He abruptly walked away from the table and toward the door.

Everyone scrambled to stand up as fast as possible once Anson was on the move, but the captain-general paid them no attention. He moved quickly out of the situation room and was gone.

Daggert looked briefly at the rest of the faces in the room. They looked surprised, but mostly they were just tired. War is exhausting in the best of circumstances, but a losing war eats away at those who command it, body and soul. Anson's bluster could be annoying and time-wasting, but you could not listen to him for long without feeling at least a touch of his outrage, and that anger had been fueling his military commanders for much of this war. Now they were left empty, and they slowly shuffled out the door to their duties.

Daggert returned to the black hexagonal hallway. His bearing was exactly the same when he left the meeting as it was when he arrived. He carried all his burdens in his long, deceptively fast stride.

"Is he in a meeting with someone else?" Daggert asked.

Carol, Anson's appointment secretary, sat very still behind her immense desk. She looked like a small duck floating behind a barge. "No," she said. "There's no one else in there."

"Then I can just go in." Daggert tried to make it clear that this was not a question.

"No. No, I'm sorry, you can't," Carol said. Her brown hair was pulled back so tight that the corners of her eyes seemed stretched. "I can't let anyone in until he says it's okay for them to come in. The captain-general has made himself very clear on that matter."

Daggert, in a chair opposite Carol's desk, uncrossed his legs, then crossed them the other way while trying not to yell at her. She was only doing her job.

He breathed deeply a few times and remained calm, mainly because that was what he did when he waited. The chair was comfortable enough, with its brown leather cushions, though it had those annoying round armrests that never allowed you to get your arms set in the right place. If Anson required him to wait, he could wait.

There was a low murmur in the room. Daggert had heard it when he walked in, but had thought it was just the sound of his blood pumping in his ears. He had been sitting for a while now, however, and his heart rate should have dropped. This had to be something else.

"Do you hear that?" he asked.

Carol looked up, startled. Daggert wondered if she had always been that way, or if years spent in close proximity to Anson Marik had conditioned her to be skittish. "Hear what?" she said.

"That noise. That murmuring, or thumping."

Carol tilted her head. "Oh, is that still going on?" She paused. "So it is. That's nothing. Just the protestors."

"The protestors? What are they doing?"

"Drumming," Carol said, her head bobbing this way and that. "Just below the legal noise limit. They've been at it for weeks."

"Really?"

"Yes. They're very . . . intrepid. Apparently there's a few engineers in their numbers, and they've managed to figure out the best location in which to drum for the sound to carry into these offices."

"Why doesn't he have them arrested?"

"They're not breaking any laws."

"That hasn't stopped him before."

The corners of Carol's mouth twitched. "Of course. To be honest, I don't know why he has tolerated them. They've been quite aggressive. At night, they move so it carries better into the captain-general's private chambers." She smiled, a quick, hesitant expression. "What they don't know is that the captain-general hasn't been to his private chambers in weeks."

"He hasn't?"

"No. He's generally here. At least, I think he is. He's here when I arrive in the morning, here when I leave at night and the security detail says he doesn't go anywhere. Someone brings him a fresh change of clothes each morning."

"He's sleeping in his office?"

Carol shook her head seriously. "Oh no. I don't think he sleeps much."

Daggert looked at the door. "Maybe I should go in."

"He wouldn't like that," Carol said.

Daggert stood. "I think I should go in anyway." He walked toward the door. It could be a short trip—if Carol decided he shouldn't go in, she wouldn't press the button to unlatch the door, and he'd be stuck out here. But as he walked by, she stared at him, eyes wide, jaw clenched, and pressed the button.

Anson was at his desk. He was motionless except for his right index finger, which tapped rhythmically on the edge of his gunmetal gray desk. It beat out the same rhythm as the distant protest drums.

"I apologize for walking in like this, my lord, but I thought since we had a scheduled appointment, you would not mind me coming in."

Anson said nothing. The captain-general did not acknowledge his presence.

"I've talked to a half dozen survivors of Helm," Daggert said, "including one who just regained consciousness this morning, Captain Zeke Carleton. He's still quite disoriented, but from what I could piece together his story confirms General Cameran-Witherspoon's theory of a failure of morale. It was a difficult situation for all the troops. I blame myself for that, since it was my planning that put them there. I accept full responsibility for their failure to follow orders."

"You can't resign," Anson said. The words came out like bullets, as if Anson had to force them, one by one, through his teeth.

"Yes, my lord, you made that clear back on Atreus. I leave it to your judgment what the most appropriate response to my failure should be."

Anson said nothing. He still stared straight ahead at nothing in particular. Daggert shifted his stance a little, trying to get in the line of Anson's gaze, but it was clear that the captain-general was not looking at anything in the room, and that he would not see Daggert no matter where he stood.

"I've been able to piece together a semicoherent narrative of the events leading up to the massacre. If you'd like I could walk you through it."

He waited for a response. Again, none came.

"The units left on Helm followed the plan for the first part of the battle," Daggert began. "They used their artillery to slow the initial Lyran advance, then backed toward the center of Helmdown. By the accounts I have heard, the pressure by the Wolves to the east was—"

"How many were killed?" Anson said.

"My lord?"

"This massacre. How many."

"It's difficult to say. There were many troops that fell in the battle, and the massacre occurred just after the last of the fighting troops fell. It's difficult to draw a line between those who were killed as part of the massacre and—"

"Give me a number."

"With the limited information I have and the uncertainty of—"

"Give me a number!" Anson yelled. Daggert quickly looked at him to see if the anger had made the captain-general's eyes finally come to life, but it hadn't. His voice sounded lively, but the rest of him looked dead.

Daggert pulled a number out of the air, a wild guess based on incomplete and contradictory information. "Between fifty and one hundred troops, my lord. Including supporting personnel."

The drums continued to beat as Anson absorbed this information.

"Small," Anson said. "A fraction of an army."

"Yes, sir."

Daggert waited for Anson to continue his train of

thought, but it seemed that was all he had to say. The captain-general fell quiet again.

Daggert didn't know what else to do, so he continued his narrative. "The troops then tried to make their escape to the south, but a Lyran unit, the First Steiner Strikers, had managed to run all the way around the city and head them off. At this point, the commanding officer of—"

"That's enough."

"My lord?"

"I said that's enough. I don't want to hear any more."

"I understand this is a difficult subject, my lord, but the information points to a serious breach of international protocol by—"

"I don't care. I don't want to hear any more."

"You don't care?"

Anson didn't answer. He continued to stare at nothing.

"Perhaps we should review the current troop deployment here," Daggert said after a moment's silence. "Your generals have served you well so far, but there are a few possible improvements I could—"

Once again, Anson interrupted him. "No. I don't want to talk about that."

"My lord, the Lyrans and Wolves are certainly preparing to come here. Our time is very short, and I believe—"

"I'm not going to talk about that right now."

"Yes, my lord. Perhaps we can schedule another session later so I can—"

"No."

Daggert stood over Anson's desk, bewildered. He never would have believed there would be a day when he would wish for Anson to exhibit one of his trademark displays of anger. This shell that was sitting behind the desk, this machine that could only offer contrary remarks, was of little use to anyone.

Frustration came over Daggert in a wave. "Damn it, Anson, why didn't you just let me resign?"

Again, the captain-general did not respond.

"Did you really need me to go down with you? If

you're intent on sitting here and doing nothing, you could have done that without my help! Why not accept my resignation and just let me go?"

Nothing.

Daggert wanted to reach across the desk and slap Anson Marik good and hard, hard enough so that his heavy jowls would shake for hours. Hard enough to unleash decades of stored-up aggression. Hard enough to make the man *move*.

But he didn't. He took a deep breath, and once again he was himself.

"I am going to leave," he said. "I am going to bring my recommendations to the generals and tell them they have your approval. Then I am going to keep talking with them and keep working to save this planet. You can sit at your desk for as long as you want, but the rest of us will be doing the actual work that you apparently can't!"

His words were designed to hurt, but they bounced off Anson with no discernible impact. Daggert stayed still for a moment more. Then, when Anson still did not speak, Daggert turned and left the office.

Carol looked like she had moved her chair to her right, taking her away from the office door, giving her more distance in case Anson came out in a rage. Daggert saw her flinch when the door opened, then relax when she saw it wasn't Anson.

"Is everything . . ." Carol said. "Is he . . ."

"I don't think he'll be coming out," Daggert said. "It turns out the whole thing was my mistake. The captain-general had no desire to see me."

He did not bother to answer her puzzled expression as he walked away.

= 17 =

Helmdown, Helm
Lyran Commonwealth
13 May 3138

"Come on a walk with me," Alaric said.

He saw the surprised look in Verena's eyes. "What?" she said.

"I want to walk through the city one last time before we leave. I want you to come with me."

Verena stood, leaving one of his uniforms unfolded. "Forgive me for saying this, but that sounds oddly sentimental."

"It is nothing of the kind," he said. "This is conquered territory. It used to work for Anson Marik. Now it works for us. I need to make sure it will function when I am gone. Nothing more."

"When you say 'us,' do you mean both the Clan and the Lyrans or the Clan alone?"

Alaric smiled. "That is one of the details to be worked out."

Alaric wore his full dress uniform, and Verena wore a plain jumpsuit. It was appropriate—both of them dressed to their station.

Once the defenders had been completely defeated, Alaric had considered taking over some of the buildings and using them for his new base camp. The sad fact of the matter, however, was that a large number of the buildings in Helmdown were too damaged to use, and many of those that were intact were grubby little buildings that were no better than the temporary quarters the Clan brought with them. Rather than scour the city for decent accommodations, Alaric had simply ordered all his ground units to come into the kilometer-wide swath of the city his bombers had cleared and set up camp there. In short order, they had a new subcity within the capital of Helm.

The ground had finally dried from the April rains, though the air did not seem to have grown any warmer. Winds still blew cold from the northern mountains, but the occasional appearance of the sun took the edge off. Alaric enjoyed the cold—it inspired motion. Cold was a reminder that sitting still was not a good way to survive.

As might be expected, Helmdown had been slow to heal in the two weeks since the battle. The local and planetary officials were either dead or missing, and Alaric had no desire to track down the survivors. They were right to hide—if they showed up in town, they would be imprisoned or executed—but they were not so important that Alaric needed to spend his troops' time and energy to find them. If they remained in hiding, they could stay alive and stay out of Alaric's way, which, as far as he was concerned, was best for all involved.

Duke Vedet had established some sort of provisional government, and Alaric did not interfere. Alaric was confident that he could get what he wanted from this planet without having to go through the ponderous mechanisms of government. That was one of the points war made for you—it convinced people that it was in their best interest to accede to your will, whether you established a bureaucracy or not.

Like the government, business within Helmdown had ground to a halt during the stalemate before the battle and had not yet recovered any significant momentum.

However, focusing the battle on Helmdown had its advantages; some industrial concerns in neighboring areas had not been touched by the fighting and were able to resume operations as soon as the firing had stopped. Metal was once again being extracted from the mountains around Helm, and some of it was even being processed. It was far from a king's ransom, but Alaric intended to make the planet pay a significant price for the damage his troops had suffered.

There was one form of commerce, however, that was in full and profitable operation, a business that never ceased during wartime. The war profiteers were active and looking for a way to benefit from the fighting, and of all the people in the city they had the least difficulty switching their loyalties. Their cravenness inspired Alaric's contempt, but he knew it was not important for him to like these people—he only needed to know how to use them to his benefit.

He led Verena out of the bombed-out area and into one of the taller buildings in town, a six-story building whose top two floors were currently uninhabitable. On the third floor there was an office that had a metal desk, a wooden chair, a lot of sawdust and some scattered two-by-fours. Alaric didn't know what this office had been two weeks ago, but it was now the office of Betty Brillat, the most capable of the Helmdown scavengers Alaric had met.

He led Verena up the dimly lit concrete stairs to Brillat's office. Brillat was waiting inside, filing her nails. She had short black hair that stuck tight to her head, curving down her jaw almost to her chin. The style made her round face look a little longer, a little harsher. She leaned back in her chair, and stayed reclined even when Alaric entered. The exaggeratedly casual air Brillat affected did not impress Alaric, but if it was what she needed to do to feel comfortable and do her job, then so be it.

"Mr. Wolf," Brillat said in greeting. Alaric did not know if her ignorance was genuine or intentional, and again he did not care. He would be off this planet soon enough, and he could put up with minor annoyances until that happened.

"Time is pressing," he said, skipping any formalities or small talk. "I assume you are close to delivering on the items we discussed."

"You assume right," Brillat said. "Most of it's coming from out of town, you understand. Nothing personal, but you and your Lyran friends did a pretty thorough job of trashing anything valuable in this area."

That was a lie, of course. They had inflicted a lot of damage on the city to be sure, but in a city as broad and sprawling as Helmdown, there were certainly some areas that had been untouched. On the other hand, without any government presence in the city, looters ruled the day, so Alaric understood why Brillat had to look for goods out of town.

"I need it before I leave," Alaric said. "Our repairs cannot wait."

"Right, right, right. Well, I'll tell you what, you can pick up the first shipment tomorrow. Right here. Bring a truck."

"Fine. I will also provide my own security. What do you think I should expect?"

Brillat smirked. "Expect trouble. Word will get out about the stuff you want, and most people will be able to guess who it's going to. And they don't like you much." Brillat paused, as if waiting for Alaric to react to what she said. Since she was not telling him anything he did not know, he remained silent.

"Word's gotten around that some of the Silver Hawk Irregulars wanted to surrender, but you wouldn't let 'em. There's all sorts of stories about what you said to them. They've given you a lot of good lines. They say the Silver Hawks were practically begging for their lives—which I don't buy, that doesn't sound like the Silver Hawk Irregulars, but I guess some people think that makes a better story—and you said 'The only reason I might consider letting you live is so you can beg a bit longer.'" Brillat chuckled. "I'm pretty sure that's a line from a holovid released in the last century. And there's another story— this one's good because it's just too cheesy to be believed. They say the Silver Hawks offered to surrender, and you said 'No. You are going down with Helm.' Get it? Down with Helm? Helmdown?" She shook her head. "That's just stupid."

None of this surprised Alaric. He was very familiar with the deep-seated need of people in the Inner Sphere to cast the Clans as villains in whatever drama was unfolding in their heads. If Alaric was at all concerned with winning the hearts and minds of the people of the Marik-Stewart Commonwealth during this campaign, he would have pondered the matter in more depth. Since he was not, though, he knew it was easy to let them hate him while he spent his time on tasks that were worth his attention.

"There will be enough security here tomorrow," he said.

"Oh, I'm sure of it," Brillat said with a wave of her hand. "To be honest, the people don't like you, but I think most of them are all talk. Deep down, they're mostly afraid of you. You're the wild card, you know. They never know who you're going to massacre next!"

Brillat may have intended that line to be offensive, or it may have just been a weak attempt at humor. Again, though, Alaric did not care enough to do anything about it.

"Tomorrow, then," he said, and he turned to leave.

He heard Verena following close behind. When he spoke to her, he did not turn to her, not even his head. He expected her to keep up if she wanted to hear.

"All these games the Inner Sphere politicians play," he said. "All their efforts to preen and promote themselves, to make themselves seem powerful or intimidating, are nonsense. Their games are unnecessary. All that is needed is action. Show what you are capable of doing, what you are willing to do, and people who are accustomed to weaker leaders quickly fall in line." He walked silently for a moment. "This is Duke Vedet's great weakness. He wants power, but he is not willing to do all that it takes to get it. He is too restrained by his Inner Sphere conditioning."

"Forgive me, Star Colonel, but who are you talking to?" Verena said.

Alaric stopped and turned to her.

"You," he said. "Who else?"

"It sounded like you were trying to convince me of something," Verena said. "Though I do not think I disagreed with you about anything."

"These are principles of leadership," Alaric said. "You would do well to learn and understand them."

"I was a commander before you captured me, remember. I have been a leader before."

Alaric frowned. "You came out on the losing end of that fight. I thought you might benefit by hearing advice from the commander who beat you."

"Victory makes you feel pretty good about yourself, *quiaff*?"

He didn't twist his torso. He just let his left arm fly up quickly, catching Verena in the jaw with the back of his hand. Her head snapped back, but she stood her ground. He glared at her, and she glared back. Then she brought her hand to her chin and dabbed the cut Alaric had opened on her face. "My apologies, Star Colonel."

"You have been getting too comfortable, Verena. You might take some time to remember where you were when I took you as my bondservant. You are now part of a conquering army—an army I command. Humility would suit you."

"Of course, Star Colonel."

He could see defiance and anger in her eyes, but she was controlling it. As she should.

He turned away from her and continued striding through the streets of Helmdown.

By the time he had returned to his quarters, his anger at Verena had mostly dissipated. He had not been precisely certain of its source—it seemed to flare rather quickly, and he was usually better able to ignore insolence. Whatever the reason, it had passed, and he helped Verena clean and bandage the wound on her jaw. He could see that she was not entirely appeased, but that was a small matter.

"Our repairs are almost complete," he said. "We should be ready to make our next move soon."

Her mouth opened slightly, but closed, and her jaw clenched. She clearly had something to say.

"Say what you want," he said. He was confident she had left her insolence behind on Helmdown's streets—for the time being, at least.

"I thought the next move was already chosen. I thought we were going to Stewart."

"That would seem like the wisest move—it is a crucial planet in this war, even if Anson Marik does not hold dominion there. For the moment, however, our decision is not official. The Lyrans have not shared their plans with me, and of course I did not feel the need to confide in them. We are not a unified force, and I have no desire to be one, but I should not be so stubborn that I punish our forces. We will do much better landing as part of a three-pronged assault than as one part of three separate invasions. At some point, coordination will be necessary."

"It does not seem like coordination should be so difficult."

"It should not be. But Vedet may be stupid enough to attempt an invasion on his own simply out of spite."

"I assume you have not spoken with him."

"Not since his visit on the morning after the battle," Alaric said. "Avoiding each other seems like the best approach."

"Then what do you do? Just leave and hope he follows?"

"No. He will not be able to move that fast."

"Steiner," Verena said, speaking a little faster now. "Trillian Steiner. She will try to make all the commanders on the planet work together. You have been waiting for her to meddle."

"She, of course, would say she is just doing her job as assigned by the archon."

"Of course she would," Verena said.

"The meeting will come soon—I thought she already would have called for it by now. I cannot see any reason to continue to wait." He lowered his arms to his sides and tapped his mattress. "But I still have not decided the best way to take advantage of the situation."

"I assume you mean the situation in which everyone involved hates you."

Alaric allowed himself to smile. "It is not so much the hate as the anger. Anger tends to make commanders sloppy. I do not like sloppiness in people who are supposed to be offering support for my troops. Not that Duke Vedet would ever admit to serving as support for the Wolves, but as long as he is occupying our enemies, he is offering support."

"But he hates Anson Marik more than he hates you, *quiaff*?"

"*Aff.* But that just makes him even more likely to make more mistakes."

"Then position him so his mistakes help us."

Alaric sat up straighter. "Be ready for him to overswing . . . yes. But we would need to make sure he enters battle in the proper frame of mind."

"I imagine that would be your job during the council of war. As long as you are not above that sort of petty manipulation."

Alaric raised an eyebrow—it was little more than a twitch, but still more expression than he typically displayed. Then he decided Verena was not making fun of him, or if she was, it was not overly insubordinate.

"Playing political games is one thing," he said. "Positioning ourselves for victory on the battlefield is another. The Silver Hawk Irregulars should already be in the proper state of mind. It should not be difficult for me to make sure Vedet is too."

18

Helmdown, Helm
Lyran Commonwealth
13 May 3138

Trillian did not go outside much. The streets were grimy and drifted with ash, and there were certain alleys that never seemed to dry, no matter how long the city went without rain. And it never went that long.

The problem was, every street, every alley, looked like that one spot in Zanzibar City. Every single damn one of them. Every time she turned a corner, she thought she would see the body of the policeman lying there, huge and limp. The policeman she had killed.

She had been thinking about that almost every day, and she blamed Helmdown. The city was nowhere near as large as Zanzibar City and, truth be told, not architecturally similar at all. But there was something about it—maybe it was the rain, maybe it was the angle and intensity of the light—that made her think of Zanzibar City everywhere she went. So, to counteract that problem, she didn't go anywhere.

Klaus went. She had Klaus running around the city like a jackrabbit, working whatever contacts he had made since they arrived here: information-gathering was a particular skill of his. He came back once or twice a day and updated Trillian on what he had found. Trillian remained in her cramped quarters behind her white plastic desk, reviewed the information Klaus brought her and tried to make sense of the situation. It was the most complicated, least satisfying military victory she had ever been a part of.

She looked forward to Klaus' visits. She didn't have too many people to talk to—she didn't know many people on Helm, and those she did know didn't come to see her very often. Klaus helped ground her, keeping her in touch with the world she did not choose to visit.

But when he walked in today, Trillian had the distinct feeling she would not enjoy the conversation.

He looked as polished as always. Klaus wore his uniform like other people wear pajamas—with complete comfort, though in his case without a hint of sloppiness. He looked effortlessly immaculate.

"How are the streets of Helmdown today?" she asked.

He twisted his mouth into a kind of wavy line. "As wet and grimy as ever," he said. "As usual, you're not missing anything."

"How is it you walk around out there all day and never have a spot of mud on your uniform?"

"My uniform is clean because my heart is pure."

"That makes your uniform clean? Then what is it that gives you the strength of ten men?"

"Same thing," Klaus said. "Pure hearts solve many problems."

"What've you got for me?"

"A problem, that's what I've got."

"What kind of problem?"

"A Vedet problem."

"What a surprise. What's he up to at the moment?"

"He's apparently decided that Clan Wolf no longer has a role in this invasion, and that they'd be better off somewhere else."

"Since that's not his decision to make, that doesn't worry me too much," Trillian said.

"It should," Klaus said. "He wants to go public."

Trillian dropped her head into her hands and rubbed her temples. "Go public?"

"With what he knows about the battle. He's already taken to calling it the Helm Massacre, and he's quite content to put all the blame for it on Clan Wolf. If he can paint them as bloodthirsty barbarians . . ."

She saw it, like a path of stepping stones floating right in front of her. "Then the archon's decision to bring them in looks pretty bad."

Klaus nodded. "He will also, of course, try to portray himself as valiantly trying to stop the massacre. He'll say he had the battle won, and the Clanner committed cold-blooded murder because he wanted to."

"Aside from a few nuances here and there, that's not really too far from the truth."

"I'm not sure that the truth of the matter is exactly our concern right now," Klaus said.

Trillian leaned back in her chair and looked over Klaus' shoulder out her small window. She saw only gray streets under a gray sky. "I'm gonna have to go out there to take care of this, aren't I?"

Klaus looked around the small, sparsely furnished room. "I'm not sure the luxury of your quarters will convince many people to come here. Besides, it wouldn't be good for you to become agoraphobic."

"I'm nowhere near an agoraphobe," she said. "I'm a Helmdown-phobe, that's all. Like anyone wouldn't be in this miserable place."

"Whatever your neurosis, I don't think Duke Vedet is going to care. And I don't think he's going to go out of his way to visit you."

"All right. Do that thing where you just announce that I'm coming instead of scheduling an appointment. Then you can blindfold me and take me to his office."

"Seriously?"

Trillian sighed. "Only the first part."

While Alaric and his Clan were squatting in temporary quarters in a bombed-out section of the city and Trillian

was making do with a back office she'd selected mainly
for its lack of windows, Vedet had set himself up in quarters worthy of a duke. The abdication of the local government had emptied out most of the offices in the
middle of the city, and while some of the nicer quarters
were too charred to use, Vedet had found a room that
had belonged to the Helmdown minister of agriculture,
a broad room with rich green carpet and floor-to-ceiling
shelves on practically every wall. Vedet sat at a desk in
front of a large bay window with a view of a section of
the city that only recently had stopped smoking.

Trillian was glad Vedet had found this room. She
found its formality far more comfortable than most other
parts of Helmdown, as long as she didn't spend too much
time looking out the window. Since she intended to
spend most of the meeting glaring at Vedet with a steely
intensity, the view should not prove much of a
distraction.

She was happy to find him waiting for her—she half
expected to find an empty room, which would not say
good things about Vedet's respect for the Steiner family.
He might be attempting to maneuver his way into Melissa's position, but he wasn't so arrogant that he would
fail to show up when a high-ranking Steiner summoned
him. At least, not yet.

"Lady Steiner. You're lucky to have caught me,"
Vedet said when Trillian walked in. "I have plenty of
preparations to supervise."

"Preparations for what?"

Vedet produced a smile that oozed across his face.
"Our departure, of course. We've been on Helm long
enough. We need to continue the campaign before
Anson Marik manages to create another regiment of the
Silver Hawk Irregulars."

"Of course. Have you chosen a destination yet?"

Vedet tilted his chair back and slouched a little, looking all too comfortable. "Yes."

"And will you share it with me?"

"I'd like nothing better. However, that might not be the most prudent action at the moment."

"And why is that?"

"You know just as well as I do that it's generally wise to limit the amount of information you give to people you do not trust."

"Are you referring to Alaric Wolf or to me?"

Vedet only grinned broader.

This wasn't good. She'd thought his presence here was an indication of some reserve of respect, but it looked like she'd read it wrong. He had stayed in his office to meet her because he wanted a chance to bait her. His arrogance had clearly prospered in the past two weeks, and he thought he now had the situation on Helm completely under his control.

At this point, instilling some humility in him was not just a good idea—it was her duty. The fact that she would enjoy her duty was just a happy side effect.

"I didn't think you'd be ready to leave just yet," she said. "I thought you'd need at least three or four days, maybe a week."

"I suppose you'd like me to sit down with the Clanner and swap strategy?" He waved a hand dismissively. "That's a pipe dream. Both of us would be more than happy to go our separate ways. Even if we end up on the same planet, I don't think either of us will be too concerned about talking to the other. We'll be best off on our own."

"No, no, no, that's not what I was talking about. A good communications strategy takes time—you need to know what messages you want to send out and who to send them to. And of course, when you're working the media, it's a good idea to keep yourself available. Media people have a habit of asking questions, and the more questions you can answer, the more your wonderful thoughts and words can be disseminated throughout the Commonwealth." She layered plenty of scorn into her voice to make sure Vedet would not be able to miss it.

Vedet blinked innocently. "Communications strategy? I'm afraid I don't know what you're talking about."

Trillian walked forward, slow paces toward the window like she just wanted to take in the view. When she passed the desk, she spun lightly on her front heel and faced the duke. "Of course you don't. You haven't assigned any of your people to work on getting out the story of Alaric's actions here. You haven't prepped some of your officers on how to answer questions from the media and what to say to put you in the best light." This second item was a guess, but Trillian was fairly certain that she knew what Vedet would be up to. A small flicker of his eyes when she was speaking told her that she was right.

"I haven't done anything of the kind," he said, in a voice so flat and so different from his normal tones that anyone listening would know he was lying.

"Oh. Good," Trillian said. She took a single step closer to him. "That will save me a lot of work."

He didn't want to ask. He sat still, hands resting on his stomach, waiting for her to offer more explanation. But Trillian could see the interest in his eyes, and she knew that all she needed to do was wait.

It took a little longer than she thought it might, but after a period of uncomfortable silence, Vedet finally licked his lips and said, "Fine. I'll ask. What kind of work?"

She was above him now—he had to look up to make eye contact with her. "Monitoring the press activity surrounding the conquest of Helm," she said. "You see, I'm fairly certain that if one version of events comes out, the media, being creatures that thrive on controversy, will look around to see if the first accounts of the Battle of Helmdown are truly accurate. And I would suspect, after some routine work, they will find another account of what happened here."

"Really?" said Vedet, sitting up straighter so he'd be taller in his chair. "And I don't suppose you have an inkling about what that other account might be?"

Trillian spread her hands. "How am I to know? There

are so many people out there, telling so many stories. Who knows which ones the media will latch on to?"

"Perhaps you could guess," Vedet said, layering scorn into his own voice.

She stepped back and resumed pacing slowly as she talked, making a short trip in front of the glorious picture window. "Oh, the media are such unpredictable, resourceful beasts. Who knows what they'll turn up? But if I had to hazard a guess, I imagine they will find some people who will claim that there was no official surrender agreement with the Silver Hawk Irregulars on Helm-down. In fact, these sources might say that the surrender was being negotiated at the very same time that some Silver Hawk troops were charging Clan Wolf lines."

"I don't see how that story is at all compelling."

"Then pay attention, because it gets better. These sources might also say that no one other than a certain Lyran commander knew anything about this so-called surrender, and that since the Silver Hawks were in the act of attacking during negotiations, the surrender was worth absolutely nothing."

She was walking toward him now, getting closer with each slow step. "This turns the battle into a tale of two commanders. One of them, battle-weary and gun-shy, claims the existence of a phantom surrender simply as an excuse to stop fighting. The other, a commander who is a *fighter*, keeps going until the battle is completely won. He will not be fooled by the Silver Hawk Irregulars' ploy of pretending to negotiate surrender. He does not concern himself with talk. Instead, he moves on and decisively ends the battle." She was looming over him again, daring him to lean away from her. "It should make an interesting story, don't you think? That talker-versus-fighter image should make for some fascinating head-lines, along with a number of interesting debates throughout Lyran space."

The first crease in Vedet's forehead had appeared early in Trillian's story, and was soon joined by another, two folds a few centimeters above his nose. Then other furrows appeared on the sides, until Vedet's head appeared as rough and uneven as the rocky land north of Helmdown.

"You're insane," he said.

"Me?" Trillian put her hands on her chest, fingers splayed. It was becoming one of her favorite gestures to indicate her innocence. "*I'm* not *doing* anything. I'm simply giving you my best estimate of what kind of stories the media will find if they go looking for them."

"You want to portray Alaric bloody Wolf as a hero of the Lyran Commonwealth! As a fighter! Good hell, who do you think is the bigger threat to the Commonwealth, him or me?"

Trillian made a show of thinking. "Hmmm. You know, I'm not sure I could answer that question right now."

Vedet jumped to his feet and slammed his hands on his desk. She had to jump back to keep his head from slamming into hers. "Get out! Get out now!"

Trillian waited before she moved, making certain she did not appear rushed. "Certainly. I'm sorry our discussion has left you upset."

The next remark needed to be timed just right. She took five slow, even steps toward the door. Then stopped. Waited a brief moment. Then turned. Then spoke.

"It's a shame," she said, "how plotting against the archon can put a stain on your reputation, isn't it?"

"Out!" Vedet thundered. With her same casual stride, Trillian left.

Outside his office, her pace quickened. She felt better than she had since the battle had ended. While she hadn't done anything to win Vedet's affection for the Steiner family, she had successfully checked him. And since she didn't care much for the duke anyway, the fact that he didn't like her carried no sting whatsoever.

The streets of Helmdown were still gray, still empty, but for some reason that wasn't bothering Trillian now, and the compulsion she had been feeling for the past two weeks to get indoors and stay there had vanished.

It was liberating—she was free to go anywhere she wanted, see any part of the city.

It was a shame, then, that Helmdown did not contain any places for her to go.

And even though she felt more confident, it was probably not a good idea for a Steiner to casually go strolling around on a planet that her nation had just conquered. There were a few safe places for her, and for the time being she should stay in them.

She ran through the list of those spots. She didn't want to go back to her quarters—she'd spent enough time there. It also didn't seem to be a good idea to stay with the First Hesperus Guards, as Vedet would not want to see her again today and his subordinates weren't too friendly either. Since she had no desire to be around Clanners, that narrowed her options even more.

There was only one choice, really. So she climbed in her vehicle and went there.

"I've never seen a line give like that when it wasn't a trap. We tore through them, and *fast*. I mean, we were moving so quick we almost ran right into the Hesperus Guards. That wasn't a defensive line they had—that was a speed bump."

Jamie Kroff had a full mug of beer sitting next to her. She had ordered it about half an hour ago, taken one sip when it arrived and hadn't touched it again. Trillian had asked her about her experience on Helmdown, and Kroff had been talking ever since. As she spoke, her hands darted this way and that, trying to duplicate the movement of each 'Mech in the battle. Trace Decker sat at a small round table with the two women, smiling and not saying much.

"And they've done that sort of thing before, from what I've heard," Kroff said. "I've talked to some of the Hesperus Guards who were chasing the Silver Hawks all over Danais, and they said they love that sort of thing. They bait you into charging too hard, into overcommitting your forces. They let the first groups through, then harden their lines and all of a sudden, whoops, your fastest 'Mechs are cut off. I hear Vedet eventually told them to stop all charges—he had them slogging around the planet like the whole thing was covered in three meters of water."

"That doesn't seem very imaginative," Trillian said. She was more than ready to join in on some criticism of the duke.

But Kroff only tilted her head. "Maybe. But sometimes imagination can be overrated. You can get too caught up in your own brilliance when you'd be better off just grinding it out and wearing down the enemy."

"Good hell, Kroff, we've been serving together too long," Decker said. "I'm starting to rub off on you."

"No, you're not," Kroff said. "I said *sometimes* imagination is overrated. I didn't say imagination is not allowed—that's your line."

"Turtle and the hare," Decker said. "Besides, the only reason you need imagination is because you don't know what actual victory looks like, so you have to guess." He took a long drink, then pounded his mug to the table. "I've been there. All I have to do is remember."

Kroff smiled and lifted her mug. "To plodding our way to victory!"

Decker lifted his in response. "To dreaming up harebrained tactics so we can have them named after us in military textbooks!"

Kroff lowered her mug. "Hey, I was nice to plodding. Now you have to be nice to creativity."

Decker rolled his eyes. "Fine. Here's to taking insane risks and getting away with them!"

"Now, that I can drink to!" Kroff said. They slammed their mugs together so hard that Trillian thought they would break; then both soldiers drank deeply.

"I've always wondered how the two of you came up with your tactics," said a voice behind Trillian. "Now I know—you do it when you're drinking. Suddenly, your strategies make a whole lot more sense."

Trillian didn't need to turn around to know it was

Roderick. Running into him was the risk she took by coming to the First Steiner Strikers' camp. She couldn't avoid him forever, and at least now she could face him when she was feeling pretty good. When she finally turned, she was able to smile and have it look natural.

"Hello, Roderick."

He nodded. "Hi, Trillian. Good to see you out of the office."

"Can you join us?"

"For a minute," he said, and sat at the table with them. He waved off a server before he came to their table, then looked at Trillian.

"Have you heard from the archon?" he asked.

"Yes. She congratulates you on a well-earned victory, and says that your efforts will contribute to the safety and security of the Lyran Commonwealth for years to come."

"That's very kind," he said, then paused. "Did she have a clerk write that, or did she just copy and paste a standard form?"

Decker and Kroff both chuckled, and Trillian smiled crookedly.

"If you conquer a few more planets, I'm sure you can get a commendation with a genuine autograph from the archon," she said.

"Will it have an embossed seal?"

"Of course."

"Well, that's what it's all about, isn't it?"

Trillian could hear a slight catch in Roderick's voice, and she knew his banter had an edge to it. But he was trying to be jocular, and she was in no mood to provoke a confrontation. So she played along.

"Embossed certificates, colored ribbons and shiny medals," she said. "The substance of glory."

"I'll drink to that," Decker said, and he and Kroff both took a few more swallows.

"But no medals for Decker," Kroff said. "Unless there's an award for running around in circles while everyone else is fighting."

Decker held up an index finger. "One circle," he said. "I ran in one big circle. And I was so scary when I did it that the Silver Hawks could only watch me instead of paying attention to your dainty, ladylike charge."

"Yeah, and I'll charge my ladylike boot right up . . ."

The two company commanders jawed at each other for a while, smiling broadly and ordering more drinks the whole time. Roderick sat back in his chair and smiled, clearly enjoying the chance to just sit back and do nothing. After sitting quietly for a while, Trillian leaned over to him.

"Your people have honor," she said, "no matter what else is going on around them."

He nodded. "Thanks," he said. "That's why I worry about what they get thrown into." But he smiled a little and patted her shoulder and didn't get up to leave, so she figured this counted as progress.

19

Marik Palace
New Edinburgh, Stewart
Marik-Stewart Commonwealth
20 May 3138

The common consensus around the palace was that the new Anson Marik was an improvement. Servants brought him his food and kept his quarters orderly, secretaries took care of his personal affairs and staff disturbed him for long enough to get his signature on various items. Through all of this no one had to endure a single outburst of temper. In fact, for the most part, no one heard the captain-general say anything at all. He grunted occasionally and offered simple answers to straightforward questions, but other than that he remained silent. Often, people who were in his presence said they had the impression that the captain-general didn't know they were there.

Daggert didn't like this state of affairs one bit. The Lyran armies were preparing for invasion, and no matter what he did to help the Silver Hawk Irregulars and the Stewart militia prepare for the coming attack, it didn't feel like it was enough. He tried to think in terms of victory, not in terms of holding on as long as possible, but a scenario for victory was elusive. He did not want to say that victory was inconceivable, but since he hadn't yet conceived a path to victory, that description seemed apt.

After a week of seeing and hearing stories about the subdued, withdrawn Anson, Daggert decided it was time to see what could be done to bring the captain-general back to life. He had to check five different rooms before he found Pavel Krist sipping a mug of tea in the private palace library. The room held few books—most of the walls were covered with original art, including a photo from the 2-D revival of the 3080s that Daggert liked. It was a picture of a street market, a lively collection of temporary booths and tents along New Edinburgh's Edwards Street. The street had been completely redeveloped after the Jihad and was now a series of faceless apartment buildings that was far quieter and allegedly safer than the open-air market. But whenever Daggert looked at the picture, he found himself wishing the market was still there, and that he could be anonymous enough to walk freely in it.

Most of the library's holdings could be accessed via a series of terminals spread around the room, which connected to a tremendous bank of servers in an underground bunker. The terminals were built into couches and overstuffed chairs, and the room was free of the bold, harsh lines prevalent in much of the rest of the palace. And, since most members of the staff had tasks other than reading to occupy their time, the room was usually empty—except for a few researchers, who were easily ignored.

Krist did not look at Daggert when he walked into the library. He didn't even look at Daggert when he sat down next to him, or gently cleared his throat. Daggert didn't bother to get irritated, as this sort of treatment had been consistent since he had first submitted his resignation. No one was supposed to know about that besides Daggert and Anson, but information had a way of getting out.

"Pavel," he said.

Krist looked up, his wide-set eyes crinkling in surprise. "Cole! I'm sorry, I had no idea you were here. I'm afraid I was a little wrapped up in my work."

Pavel Krist could listen to three conversations simultaneously and not miss a word of any of them, but again, Daggert decided not to make an issue of it. If being on Anson Marik's staff taught you anything, it was to not rise to every bit of provocation.

"I was wondering if I could have a moment of your time," Daggert said.

"Of course," Krist said, though his eyes returned to his terminal screen.

"I'm concerned about the captain-general."

"Really? Why?"

"Hasn't he seemed different to you?"

Krist touched his screen briefly, and Daggert could see he was just turning a page, not closing anything.

"He's seemed unusually focused," Krist said. "Is that what you mean?"

"Unusually focused?" Daggert said. "Is that what you call it?"

"Of course. What do you call it?"

"Clinically depressed."

"Oh, no no no," Krist said, shaking his head. "Not at all. Listen, Cole, you know as well as I do that there are a lot of trivialities that take up a good amount of any ruler's time. I believe all you are seeing is that the captain-general has focused on the existing emergency to an extent that the attention he might give to other, less important matters has diminished. That's all."

"But, Pavel, I'm the one trying to address this crisis! He should at least talk to me!"

"With all due respect, Cole, we are *all* focused on the crisis. Your tactical knowledge is vital, but you are hardly the only person dealing with the problem."

Daggert sighed quietly. It was the nature of so many conversations with people in politics—conversations all too quickly shifted to matters of credit and blame. But power tended to be held by the people who want it, and they knew the mechanics of getting and keeping it. They couldn't change their nature just because Daggert wanted them to, so he had to put up with their quirks—while remembering that some of those quirks were his quirks too.

"Of course. I know it's consumed us all. I suppose that's why I'm worried about the captain-general. We're all doing everything we can to head off the coming crisis, and he seems rather . . . inert."

"It's nothing for you to be concerned about," Krist said. "Think of it as the calm before the storm. Before you know it, the captain-general will erupt into a positive riot of activity."

"I hope you're right."

Krist smiled reassuringly, but he still wasn't looking at Daggert. "I am. If you knew Anson Marik as well as I did, you would understand."

And with that small poke at Daggert, the conversation was over.

After Daggert left the library, his day became a blur. He was walking to this place, talking to that person, looking at one terminal screen and then another, analyzing updated estimates of the strength of the Lyran and Clan Wolf forces, reading through the latest intelligence on the battle tactics of the commanders and their likely approaches to Stewart, conferring with multiple generals and often speaking authoritatively on topics even though he didn't feel like he had a grasp on anything that was going on.

He wasn't sure how he found himself back in Anson Marik's presence. His conversations with Anson had become as frequent as they were one-sided—Daggert would find himself walking briskly into the captain-general's office, sharing a bit of information, waiting for a response, getting none, then leaving, wondering why he had bothered to come. That had happened somewhere between ten and twenty times over the last week.

And here he was again. Anson still sat motionless behind his desk, staring at nothing. His jowls hung heavy, pulling his entire head down with their weight. Daggert could not immediately recall what he was supposed to say while he was there, but it must have been important or he would not have bothered to come. He looked at his noteputer to jog his memory.

Oh.

He couldn't start with that piece of information. The first thing he saw on his noteputer was the type of news that, in ancient Terran days, tended to get a messenger's head separated from his shoulders, no matter how uninterested a ruler appeared. He had to build up to that, find some sort of cushion, *any* cushion.

No other items appeared on his noteputer. So he quickly reviewed the events of the day to this point and threw out something he hoped would seem interesting.

"The supply JumpShip from Keystone is preparing to leave the Bedeque system," he said. "We anticipate its arrival in about a week. It does not have all of the supplies we requested, of course, but every bit helps, and its landing will help shore up our defenses. Since we have not detected any invaders arriving in-system, the supply ship should arrive well before they do."

Unsurprisingly, Anson said nothing. He continued to stare into empty space. Daggert, as had become his habit, glanced down at the captain-general's chest to make sure he was still breathing. He detected a gradual rise and fall, so he continued with his briefing.

"Other news from rimward territories is not as good," he said, then took a deep breath. "We have intercepted a message from the planetary government of Ariel. They have asked Jessica Marik to help them defend their planet from possible harm."

He waited. No reaction. His first instinct was to relax, since the expected explosion didn't erupt from Anson, but then he immediately became even more tense. This was the type of news that should send even a mild-mannered ruler into a rage. If Anson could not bring himself to react to it, something was truly wrong.

He went ahead with the rest of the news from Ariel. "We have not received any declarations—or any communications at all—from the Ariel government, and there is no record that they have taken an official position. However, it is worth noting that, in their message, they refer to Jessica as 'Captain-General Jessica Marik.' "

He stood silent again. Anson did not so much as blink.

"That's all I have for the moment. You can always summon me if I am needed." He turned and took three steps toward the door.

"Say that last part again."

Daggert stopped in his tracks. The voice rumbled like Anson's, but with a creak, either from age or from disuse. He slowly turned. Anson looked like he had not moved, but then Daggert looked closely and saw his eyes had shifted a bit to the left. Instead of looking at nothing, Anson Marik was gazing squarely at him.

"What was that, my lord?"

"Say that last part again," Anson repeated.

"I said that that is all I have for the moment, and you can always—"

"No. Not that. The part before it."

Daggert reflexively took a step backward. "In their message, the leaders of Ariel call Jessica 'Captain-General Jessica Marik.' "

For a moment, Daggert thought he had lost the captain-general again. There was no movement, no more words. He stared at Anson, waiting for a sign of life, but he didn't see anything.

Then there was a crack, sharp and loud. Daggert jumped backward, shielding his head with his arms. But nothing hit him. He lowered his arms and looked around to see what had happened.

A strip of Anson's desk, a piece of wood about a meter long, had snapped off in Anson's hand. It left a gaping wound in the desk near Anson's stomach. The captain-general was still for a moment longer; then he abruptly pushed himself backward, his chair rolling quickly and hitting the wall behind him. As it did, Anson lowered the piece of wood he was holding to his knee and snapped it in half with another loud crack. His chair bucked with the impact against the wall, and when it settled back on the floor Anson leaned forward, then stood. He pulled himself to his full height, raised the pieces of the desk he held in his hands above his head and threw both of them across the room. The one from his right hand passed within a half meter of Daggert's head, whistling quickly, then slamming into the opposite wall. One of the pieces hit a screen that showed a rotating series of images, and the screen shattered. The piece of the desk thudded to the floor as glass fragments showered on top of it.

"Bloody *hell*!" Anson yelled, his voice shaking off rust like machine gears that had been long idle. "Goddamn that woman and her shit-brained family and her bloody advisers and her worthless, piss-brained people! I would cut out her eyes and fill her skull with maggots if she was here! She is a blight, a boil, a festering *pustule* on the Marik name! Damn her and her worthless children straight to the hottest hell there is!"

"It's good to have you—" Daggert started to say, but Anson Marik was not done.

"Children!" he said. "Stupid bloody children playing with toys! Playing stupid goddamned bloody games! What are they worth? What the hell are they worth? They are useless as rulers, useless as human beings! Rip off their limbs, grind their goddamned bodies into paste and feed them to pigs, because that's all they're good for! What are they? What in holy hell *are* they? Infants! They're all infants! Infants crying for their toys, infants complaining if they don't have their bloody way! That's how this place is run, that's how every bloody place everywhere is run! By infants! There are millions, there are billions of bloody people out there, and they're nothing to them! They are grist for the mill! They are bloody pavement stones for these arrogant pieces of shit to walk on! They pave the Inner Sphere with the bodies of these people, then call themselves great. What have they done?

They kill and steal, they play their games and they call themselves noble! They call themselves heroes! And they talk to their people, and they tell those idiots, those sheep, that they're doing it all for them! They make the goddamned fools believe it! And they rejoice, the idiots and the morons and the bloody goddamned infants they call their leaders, they rejoice because some of them get to kill, and some of them get to die, and all so they can put a piece-of-shit *name* on a piece-of-shit *planet*! And that's what they do, playing their games, working on their reasons, always telling themselves we need to do this, we need to do this. Always creating their need, always finding an excuse, always making like they're bloody sorry to be at war when the one thing, the only thing these rotten pus-brained dirtbags fear is peace. They hate it! How do you give out medals in peace? How do you prove who warriors are in peace? We can't have peace—we don't have any bloody idea what it's worth! We don't know how to survive it. We only know how to kill, we only know how to tell other people to die. We'll tell ourselves to die if we need to, because that's what we do. Because we're bloody children. Because we have never, ever discovered anything to do besides fight over our goddamned toys. To make the Inner Sphere a gigantic damned toy box, and pull planets back and forth between us. We think it's all a game, we think we can bloody win! Kill enough people, and you win! But those people want to kill you, and they want to win too, and everyone wants to kill everyone else, and that's the way it's been for centuries and that's the way it is now and that's the way it will always be because we have no goddamned idea how to do anything else. We act like we are the cream of the goddamned crop, the best people there are, the only people with the vision to lead the idiots under us. What vision do we have? We have visions of death. We have visions of killing, of killing, of killing, of killing enough to get what we want. That doesn't make us *noble*. That doesn't make us *brave*. It makes us cowering goddamned bloody *animals*!"

Daggert didn't realize his mouth was hanging open until midway through Anson's tirade, and even when he noticed it he didn't get around to closing it for a few moments. Anson's anger built like a whirlwind, his voice echoing and swirling around the room and gaining power with each word. He roared in a way Daggert had never heard, even though he thought he had encountered every bellow the captain-general had in him. But there was something in Anson's voice that Daggert had never heard before, and he didn't place it until just before the captain-general finished speaking. It was something very like grief.

Daggert didn't speak for a few moments after Anson fell silent. He waited for the room to be silent again, waited for some of the ringing in his ears to fade. When he spoke, he spoke quietly, in a conscious effort to balance the volume of Anson's rage.

"You are unfair," he said. "Wars in the Inner Sphere have been fought for every reason there is, the noble and the ignoble. There are leaders of greatness, and leaders of weakness. It is not all as you say it is."

When Anson replied, his voice was petulant. "It seems that way to me."

A reply jumped to Daggert's lips, but his sense of decorum stopped it. Then he remembered that he wanted to quit anyway. He had more freedom to speak than anyone under Anson Marik ever had. And freedom was quite useless if it was never employed.

"The reason it seems that way to you," Daggert said, "is that is all you have ever been. You have always ruled as a child, and so you can't understand that other people have ruled in other ways. Most of your anger, most of your words, are directed at yourself."

Anson was silent for a long while. When he finally spoke, it was with a weight of authority.

"Are you trying to get yourself fired or executed?"

Daggert smiled wanly, in spite of himself, in spite of everything. "Fired, preferably. But firing me or killing me won't change anything either of us said. You know why you said it. And you know what you were thinking when you did."

Anson was quiet again. He wiped his hand across his forehead, and left a trickle of blood smeared there. He had damaged his hands in tearing apart his desk.

"I can only rule the way I've ruled," he said. "I only know what I know. Fight for my name. When we are hit, hit back. Keep your enemies in fear. That's all."

"That's not enough."

Anson laughed, a short, bitter, joyless sound. "Nothing is going to be enough. You know it as well as I do. We can make all the preparations in the world, and it's not going to be enough."

"We don't know that," Daggert said, and he tried to sound confident.

"Listen, Daggert, if I need someone to blow smoke up my ass, I'll call in Krist. I kept you on because you always give it to me straight, and I figured you'd be even more blunt when you didn't have to pretend you liked me. Don't act like the impossible is possible. Don't stand there and lie to me."

And then, suddenly, in a burst of light that no one else could see, Daggert understood. He understood everything. He knew why he was there. He knew why he hadn't been allowed to resign, and the reasons had nothing to do with Anson Marik. There was something else directing his path—fate, destiny, God, whatever—and Daggert finally understood what it was up to. He knew what he had to do, and he knew exactly what he had to say to Anson Marik.

He looked the captain-general square in the eye, and he saw a little surprise flash on Anson's face. He had likely never seen such intensity from his tactical adviser before.

"We can win this battle."

Anson was not easily swayed. "You're full of shit," he replied.

"No. I'm not. We can win. It will not be the victory you might expect, or the victory you want. But you have a chance. A new opportunity. You can grab a victory no one will be expecting you to grab."

"I have no idea what the hell you're talking about."

No, I wouldn't expect you to, Daggert thought. Aloud, he said. "Give me some time. I'll explain it to you as soon as I understand it myself."

"Fine. Do whatever you want," Anson said. "If you think we can win, I'll listen."

"Thank you, my lord," he said. Then he left.

He would have to hurry. There wouldn't be much time to sleep or eat. The education of Anson Marik had begun. And Daggert only had a week or two to finish it.

20

It had been at least four days since a unit commander had last told Trillian, "We'll be leaving in a day. Maybe two." A seemingly unending series of supplies had been packed into DropShips, 'Mechs had been repaired and rerepaired and then polished a few times, and the soldiers on the ground had convinced themselves, as soldiers tend to do, that the terror and chaos of the battlefield were somehow preferable to the interminable waiting.

There was no question what the next destination would be. Not since word had gone out that Anson Marik had bought his way onto Stewart, and that he was trying to rally his troops around him. The leader of the Marik-Stewart Commonwealth was waiting for them a single jump away—where else should they go?

All three commanders now knew they were going to take their respective armies to Stewart. There was no mystery. But still, no one left.

Trillian was as tired of sitting around as any of the grunts. The political situation on the planet was stable.

It seemed certain that the forces would attack Marik troops before they attacked each other, and that was about as good as things were going to get. If they got off this bleak gray rock and did some fighting, there would be winners and losers and a whole new political situation for her to play with. She had spent enough time waiting for the movement to happen; the time had come to push things forward. So she started with the one commander she trusted.

"Why are you still here?" she asked.

Roderick looked around her small, dingy office. He sat in a plain wooden chair, slouching like it was actually comfortable. "Because you asked me to come here."

"No, no, no, not here, *here*." She pointed out her window, which provided little more than a view of a dingy brick wall of a neighboring building. "On Helm."

"Because no one else has left yet."

"So?"

Roderick twisted his chair lightly from side to side. "It doesn't make much sense for us to go there alone. Why face the Silver Hawks and whoever else they've lined up by ourselves, when we could do it with two other perfectly capable armies?"

"That makes sense. Have you asked Vedet and Alaric when they're leaving?"

"Yes."

"And what did they say?"

"They wouldn't give me any specific information."

"Why the hell not?"

Roderick shrugged. "I don't know. It might be an ego thing. Each commander wants to be the one to order the charge forward, and if they adopt someone else's departure date, that will make it seem like they're following someone else's plan."

"That's ridiculous."

"And also highly probable."

Trillian dropped her head, letting her forehead rest in her hands. "Is this the way grown-ups fight wars?"

"Grown-ups avoid wars," he said. "But when they're forced to fight them, the truth is, yes, it often ends up this way. Occupational hazard, I guess."

"Great. All right, for the record—if I could get one or both of the others to settle on a date to leave, you would be able to somehow set aside your ego and leave on the date they chose, right?"

"In a heartbeat."

"And I can quote you on that?"

"Feel free."

"Okay. Would you like to come with me to talk to the others?"

Roderick smiled and slouched a little more. "Not on your life. But you can tell them I said hi."

She smiled wanly. "Great. Okay, you can go."

He stood, and a little of his nonchalant demeanor went away. "I know you're in a vise here, Trill. I know you've been put right in the middle. Honestly, if I thought there was anything I could do to help, I would."

"Yeah, yeah," Trillian said. "You're the nice one. Got it."

"Just so long as that's noted," he said. "Good luck."

She watched him go, then frowned at dust dancing in the faded sunlight pushing its way through the small, thick window to her right. This all felt like déjà vu to Trillian—cycling between the three camps, trying to track down each commander to convince him it was time to move. Vedet and Alaric had a deep and understandable mistrust of each other, and getting them to collaborate, to work together and trust each other, was a task that seemed impossible at best. . . .

She jumped to her feet. "Good *hell*!" she said out loud. How could she be so dense? Why had it taken her this long to figure it out?

She stormed out of her office, cursing herself as she walked. It was so obvious, now that she understood it.

She'd been trying to get Vedet and Alaric to trust each other, but that wasn't her job. Her job was to get them moving while hopefully keeping them from killing each other. That was it. And in diplomatic work, it was always better to work with the tools you had in front of you than to try to forge new ones.

She had the two men's mistrust. It was beautiful in its consistency and completeness. And she had failed entirely to use it.

She kept cursing at herself as she made her way to the Clan Wolf camp, but at least she knew the campaign would continue before the week was out.

A good intelligence officer gets his operatives to give him the information he wants. A great intelligence officer can do the same thing without the operatives ever knowing who they were working for or just what they were doing.

Trillian was not an intelligence officer, but she'd spent enough time in the information arena to know some of the tricks. It helped that she wasn't gathering information—she was planting.

The air smelled cleaner, fresher to her. She walked with a new spring in her step. Being freed from the burden of making people like you or trust you was liberating; being disliked was so much easier.

She looked for Clanners with the Alpha Trinary insignia on their uniforms. She didn't want to use Star Captain Xeno for this particular task—she wouldn't say they trusted each other, but her relationship with him was less hostile than with any other member of Clan Wolf. It wouldn't do to have that relationship destroyed too quickly.

So she looked at some of his subordinates. She didn't need to know their names; she just needed them to walk slow enough to let her talk at them.

She caught up with the first one she saw, a woman whose chin was level with Trillian's forehead. Trillian didn't bother with a wave or a smile or small talk. She plunged ahead as if they knew each other and had already been talking for a while.

"Securing New Edinburgh will be a bitch compared to this, right?"

"We are not there yet." The voice was flat, dismissive, trying to end the conversation before it started.

"But it's good to plan ahead, right? I mean, *quiaff*?" The Clanner responded with a cold glare, and Trillian felt the familiar thrill of successfully being underestimated.

"The thing is, it's going to be a question of supplies as much as anything. You invade a city, you tend to break it pretty good. If you want the people you just conquered to relax a little, to feel, you know, positive toward you, then you need to fix what you broke, and hopefully fix it right. That's not the kind of supplies we normally have, right? Fighting supplies are different than fixing supplies."

The Clanner was walking faster, and Trillian was almost jogging to keep up.

"I still do not have a reason to be interested in what you are saying," the Clanner said.

"Well, it's a matter of timing, isn't it? Look, if you go from the start and say you're leaving in two days, then estimate the initial invasion will take . . ."

She saw the expression on the Clanner's face and knew the fight was almost over. "I'm sorry," Trillian said. "Did I say something I shouldn't?"

"The timing of our departure has not been decided yet," the Clanner said.

Trillian kept her face blank and blinked a few times. "Oh, right, right, you probably haven't heard. Well, information gets out slowly sometimes. But look, assume I know what I'm talking about. Now . . ."

The conversation didn't last much longer. The Clanner had clearly become distracted, and she hadn't been that interested in talking to Trillian in the first place. Trillian let her walk away, and turned her sights on another member of Alpha Trinary.

Spreading rumors would be a lot easier if the Clans liked gossip, she thought.

She was ignored many times, dismissed almost as many, but eventually she—and Klaus, who was also wandering through the Wolf camp—planted their seed in enough Clan minds to fulfill their purpose. People would be talking now, and some of them would be convinced that they knew what they were talking about. Now all she had to do was make sure someone was listening.

She had styled herself in what she always thought of as her executive domanitrix look—shiny leather boots, high-collared, uniform-like blue blouse and hair slicked back and pulled tight. She always wanted to carry a riding crop when she dressed like this, but she thought that would be over the top.

The look suited her purposes perfectly—the duke would think she was trying to order him around, but would still assume she was a lightweight and would be dismissive. His arrogance would play right into her hands.

When she walked into his office, his face showed only dismay. Which was just fine. She walked toward his desk and stood across from him.

"Duke Vedet, I'm here in an official capacity as a representative of the archon. It is time to move to Stewart, and she requests that you tell her exactly when you plan to depart."

"I haven't decided the date of our departure yet," Vedet said primly.

"Right. And the archon's telling you to do it. *Now*."

Vedet clearly did not like looking up at her, so he stood as well and moved from behind the desk, walking closer to Trillian. "The archon has been in power long enough to know that when she doesn't have the power to enforce an order, it's usually not going to be followed."

Trillian spoke harshly, trying to punch each individual word out of her mouth. "So you will not choose a date?"

"Not one that you'll know, no."

Trillian spent a moment putting on a show of fuming. Then she slowly smiled.

"You realize that will put you on the planet behind Alaric Wolf's forces," she said.

Vedet put his hands on his hips and looked briefly like

a military statue of himself. "I know nothing of the kind. Alaric Wolf has not shown any indication of leaving."

"If that's what you think, you're behind the news. You might want to check your intelligence more frequently."

"Really?"

"I assume you've developed sources within the Wolf camp."

Vedet frowned, apparently trying to take his measure of Trillian. "Why should I bother developing sources in my ally's camp?"

Trillian turned her back to him, walking toward the bookcase behind her, pretending to look at the titles some Helm bureaucrat had left behind. Her steps were slow and casual. "You're right," she said briskly. "You shouldn't. You definitely shouldn't find out if they have heard any interesting chatter around camp." She turned back toward him, snapping her heels together as she did so. "Thank you for your time."

She left feeling quite content.

Later that night in her quarters, Trillian had Klaus crack open a bottle of wine and pour a couple of glasses. If everything went as planned, she would never go back to her dingy office again, and in a week it would be used by some greasy Helmdown bookie.

Her quarters were plain, without so much as a single picture on the wall, but they were orderly since she had barely used them. She sat with Klaus by a metal table with a white tile top. The wine, which Klaus had rooted out of a Helmdown wine cellar at some point in the past two weeks, was probably more expensive than all the furniture in her living space combined.

"To mistrust," she said, "and may I never forget its value again."

"Amen," Klaus said, and they clinked glasses.

The wine was excellent, full and fruity, with a nice hint of black currant. She took a sip small enough that a single glass could last a full week if she kept herself under control.

They talked. They didn't talk business, or politics, or war. They talked about wine, and holovids, and the type of things that people talk about when they're living normal lives. It was enjoyable, made even more so because Trillian knew exactly what was going on in the Lyran and Clan Wolf camps, and it was what she wanted to happen.

It didn't take long. She and Klaus had about an hour before both of their comms beeped with message after message after message. They all had different words, but they said the same thing.

All three armies would be set to leave Helm in two days.

21

Marik Palace
New Edinburgh, Stewart
Marik-Stewart Commonwealth
22 May 3138

The world had changed. That much was clear. Anson was surrounded by familiar people, with all the familiar trappings he had brought with him to Stewart. He'd wanted people, including himself, to get to work right away without wasting time on making the place feel like theirs. So it all should have been the same. But it wasn't.

He didn't spend a lot of time trying to decide how it was different. Maybe the air was dirtier, maybe the cleaning staff had been less than diligent, or maybe his eyes were just failing. It didn't matter. Things looked different, but he could adjust. He could function.

The one place where he still didn't feel comfortable was his office. Every time he sat behind the massive gray desk, he could feel inertia in the air. It only made sense—he'd spent almost all of one week sitting there doing nothing, and that atmosphere did not vanish easily. He felt as if he aged twenty years the minute he set foot in that room. So he had spent a lot of time wandering the palace, looking for a room that suited him better.

He knew where not to go. His staff had their section,

the serving staff had their section, and the large group of people who were continuously busy on tasks Anson did not know or care about had their section. He didn't want to be too near any of these people, mainly because he was not in a mood to be easily found.

So he traveled back corridors and dim hallways. There were entire sections of the palace that had been forgotten, parts that had been hastily built decades ago when Stewart had been an important planet in the Free Worlds League and the demands of the nation required more staff, more space. That space had stopped being used when the League crumbled and the Marik-Stewart Commonwealth constricted into a nation that didn't need a seemingly infinite bureaucracy. Some of these rooms were crammed behind, between and beneath existing structures, and they were usually simple spaces, plaster walls and gray carpet in uniformly rectangular rooms. Most of them didn't have windows.

They were quiet, though. Anson was certain his security detail would have a fit if they knew he was wandering around in unmonitored areas. They were under firm instructions to leave him the hell alone when he was in the palace, and they only agreed to his demands because they could post guards in every known corridor. But they apparently didn't know about these hallways, or didn't think anyone, particularly Anson, would bother with these areas. But here he was, the captain-general of the Marik-Stewart Commonwealth, walking through dim passages without a guard in sight. It made him love this part of the palace.

Most of the rooms weren't usable, though. They had been stripped of furniture, and Anson couldn't even be sure that electricity was still flowing to them. He didn't envy the drones who had been stuck down here when these rooms had been in use.

Even though the rooms were empty and generally unpleasant, the walks did Anson good. He hadn't liked what Daggert had come up with at first—his plan for victory did not fulfill any definition of the word Anson was willing to acknowledge. But the time he spent alone gave him time to reconsider. That didn't mean he liked the plan, but at least he had started to understand what the hell Daggert had been talking about when he first outlined it.

The second day he walked through the abandoned hallways, Anson found something besides empty offices. The palace had not only hosted many more bureaucrats in the past; it also provided space for many diplomatic visitors. There were still plenty of empty rooms in the main section of the palace, waiting for foreign dignitaries, but Anson found a group of rooms in one section of the basement that had been housing for second-tier diplomatic guests. They were close enough to the surface that a line of windows near the ceiling let in some natural light, and there was one room in particular that caught Anson's fancy. It had obviously been designed with Draconis Combine fashions in mind, possibly to make emissaries from that nation feel comfortable. It had a low table and several long benches around the walls covered with silk pillows. The benches didn't interest Anson much, but the table was the perfect height. With a few pillows thrown on top of it, it made a perfect ottoman for an armchair that he dragged in from a nearby room. With a comfortable place to sit, warm, even light from paper lanterns and holoart on the walls showing craggy mountains and high, narrow waterfalls, Anson was comfortable.

It was with great regret that he told key members of his staff about his new hideaway, but he knew that simply disappearing for long stretches of time was not an option. Krist and a few other senior staff members knew where to find him, which meant his daily briefings continued.

Cole Daggert, for one, barely seemed to notice the new surroundings. He was there now; he had just walked into Anson's new room, standing stiff and firm, looking Anson directly in the face, just like he did in any other room. Anson briefly wondered if Daggert was ever comfortable anywhere.

Maybe he would have been comfortable if I had let him resign, he thought, and laughed harshly to himself.

"What do you want?" he said, with more spite than he felt. He had been feeling oddly calm since his outburst of two days ago, but he had an established pattern of how he communicated with his staff and he didn't have the energy to change it.

"There is a message from Lester Cameron-Jones I thought you'd be interested in."

Anson rolled his eyes. He couldn't think of anything the old man of the Regulan Fiefs would have to say that he'd find interesting. "All right, go ahead."

"In the interest of countering other powers that are gathering in the area, he has a proposal for you—he thinks it might be wise for you to make him your heir."

Anson took his feet off the table and leaned forward. "He thinks *what*?"

"That he should be your heir."

Anson felt a rumble deep in his chest. He didn't have to force it—it came out fast and smooth, all on its own. But he was surprised when he opened his mouth and heard a laugh, not a roar.

He laughed. For a solid minute he laughed. Daggert stood, spine straight, while Anson Marik doubled over in laughter. When Anson composed himself enough to look at his tactical adviser, he thought he saw a slight smile playing on the corner of his lips.

"Lester wants to be my heir, does he? Good hell, he's finally gone delusional. Heir to what? What does he think I'll be leaving behind me when I'm gone?"

Daggert looked at his noteputer. "He's not specific about that," he said dryly.

"All right, send him a reply. Tell him no, for two reasons. First, there's a damn good chance I'm not going to be leaving much behind me when I go. Second, whatever I have to pass on sure as hell is not going to him. And that's all."

"Yes, sir."

"Anything else?"

"Yes. Force Commander Cameran-Witherspoon is ready to talk. Where would you like to meet him?"

"That's today?"

"Yes, my lord. We agreed it should happen as soon as possible."

Anson stood. Suddenly, the room seemed much less inviting and comfortable. He took a few steps, then stopped in front of a holoimage of a mountain peak poking through a thick layer of clouds. The image was sharp and crisp, and Anson could almost feel the cold winds that carved the stone streaming out of the picture. He opened his mouth, but he couldn't summon the words for what he wanted to say, so he closed it.

"Sir?" Daggert said. "Is something wrong?"

"No." He turned to Daggert and pulled himself to his full height, arms folded across his chest. "Nothing at all."

"Should I bring him here?"

"Yes. That will be fine. Go get him."

"Thank you, my lord." Daggert bowed quickly and walked out of the room.

Anson remained standing for a while after he left. He knew what he wanted to do with Force Commander Cameran-Witherspoon. He wanted to yell, to put the fear of God and Marik into him. He'd make him fight with everything he had because he'd be scared of what Anson would do if he didn't. That was the way Anson worked. That was what he was comfortable doing.

But that wasn't going to work anymore. He and Daggert had talked, they had agreed on a plan, and if it was going to work he had to operate in a new way. Whether he felt like learning new tricks or not.

He had a few more minutes before Cameran-Witherspoon arrived. He tried to remember how Daggert had explained it. He tried to believe that it made sense, and that it would be worth the effort.

Daggert led Ian Cameran-Witherspoon through the disused corridors of the Marik palace. If he was curious about the path they were following, he gave no indication. Cameran-Witherspoon was tall and matched Daggert's stride with ease as they approached Anson's new retreat.

Daggert wondered if Anson would still be standing in the same spot where he had left him. He found himself looking repeatedly at Cameran-Witherspoon as they approached Anson's room, trying to gauge his mood. He hoped the force commander would be patient with Anson, as he was not sure how well Anson would be able to make the intended point—or if he would just give up and fall back into old habits.

He could feel his heart beating as he opened the door to Anson's room. He probably shouldn't be nervous—in one sense, this was a meeting mostly for morale, a conversation that would be longer on rhetoric than on specifics.

In another sense, though, this meeting carried perhaps their only hope of ultimate success.

Anson was still on his feet, but he was no longer staring at the picture on the wall. He was instead near one of the high windows, the bottom of which was at the level of his chin. He was looking up and out the window, likely seeing nothing more than the black exterior walls of the palace. But he was staring at it like it was a great work of art.

Though, come to think of it, Daggert could never remember Anson Marik ever showing any interest in art.

"Captain-General Marik," Daggert said. "Force Commander Cameran-Witherspoon is here."

Anson turned. His face was flushed, his brow creased, the way he generally looked when he was preparing to deliver a shout that would tear his lungs in half. He was breathing heavily, practically panting, like he had just climbed a thousand stairs.

"Force Commander Cameran-Witherspoon," he said. "Who do you serve?"

Cameran-Witherspoon looked calm but curious, his blond curls looking tousled as always. He looked quickly at Daggert with a raised eyebrow. Daggert tilted his head toward Anson, indicating that Cameran-Witherspoon should just answer the question.

"I serve you, Captain-General," Cameran-Witherspoon said.

"No, you don't," Anson said.

Cameran-Witherspoon looked at Daggert again, then at Anson. "Are you questioning my loyalty?" he said. Daggert noted the lack of an honorific—Cameran-Witherspoon was not one to sweet-talk his way through a conflict.

"No," Anson said. "I'm telling you if you think you're loyal to me, you're wrong. You shouldn't be."

"Then who should I be loyal to?"

"You command the Silver Hawk Irregulars. You're supposed to defend the Silver Hawk Coalition. You're loyal to them, first and foremost."

Cameran-Witherspoon's mouth became a diagonal line. "Then what the hell am I doing on Stewart?"

Anson's face reddened, he took a deep breath—then he smiled. "Right. Good point. You're here because the biggest threat to the Silver Hawk people is coming here. It doesn't matter if this was never a Silver Hawk planet. You want to defend them, and the fight is here. That's what you're doing here."

Cameran-Witherspoon didn't respond, and there was an uncomfortable silence. Anson looked at Cameran-Witherspoon, Daggert looked at Anson, and Cameran-Witherspoon kept looking back and forth between the two of them, apparently trying to figure out what he was doing there.

Finally he spoke. "What am I doing here?"

"You're getting your priorities straight," Anson said. "You serve the people of the Silver Hawk Coalition first. Them before anyone. You need to understand that."

"Fine. I understand it."

Anson frowned and rubbed his forehead. "I'm not sure that you do."

"What exactly do you want from me?" Cameran-Witherspoon said. "Bring in someone from one of the

Silver Hawk planets and I'll bow down in front of them if you'd like. Would that help?"

"Don't screw around with me!" Anson barked.

"I'm just not sure what you're trying to tell me."

"How much more plain can I make it?" Anson started to take a step forward, then stopped, legs and hands both trembling. "Your first duty is to your people. Your *people*. Not me. Not any other politician. Your goddamned *people*."

"All right, fine," Cameran-Witherspoon said. "I serve the people. So if some of my people fall to the Elsies, or the Wolves, does that mean I'm Lyran? Or a Clanner?"

This time Anson couldn't stop himself from stepping forward, two quick strides. But he managed to stop short of bowling into the force commander. "Damn it, Cameran-Witherspoon, are you listening to what I'm saying, or are you just dumb? Your *people*. You serve your *people*. Do you think it's best for your people to become Lyrans? Or, God help them, Clanners?"

"No."

"Then don't become a thrice-damned Clanner! You are a Silver Hawk. *Be* a Silver Hawk!"

Daggert looked at Cameran-Witherspoon. It didn't appear that he understood what was going on any better, but he had decided not to fight it anymore. "Yes, my lord. I will."

"That's it, then. We're done." Anson stepped back and returned his gaze to the window.

Cameran-Witherspoon walked out quickly, and Daggert scurried to keep up with him. It wouldn't do to have him lost in these corridors.

"What the hell was that?" Cameran-Witherspoon said, and Daggert wasn't sure if the force commander was talking to him or himself. "What in the hell was that about?"

"It was something the captain-general felt needed to be said," Daggert replied.

"Why? Is he dying or something?"

"Not that I'm aware."

"Then what's going on?"

"The defense of the realm."

"Crap, you two must be sniffing the same fumes. Neither of you is making much sense. Look, I'm going to do what I do. The Lyrans and the Wolves are going to come here, and I'm going to try to kick their asses. I don't know what Anson expects me to do."

"Then think it over," Daggert said. "Maybe you'll come up with something."

Cameran-Witherspoon rolled his eyes. "Right. Listen, let's get you two a mountain to sit on and you can be as oracular as you please. Until then, though, as long as you're here around us mortals, it would be nice if you could make some sense."

"Sorry to let you down."

"Now, *that* I understand," Cameran-Witherspoon said.

Daggert was worried the meeting, brief as it was, had been a total loss. But then Cameran-Witherspoon spoke again and showed he was already turning some of the meeting over in his mind.

"And another thing," he said. "What was all that 'serve the people' bullshit? Since when has Anson Marik put the people at the top of anything? Don't get me wrong, I love the Silver Hawk Irregulars, and I'll forever be in his debt for giving them to me, but I don't think you'll ever find anyone who says that Anson's top priority is anything besides himself. Since when is he a man of the people?"

"I don't think you need to worry about that. Just worry about what he said, not what he's done in the past."

"Yeah. I'm sure he'd like that."

The rest of the walk was made in silence.

22

The word came. It filtered down quickly, because it needed to. Aero units stationed in the city and surrounding towns, impatient MechWarriors waiting in scattered hangars, artillery units in well-stocked bunkers and infantry units tired of purposeless marches through the city all got the news, and they received it with a combination of anticipation, excitement and stomach-grinding dread.

The combined Lyran/Wolf forces would arrive 4 June. Give or take a day. Drill time was over.

There had been some migrations from New Edinburgh, but by and large life in the city had continued approximately as normal. Until now. Suddenly, departing DropShips were full of people who had the means and the desire to depart. Businesses started shifting activities off-world where possible, and they didn't lack for volunteers to scout new locations. In a matter of days, downtown became much quieter, and the people who remained grew increasingly edgy.

On the plus side, Daggert thought, traffic in the city was getting much more manageable.

Which was good, because Daggert had an order sitting in front of him, waiting for Anson Marik's signature, that would impose military control over just about every aspect of the city, including traffic. The fewer cars they had to direct, the easier their task would be.

Daggert hadn't slept much since he'd learned about the departure of the invading host, and it felt like he'd spent the great majority of his waking hours staring at a map of the city and the land around it. The preparations he'd made to this point were quite detailed, but he could always do more. He *had* to do more.

He focused on the perimeter. He didn't want the Lyrans and Wolves to beat his own forces into the city, and it would be best if they stayed out altogether. Street fighting might keep the defenders of Stewart from being overwhelmed, but it could also damage the core of New Edinburgh beyond feasible repair, and the Commonwealth could not afford to lose such a major economic center.

Although in the end, if all Daggert had to worry about after this battle was the economic fallout, he would be ecstatic. He was planning for worse.

He had prepared for fifteen different landing locations for the invading armies. He had looked at digging tunnels, laying minefields and putting up a giant electrified fence around the city. He'd discarded that last option fairly quickly, but the others were integral parts of his plan.

Through it all he tried to picture the coming battle as the invaders would see it. What approach would they take toward the city? How would they advance on the first troops they saw? And, most importantly of all, what *wouldn't* they see? What could he hide?

Timing would be crucial. If the complete scope of Daggert's plan became clear too early, the invaders could make the whole thing come apart. He needed to make sure the invaders didn't see anything that made them hesitate to move forward. He needed them to stick to their guns. He needed them *here*.

He leaned back in his chair. The plan seemed more ludicrous the more he thought about it. The end goal he intended to achieve—did he *really* propose that to the captain-general? And did Anson finally, grudgingly, agree to it? Did they even have the right to make the decisions they were making?

He knew the answer to that last one, at least. They were making this decision because they were the only ones who could. Whether historians praised them or damned them for what they were going to do, he hoped at least a few of them would understand why they did it, and how few other options they had.

The ceiling of Daggert's office was a rough, uneven texture, with bumps and lumps that cast small shadows over the white surface. As Daggert stared at the ceiling, focusing on this bump or the other, they seemed to take on identities. This bump was a *Vulture*, that one an *Uller*. Movement vectors appeared, and the bumps seemed to drift across the ceiling. Then he would move them back and set them on another course of action, watch them chase another possibility.

He closed his eyes, and he still saw them. He was fairly certain he would keep seeing them, whether he was awake or asleep, until the battle was finally done.

"Wake up," a low voice said. It was gruff but contained an oddly calm note as well. Odd because the voice belonged to Anson Marik.

Daggert opened his eyes. "I wasn't asleep," he said.

"Then you should be." The captain-general settled his bulk into a chair that Daggert always thought was normal-sized until Anson made it appear small and cramped. "When was the last time you actually slept?"

"I'm not sure. A few days," Daggert said warily. Anson's demeanor put him on his guard—since when did the captain-general care about his well-being?

"That's not enough," he said. Then, as if he was aware of how strangely he was acting, his tone grew harsher.

"You can't nap when the shit starts flying. You'd better be ready for it."

"I'll be ready."

"Tell me what you've done."

Daggert reviewed everything—troops placements, battle plans and the situations where they'd be used, artillery placements, mine deployment, aerial force capacity and any other aspect of the defense that popped into the captain-general's mind. Daggert had already planned this presentation, though he hadn't expected Anson to pop into his office and request an impromptu recital, and he tried to run through a large amount of material in an organized, efficient fashion. But Anson kept hindering his pace.

"How dense are the mines to the north?" he asked when Daggert was outlining the minefield boundaries.

"Medium density," Daggert said. "A little over 150,000 mines per square kilometer."

"Is that enough?"

"Enough to make the 'Mechs cautious, yes. Given that we don't have an unlimited number of mines, I believe it's the right amount."

Anson nodded curtly. He didn't seem satisfied, but Daggert couldn't remember the last time the captain-general seemed satisfied about anything.

It wasn't long before the next question.

"You've put most of the Silver Hawk Irregulars in the outlying areas and the militia troops in the city."

"Yes."

"Are they still talking to each other? Coordinating?"

"Yes. There have been regular drills, and we've gone over a number of scenarios involving troops charging into the city and the kinds of things that would require coordination between both levels of troops. The commanders have gained a workable understanding of each other's tendencies and tactics."

"Why not flip-flop them? Put the seasoned fighters in the city where they can make life hell for the invaders?"

"Because that would unnecessarily expose the less-hardy militia troops. They will need the shelter of the city to survive, and it's important that they know the ins and outs of New Edinburgh better than the Silver Hawks. And if we get the outcome we're planning for, it would be best for the Silver Hawk Irregulars to be well away from the center of the city."

Anson's eyes looked wide and vacant, as if he couldn't remember what Daggert was talking about. Then he jerked his head back, and his eyes narrowed. He had remembered.

"Right. Of course. Okay. Go on."

Daggert did. The questions from Anson didn't stop, though. The captain-general, usually completely uninterested in the technical details of war, picked through every aspect of the battle plan, poking at each detail, looking for a flaw. For a time Daggert found it refreshing—it was good, he believed, to have your ideas tested, to be forced to justify them. And having Anson be so interested in the particulars of his job was a novelty.

That lasted about an hour. After that, the constant flow of questions started to wear Daggert down, and he kept restraining himself from asking if Anson could just trust his decisions. But he knew how poorly Anson took challenges to his authority, so Daggert kept his temper in check, and Anson's questions, comments and criticisms kept coming.

"You're focusing too much on the roads. They're going to stay away from the roads, because they'll assume you have them locked down. You put too much manpower there, you'll end up wasting forces who spend the whole battle waiting for the enemy to come find them."

And then: "Don't trust so much in artillery. No one's going to be scared by it. They came here for a slugfest, and they're not going to turn back until they get it."

And later: "This isn't Danais. This isn't Gannett. Why are you still relying so much on the hit-and-run? Aren't they used to that by now?"

And still later: "Don't worry so much about the launch

points. Worry about where you're going to put the damn ships and keep them safe."

And even later than that: "The aero forces aren't secure enough. Make sure they can't take out our air units as soon as they land."

And so on and so forth. It was exhausting. Daggert didn't know if Anson was operating off some comprehensive battle plan that he carried in his head or if he was simply being contrary as often as he could. It helped that Daggert was already tired to begin with—had he lost his composure and tried to unleash his temper on Anson, his lack of energy would make his fury sound much like his normal voice. He could completely give in to anger without Anson noticing a thing.

But he kept his patience, and he kept talking, tried to cover everything until he reached a point at which he noticed that no one had spoken for a few minutes. He had presented everything he had, and Anson had given every response he had, and both of them were done.

Daggert tried to look Anson in the eye, but the captain-general's head was slumped, his chin practically to his chest. He could see that Anson was awake—the captain-general's right hand was squeezed into a fist, and he occasionally rapped the armrest of his chair with his knuckles. Daggert kept quiet, waiting for Anson to do whatever he was going to do.

Finally Anson slowly raised his head. His brow was clenched, his mouth twisted into a snarl. It was a familiar expression. But when he spoke, his voice was level.

"Is there anything we could do differently?" he asked.

"Many things," Daggert said. "But none that would take us to our goal."

Anson's expression didn't change. He was looking toward Daggert, but not at him. His attention was focused on something far distant.

"There had to be a time," he said, "when it could have been different. There must have been a way."

"Maybe," said Daggert. "But that doesn't really matter now, does it?"

"No. It doesn't."

"The situation isn't going to change. We have the tools we have, the same tools we've always had. We'll use them as well as we can. That's all we can do."

"The same tools we've always had," Anson echoed, and Daggert knew that no matter how little sleep he'd had recently, the captain-general had had less.

Daggert fell silent again, waiting for Anson's focus to return to something in the room. It didn't take long. Anson's face remained set in its angry cast, and his eyes seized on Daggert.

"We will," he said. "We'll use them in ways they'll never expect."

Daggert nodded.

Anson's fist was tight, his knuckles white. "There's one more tool. One more we should employ."

Daggert nodded again. "The operative."

"Yes. It won't be smooth—he'll probably be lost to us after this—but he's placed so deeply, we'd be foolish not to take advantage of him now."

"Yes, sir. I'll prepare some information for him to pass along."

"See if you can give him an escape route as well. He's earned the chance to survive if he can."

"Haven't we all?" Daggert said. He tried to make his voice sound light, but he was too tired to pull it off successfully.

Anson didn't answer. He stood and walked heavily toward the door.

Before the door opened, Anson stopped.

"Thank you," he said without turning around, his voice low. Then he left.

Daggert blinked a few times and couldn't compose himself rapidly enough to say anything in return.

He looked at his map again, but his eyes wouldn't focus. The adrenaline needed to make the effort of explaining the details of his plan to Anson was gone, and now he felt more drained than ever. He really should sleep.

He wouldn't go home. By the time he made it home, a hundred details that needed his attention would have popped into his head, and he wouldn't be able to sleep until they were taken care of. He would end up turning around and coming right back.

But he could sleep here. He leaned back, put his feet up on his desk and closed his eyes. For a brief time, he saw only welcome blackness.

Then he saw 'Mechs marching in formation. Battlearmor troops screaming onto the battlefield, jump jets flaring. Aero units strafing enemy lines with bombs while dodging shots from planes racing past them. And he plotted and planned and hoped that either he would plan himself to sleep or that his thoughts would remain lucid enough for the time he spent awake to do him some good.

23

Every time Duke Vedet saw anyone whom he believed might have access to intelligence about Stewart, he asked the same question. It didn't matter how long it had been since he'd last asked someone the question—he'd always ask it again. He couldn't quite believe his good fortune or Anson Marik's apparent stupidity, so he made a point of confirming it over and over.

The question was: "Is Anson Marik still on Stewart?"

Half the time he asked the question, the only answer he got was a blank stare. Vedet would quickly dismiss the person he was talking to and walk away, making a mental note that the individual in question was obviously not as informed about intelligence matters as he had thought.

A few people answered with a simple "I don't know," but most of them said the words Vedet was hoping to hear: "Yes. From everything I hear he is."

It was much easier to cut the head off a snake when the snake sat still and stretched its neck out for you, and that's exactly what Anson was doing. Rather than get off the planet before the invaders landed and find a safer haven, he was foolishly staying put, waiting for them to arrive. But maybe that's how bad things had gotten for him—maybe he was running low on safe havens.

Whatever the reason, Vedet was thrilled to have Anson there. He owed the captain-general—owed him for weeks and months chasing the Silver Hawk Irregulars, owed him for his damn obstinacy. He could repay a debt while taking a big step toward winning this whole war because Anson Marik was still on Stewart.

In other circumstances, there might have been a number of approaches to Stewart—maybe starting by storming and conquering some valuable Corean Enterprise emplacements, or possibly by cutting off food and other supplies going to New Edinburgh, starving out the capital until it fell and brought the planet down with it.

But now there was only one target, and it was holed up in the middle of a palace in New Edinburgh. The battle for Stewart, as far as Vedet was concerned, would be the fight to capture Anson Marik..

The captain-general would make quite a trophy. It was a shame that Vedet would not be able to kill the captain-general with his bare hands, but doing that would be shortsighted, though satisfying. Pictures of him standing over the captive Marik would be extremely popular in the Lyran Commonwealth, he was certain. And if Anson had a few bruises on his face and neck in those pictures— well, he didn't think anyone in the Commonwealth would object.

The challenge now was getting to Anson Marik—what was the best path to take and who would get there first? The first option to rule out was the highways leading into the city, since few defenders were dumb enough to leave the broadest, smoothest path into the heart of their city wide open. The second option to rule out was a repeat of Alaric's scorched-earth tactics. That was fine for a spread-out city of small, poorly built structures like Helmdown, but it would never work on a solid, dense city like New Edinburgh. The buildings there were built to stay.

The palace Anson had chosen as his residence was in the northeast section of the city, meaning the north or northeast approaches were likely to be heavily guarded. The industrial sector to the city's north, which included several Corean Industries facilities and suppliers, was sure to have a strong complement of troops attached to the existing garrison, while the DropShip port to the east would be closely guarded by Marik aerospace units.

But there was still the southeast approach. Two highways came from the east, one to the north, one to the south, but there was plenty of space between them. If the invading armies stayed far enough south of the highway leading to the DropShip port, they might find an approach that was guarded relatively lightly. If two or even three of the forces converged there, they might be able to surge into the city to find Anson Marik waiting for them.

There were a few hitches to the plan starting to form in Vedet's head, the main one being he had no confidence that any of the force commanders would work together. Even if he could get some of them to take the same approach to the battle, it would be difficult to convince them to drive into the city. Attacking forces were generally reluctant to charge into a well-defended enemy city, and Alaric Wolf and Roderick Steiner might choose to keep the conflict in the outlying areas.

But if he could convince them of the value of the prize waiting for them in the palace, maybe he could overcome their reluctance. In fact, he might end up with all three forces in a race to the center of New Edinburgh.

But he couldn't make final plans yet—there was a crucial meeting ahead. Vedet could talk to all the people he wanted, guess to the best of his ability about who might know what, but when his Loki liaison requested a meeting, that meant he was about to acquire information that was as solid as it got. Information that might be the center of his plan.

Even when he had been running Defiance Industries on Hesperus, Vedet had regularly met with Loki operatives. Corporate intrigue was at least as cutthroat as the

military variety, and protecting the secrets of his operations was one of the duke's most important duties. As a
result of years of dealing with intelligence agents, Vedet
knew they could be divided into two groups. The first
group were professional bureaucrats who had moved into
intelligence simply because they had found opportunities
in that area. This group tended to be buttoned-down,
efficient and quite willing to adapt their findings to the
needs of their superiors. The second group were people
who had been in intelligence their whole careers, individuals who might have been agents at some point and had
risen to the ranks of management and administration.
These people were a more wild-eyed group, given to in-
vesting their convictions in hunches and instincts and
bristling whenever anyone attempted to do anything they
interpreted as being told how to do their jobs. They had
trouble believing that anyone could know more about
their work than they did.

Vedet much preferred working with the former group;
unfortunately, as soon as he met his liaison, he saw this
woman was one of the latter. She wore a gray jumpsuit
that looked like something a mechanic would wear, right
down to the grease stains on the knees and elbows. Her
brown hair was spiky, barely longer than a crew cut on
top and shaved to mere stubble on the sides. She had
enough sense of decorum to rise when Vedet entered
the room, but she was up and down so quickly that Vedet
could not be completely sure she had moved.

He sat across a metal table from the woman, leaning
over the wood veneer that miserably failed in its attempt
to make the table look slightly less utilitarian.

"You must be Colbin," he said.

"And you must be Duke Vedet," Colbin said in a
drawling tone that made Vedet dislike her immediately,
especially after her practically nonexistent nod to respect
when he came in.

"What do you have for me?"

She smiled. "Right down to business," she said. "I
like that."

Vedet waved a hand impatiently and didn't say anything.

"Okay," she said. "I've been putting a package together. Now that we're in-system, there's certain people I can get a hold of that might have had problems getting messages to me, you know what I mean?"

"Go on," Vedet said.

"So this is what it looks like from where we're sitting. First, you've got a two-tiered defense, Silver Hawk Irregulars outside the city, planetary militia inside. To the surprise of absolutely no one, the palace is right in the middle of their formation. It's the egg sitting in the middle of a big bunch of chickens, if you get my drift."

"Sure," Vedet said curtly.

"Then along with that you've got your minefields, your artillery bunkers and shit like that. I'm not claiming I've got a map of everything they've put down—the bastards have been awfully busy lately, and we don't have enough eyes down there to watch everything. But I've got files that would give you a pretty good overview of what they're trying to do and where they're trying to do it. Tell me where to send 'em and you'll have 'em before you leave the room."

"Fine," Vedet said.

"Now, that's the definite stuff. There's something else you should know about, though."

Vedet gritted his teeth. "Tell me."

"You know that Anson Marik's on the planet, right? He came there to try to rally the troops, rally the people, be an inspiration, that sort of thing. Didn't work out too well—people are pissed at him and would rather kick his ass than listen to him—but he's still there. Captain on the sinking ship, right?"

Suddenly Vedet felt his patience for Colbin increase. He tried not to look too eager as he leaned farther forward. "And he's still there. He's still there, right?"

"You got it, Chief. But here's the thing—the reports I received say he's starting to get a little nervous. He sees which way the wind is blowing and knows that there's a good chance if he sticks around he won't be a free man, or even a living man, much longer. So he's having second thoughts about making his last stand, and planning on maybe getting out when the getting's good."

"He's leaving?"

"Easy, Chief, easy. I said 'maybe.' He hasn't left yet, hasn't decided for all I know, but what he's doing is making a plan. You see, the way it works is, Anson and his people know that when push comes to shove they might want to leave the planet fast. So what they've done is set up a temporary DropShip port on the southwest side of town, really just a tarmac next to a big hangar. If Anson starts to panic, he'll grab a few key members of his staff and haul ass to the tarmac, where a smallish DropShip will be waiting. They'll try to get off the planet before anyone knows what's happening."

A feeling of peace settled over Vedet. He leaned back in his chair and smiled, knowing that Colbin probably found the expression unnerving. Assuming Colbin had any nerves.

He couldn't have plotted a better course for this battle. The next steps were incredibly simple. In a spirit of openness and generosity, he'd share most of what Colbin just told him with the other commanders. Being intelligent men, they'd come to the same conclusion he had—that the southeast approach to the city was best. And he would leave that approach to them, so they could decide whether to charge into the streets or stay on the outskirts on their own. Because Vedet would not be there.

Duke Vedet and the First Hesperus Guards would approach Stewart from the south. He would go slowly, letting the battle come to him instead of forcing his army into New Edinburgh. He would let Alaric Wolf and Roderick Steiner pressure the core of the city until Anson Marik felt the heat and was forced to flee. Then, when Anson ran to his temporary DropShip port, Vedet would be waiting for him. Anson would never get off the ground and would fall quite easily into his hands.

It was perfect.

DropShip **Vlad Ward**

As Alaric sat at a terminal, reviewing the information from Duke Vedet, he decided he could trust it, for the most part—mainly because it fit with what he already believed would be the case. The formations of the defenders and the locations of the minefields and artillery bunkers were reflective of a solid, if unspectacular, understanding of military tactics. Alaric expected neither more nor less from the Marik troops, which gave the information the ring of truth.

He was not foolish enough to believe that he was looking at the whole truth. It was only logical to assume that Vedet was holding something back—or, on the off chance that the duke was showing all his cards, he was only doing so because he was playing another one of his games.

All of this—the information, the tactics, the gamesmanship—mattered little to Alaric. He knew what the general shape of this battle would be. As soon as he had finished off the last of the Silver Hawk Irregulars on Helm, he knew how Anson Marik would react. He would be looking for payback, and he would attempt to obtain it on Stewart.

Alaric expected the defenders to be more aggressive than they had been on other Marik-Stewart planets. He would be patient, waiting for their desire for revenge to make them do something foolish. He would find a place with space, get his troops in position and then goad the defenders into a slaughter.

To the north of New Edinburgh were rolling hills, to the west were grasslands. To the east and southeast were grassy fields and farms, perfect for wide-open fighting.

Alaric would land a good distance away from that area, make his way there and wait. He would fight the battle he wanted, and when it was over the Silver Hawk Irregulars would be shattered and the Marik-Stewart Commonwealth would be disintegrated.

He would use the intelligence from Duke Vedet to make minor adjustments to his plan, but the sweep—and the ending—would remain the same.

DropShip LCS Arm of Hesperus

Klaus Wehner was suspended in the middle of a small room, wrapped in a small cocoon attached to the walls. His eyes were closed, but he was not asleep. In truth, it was difficult to stay awake. He had spent enough time in DropShips that he almost preferred sleeping in zero-gravity bags to beds stuck in gravity. In space, your muscles were free to relax completely instead of adjusting to the surface beneath them. You could relax your neck muscles completely without having your head droop. In fact, other than cursory work by the heart, lungs and brain, no muscles in the body needed to do anything. It was, in Klaus' opinion, tremendously soothing.

But he couldn't sleep yet. He had to go over the list one more time. Or twice. As Trillian's aide, Klaus thrived on order, keeping careful records of what needed to be done when. In his other capacity, though, he could not write anything down, or record it in any way. It all had to be in his head.

The files had been intercepted and carefully edited, then passed along to the Loki operative aboard. He wished he could have changed everything—the Loki agents were good, and they had gotten a lot of information Klaus did not want to see in the hands of Vedet, Roderick and Alaric. But if he scrubbed information out of the reports and made them too weak, suspicions would be raised and his mission would fail. There were some things he had to let through.

He'd changed the time stamps on the data so no one would notice the delay. He had scrubbed the files clean so that his fingerprints, or any other sign of alteration, would not appear. He had wiped the drive of the note-puter he had used to make the change. He had packed a few essentials in a small knapsack tucked into the bottom of a footlocker. He reviewed his escape plan, step by step, right up until he was on the ground and on his own. Then he reviewed it again.

Then one more time for good measure.

Then he slept. He hoped he would dream something about his life after the invasion of Stewart, but he dreamed only of space and darkness interrupted by a few bright pinpoints.

24

Trillian always found that the relative inactivity of space travel gave her too much time to think, and this trip was no different. It was with a start one morning that she realized she had completely forgotten how normal people operate. She had some recollection of being able to talk to people simply because she wanted to talk to them, of going out spontaneously with friends because it felt like a good idea and because there were people she wanted to be with. People whose company she enjoyed. Back then, that was reason enough to get together with someone.

But now she couldn't comprehend that way of thinking. How did you get together with people without a motive? Social time is when some of the very best positioning is done. Should you go out in public, you are seeing who other people are with and other people are seeing whom you have chosen to accompany. Every choice along the way has its ramifications. Take, for example, the simple act of going to dinner. Do you go somewhere expensive or cheap? A high-profile restaurant or an out-of-the-way, hidden spot? Do you choose a place you like, or cater to your companion? Who pays for the meal? When you walk in the door of the restaurant, who goes first?

Every choice, every move, has an implication. The minuscule analysis of every single move was like dating, but a hundred times worse. And with a far smaller chance of a happy ending.

She drifted slowly around her small room on the DropShip and tried to remember what she would have done in this situation, back when she was a different person. She had a dim recollection that she would find someone she liked to talk to and go to the grav deck, where they could have a nice long meal and good conversation. But what would she talk about now? She didn't know about anything other than the war, and she was sick of talking about it. It seemed that whatever actions she would have taken in her old life did not apply to who she was now.

She should think politically, then. What alliance could she shore up? Was there anyone who had information she should know about? Anyone she should get to know better, or even meet for the first time?

She closed her eyes, shook her head and floated out of her berth. She would remember how to be different if it killed her.

She pulled herself through the corridors of the DropShip while sending a quick message to Roderick.

Come have a drink with me at Tennyson's. Five minutes.

He got an answer back to her in less than a minute. *Beats working*, it said.

When she got to the bar, Roderick was waiting for her. It was a dark room with plain brown carpet and small round tables bolted to the floor, but it at least had a grand window showing millions of stars. With that sort of view, the room could have been a collection of cardboard boxes in which people sat to hold drinks poured into paper cups and still been one of the better bars Trillian had ever been in.

The gravity was comforting, and Trillian felt like jogging a few times around the room to work her leg muscles. Instead she smiled at Roderick and they found a small table in the corner.

"Thanks for coming," she said. "Makes me glad you're on the ship." That had been another difficult job—convincing Roderick to ride on the same DropShip as Duke Vedet. From an efficiency standpoint it made all the sense in the world, but that didn't mean Roderick wanted to be there. She had talked to him for a good half hour explaining that riding on the same ship as the duke didn't mean he was admitting he was subordinate to the duke's authority.

"No problem," Roderick said. "At least, there's no problem as long as you're buying."

"You got it."

They ordered drinks and sat in silence for a time. Roderick seemed fidgety, staring at his glass while turning it this way and that. She kept looking at him briefly, trying to think of something to say, then looking away when nothing came to mind.

"So what did you want to talk about?" Roderick finally said.

"I don't know. Nothing in particular. I thought we'd just . . . talk."

"Really?"

"Really."

Roderick looked up from his glass and looked Trillian straight in the eye.

"Come on, Trillian. What is this really about?"

"Nothing!"

"You're not working some sort of angle?"

"No."

"You're not trying to get me comfortable so you can ask me to do some horrible thing?"

"No!"

Roderick's eyebrows were raised, his mouth pulled into a tight almost-grin. Then his face relaxed. "Okay. No ulterior motives." He nodded. "Good."

There was another moment of silence.

"Did you know Signus Wainright came out with another book?" Trillian said.

"Oh no. I thought he was trapped in The Republic."

"Apparently he was trapped on the outside," Trillian said. "Much to his chagrin."

Roderick took a drink, and Trillian could see tension flowing out of his body. "What's he raving about this time?"

"What else but the bane of his existence, the thing that has separated the man from a large portion of his readership? It's all about the whys and whats of Fortress Republic."

"Does he have any hard information in there?"

"No, not really," Trillian said. "Plenty of guesses, though."

"Any of them good?"

"I haven't read the whole thing," Trillian said, tapping an irregular rhythm on the table. "He's got an interesting chapter about the Word of Blake, though, from what I hear. He thinks the Fortress might be the Word's final victory. They've got Terra, and now no one can get to them."

"Ah, the old Devlin Stone as a Blakist theory," Roderick said. "Glad to see that one hasn't died."

"You'd think all the Blakists that were killed by Stone and his people would have put that one to rest."

"Reality's never been good at keeping a good conspiracy down."

Then they were quiet again. Trillian desperately flailed for something to say—for a minute there, it had felt like a real conversation. But she was back to not being able to think about anything besides the war, and she didn't really want to talk about that.

But Roderick did, apparently.

"This is going to end it," he said after he swallowed some of his bourbon.

"The war?" she asked. Something in her gut tightened.

"The nation," he replied. "The Marik-Stewart Commonwealth is going to be done as a nation after this."

"After this war?"

"After we're done with Stewart."

"I guess that's a possibility," Trillian said slowly. She looked out the big window and took in the stars, one by one.

"It's the way it is. There may be a few loose planets who cling to the Marik-Stewart name, or who carry on some illusion of independence, but it won't be real. It won't be a nation anymore."

Something about Roderick's voice annoyed Trillian. He sounded mournful, of all things. The knot in her stomach tightened, and burned, and shot bile through her whole body.

"Okay, fine, you're breaking my heart," she said. "Look, it's going to be a win, and it'll be a good one. You've got a genuine Marik nation here, and you're about to put a good chunk of it under the Lyran flag. How is that a bad thing?"

"Is that a serious question?" he asked.

"Sure."

"We're eliminating one threat that may not have been a threat in exchange for building two new threats. What do you think Vedet's going to do once this war's over—go back to Hesperus? Give all the glory to the archon and live in her shadow? And how about Clan Wolf? Are they going to stay in their new occupation zone and turn themselves into a Warden Clan, happy just to sit around and keep an eye on their territory?"

Roderick didn't wait for an answer. "You know what both of them are going to do," he said, hoarseness creeping into his voice. "Vedet wants the archon's seat, and Alaric wants . . . Alaric wants any part of the Inner Sphere he can get his hands on, for all I can tell. Was Anson Marik really a greater threat than that?"

"He was a Marik on our border and he was weak,"

Trillian said, while still not looking at Roderick. "That's always been enough in the past."

"And what has the past gotten us? We've fought all these wars mainly so we can set ourselves up to fight more wars. I know you say the archon takes her responsibilities seriously, and I believe you. I don't think she started this war lightly. But no matter how seriously she took it, it's a whole hell of a lot easier to start a war when you're commanding it instead of fighting it. It's all abstract to her, a game of planets. Get a few gauss rounds whistling past her ear and she might stop waging war just because she has a chance."

"Lower your voice!" Trillian hissed. She had caught a few other patrons of the bar looking in their direction as Roderick's arguments became more heated.

When Roderick spoke again, it was barely above a whisper. "Sorry, Trillian. You've got to understand this isn't easy for me. I'm about to win a war alongside two commanders who might turn out to be the two biggest threats the Commonwealth will face in the next few years if we're not careful. It's tough to remember who I should be shooting at sometimes."

"You don't have to worry about all that," Trillian said. "That's why I'm here. To be careful. To make sure these threats you think you see don't ever develop."

Roderick stood, leaving a half-full glass on the table. He wiped his mouth quickly with the back of his hand. "I damn well better worry about it," he said. "Because when the next fighting comes—when one of these idiots does something that makes it so the archon has to call up troops to stop them—you know I'm going to be there. I'm going to be the one fighting that war. The archon will be trying to stay in power, you'll be playing your games, but me and my men will be the ones in the crosshairs."

"Roderick," Trillian said, making her voice as calm as possible while finally looking at him square in the face. "I didn't want to talk about all of this. Sit back down. Let's talk about something else."

Roderick remained standing. "We're about to take out a nation, Trill," he said. "I'm not really ready to do small talk right now." He walked out of the bar.

Trillian stayed awhile longer and spent most of the time wishing she was drinking more. This would be a good opportunity to get good and ripped—they wouldn't land for two or three more days, after all, so she'd have plenty of time to recover. But she kept nursing her drinks instead of gulping them, and by the time she was ready to return to her berth, she was far more sober than she had planned to be.

Still, she was a little unsteady as she walked away from the grav deck, and she welcomed the feeling of zero gravity as it removed the possibility that she would fall on her face. She pulled herself toward her berth, running a series of arguments through her head. It was too bad Roderick had left—it had taken her a good portion of the evening, but she had managed to refute just about every point he had made. At least she thought she had. The drinks may have been playing games with her mind, but for the moment she thought her arguments made perfect sense.

One argument was that, while she couldn't speak for Melissa, Trillian was not as safe as Roderick wanted to believe. War had a way of reaching beyond the soldiers, and Trillian had almost gotten in over her head in Zanzibar City, and she had damn sure been in somebody's crosshairs. The soldiers, of course, bear the brunt of any war, but Trillian should never have let Roderick walk away thinking they carried the entire burden.

But if she really wanted him to understand, she would have to tell him about the policeman she had killed, and she wasn't sure she was ready to do that yet. Maybe it was better if he didn't understand how compromised she was.

She shook her head. Damn drink. Muddling her thoughts. She didn't have to tell him anything other than that he should stop complaining and do his job. She'd never heard a soldier on the verge of a major triumph complain so damn much. You didn't have to spend much time in politics to understand that victory is always, always good. People feel good about their leaders, about their nation, about life in general right after a victory. And taking a Marik away from the Lyran border—who, exactly, was going to be unhappy about that?

Maybe he was right about Vedet and Alaric, maybe there would be new threats, but who cared? Threats unify a nation. Threats give people a common cause. In the end, a threat is just the first step on the road to another victory. If Vedet and Alaric had designs on the Commonwealth or the archon's seat, well, then bring it on. People and the politicians who lead them like nothing better than a good fight. It keeps the blood moving.

She looked down the corridor. She was practically at the end. Had she gone too far? Was this even the right corridor?

She was suddenly very tired. She needed to find her quarters soon. It wouldn't do to drift off to sleep right here in the hallway.

A giggle jumped out of her mouth. *Drift,* she thought. That was funny. Drift off to sleep, drift through the corridor, float away asleep in the hallway. That wouldn't be too bad, really. A little drifting would feel good.

But then she looked at the door in front of her and realized it was hers. She stared at it for another moment before palming it open and sliding inside.

She didn't bother wrapping herself in her cocoon. She wanted to drift. She took off a layer of clothes and then just closed her eyes, spread her limbs and floated in her room. Totally directionless, totally free. She fell asleep quickly.

An hour or two later she bumped hard into the door of her closet and was jarred awake. *Damn DropShip air currents,* she thought as she rubbed her arm; then she wrapped herself in her cocoon and went back to sleep.

25

"They're landing."

The words came over an intercom, because there was no time for anyone to walk through the halls of the palace and track Anson down. He had left an order that this news needed to be delivered to him immediately, no matter when it happened, no matter what he was doing. And now it had come.

"Where's Daggert?" he said.

"On his way to see you."

"Is Cameran-Witherspoon with him?"

"Yes, my lord."

"Okay." After a pause, he activated the intercom again. "Thank you."

He could almost feel the surprise radiating out of the intercom.

It didn't take Daggert long to find him. He'd made the journey to Anson's new office enough times that he knew the shortest route. The whole secret had actually fallen apart rather quickly—there were even two guards stationed outside the room now, a development that had caught Anson by surprise. He didn't know how the guards had tracked him down, but he had known he couldn't stay hidden forever.

Anson started talking as soon as he saw the door opening.

"Are they all here?"

"Yes," Daggert said

"All three forces?"

"Yes. All on their way down."

"All right. So far so good." He turned to Cameran-Witherspoon, who seemed a little surprised at the pace of the conversation. "Force Commander Cameran-Witherspoon. Are your troops ready?"

"Yes, my lord."

"Briefed on the battle plans you made with Daggert?"

"Yes."

"And your division commanders know what they're doing?"

"Of course, my lord."

"Good. Excellent. Then it's time for you to go."

Cameran-Witherspoon blinked. "My lord?"

"Go. Leave. Get the hell off this planet. You and most of the Silver Hawk Irregulars. I want you to leave three companies behind, and the rest of you will get the hell off this planet."

"Three *companies*? My lord, that's nowhere near enough to—"

"I didn't ask if it was enough and damn well didn't ask for discussion on the matter!" Anson yelled. Old habits die hard. "You're leaving the planet because I *said* you're leaving the planet! Now get the hell *out*!"

Cameran-Witherspoon's hands were floating above his waist, wiggling this way and that in a series of incomprehensible gestures. "But . . . my lord, where?"

"Where? A DropShip port, of course. That's how you get off a planet. But use the MacDonald port—I think our own port will be watched pretty closely between now and then. I've already arranged to put a lot of movement on the highway to disguise what you're doing. I want you in MacDonald, and all but three of your companies with you, and I want you to take off. Where you go from there, I don't care. Probably should be a Silver Hawk planet." He paused. "New Hope. Go to New Hope. Take it as a damn symbol if you want."

"I don't—"

"You don't have to understand!" Anson thundered. "All you have to do is bloody well follow orders! You're a *soldier*. That's what soldiers *do*. You were in this office just a few days ago when I explained your duty to you and you said you understood it. Your first responsibility is to the people of the Silver Hawk Coaltion. Well, those people aren't here. So get the hell off this planet and go fight for your people."

Cameran-Witherspoon still didn't move.

"Get the hell out or I'll have the guards carry you out! Move your *ass*!"

Cameran-Witherspoon was talking to himself, shaking his head as his mouth moved soundlessly. Anson couldn't quite read his lips, but he was pretty sure it was mostly four-letter words with a ten- or twelve-letter combo thrown in for variety's sake. Cameran-Witherspoon was not happy, and he was confused as hell. But he was leaving.

Anson watched the door shut behind him. "Do you think he'll really go?" he asked.

"He's a fighter, so he's not going to be happy about abandoning any of his troops when a big battle is brewing. But he's also a soldier, and you're the captain-general. He'll follow orders."

Then Daggert did an odd thing. His top lip curled a bit, exposing some teeth, and the corners of his mouth edged minutely closer to his eyes. It took Anson a moment to recognize the expression as a very weary grin. "Plus, I'm sure he was impressed by the Anson Marik charm."

"Damn it, Daggert, you've become awfully familiar lately. You like yourself way too damn much," Anson said. But he was smiling as he said it.

The moment was brief; then it passed. The smiles disappeared.

"You could still go with him," Daggert said. "There are plenty of decoys available. The plan will work without you. You don't have to stay."

Anson slowly eased into his chair. He'd been noticing his own weight the past few days. He thought he felt heavy, ponderous, even awkward sometimes. His frame had always carried his weight well—at least he thought so—but now his flesh felt like it was sagging, his muscles felt atrophied, his legs occasionally shook under the burden of his weight.

"Cameran-Witherspoon was right about one thing," he said. "You shouldn't abandon your troops in battle."

"Unless you're serving a larger purpose."

"What purpose? A figurehead? Someone for the people to rally around?" He smiled again, but this time it was entirely without joy. "These days, the people only rally around me when they can light me on fire."

"That's just the protestors, my lord. It's not everyone."

"I'm staying," he said flatly. "They're coming for me. That's one of the reasons they're putting so many troops on the ground, and that's how we'll get them to stay. And I'm not gutless enough to make 'em chase a decoy while I turn tail and run. If they're coming for me, they can find me. Then let 'em figure out what to do with me."

"All right," Daggert said, and Anson knew the issue would not be brought up again. He'd just closed and latched his last escape hatch.

"There's a lot of nonsense in this plan," Anson said. "They better bite on some of it or we're going to be doing a lot of running around for nothing."

Daggert held up a noteputer. "You should probably look at this."

There was a map of New Edinburgh and the surrounding area on the display, overlaid with arrows showing the estimated landing positions and destinations of the invading troops. Anson squinted and immediately saw it.

"The duke's taking his troops to the south," he said. "Right by the tarmac, probably."

"Yes, my lord."

"He's taken the bait like a good, stupid little guppy. All right," Anson said, and he pulled on the bottom of his shirt to smooth it out. "We'd better make sure we give them the show they came to see."

Outside New Edinburgh, Stewart

Alaric, like just about anyone who had climbed into the cockpit of a 'Mech, went through a period where he started to get impatient when a lot of time passed without him discharging a weapon. A 'Mech was a fighting machine—doing anything else with it felt like a waste of time. He'd never made any of the critical mistakes that often plague young pilots, but he'd felt the itch on his finger and the jumpiness of his leg and he wanted to *fight*.

The biggest aid to overcoming his impatience was remembering that the fight was more than the exchange of weapons fire.

That didn't mean Alaric didn't relish pulling the trigger and watching an enemy stagger under the onslaught of his weapons. But he understood the big picture. The weapons fire was simply the last step in a long process that began the moment a pilot powered up a 'Mech.

That meant that even though he hadn't encountered enemy fire, even though he didn't even have an enemy unit appearing on his scanner, the battle for Stewart had begun.

Alaric was keeping his units close together. There was no reason to stretch them out and give the defenders the chance to separate one lance from another. A tight formation would keep the defenders at a distance, which was what he wanted as he walked through the grasslands and fields outside New Edinburgh.

Roderick Steiner and his First Steiner Strikers were nearby, just to the south of Alaric. Colonel Steiner had obviously seen the same things Alaric had, and had come to the same conclusion. He was a good commander, Alaric had noticed—tactically sound but not too conservative. Despite his last name, Colonel Steiner had not shown any interest in playing the power games that consumed Duke Vedet. He was here to fight, a quality for which Alaric had considerable admiration. In future campaigns, Roderick Steiner would be a worthy ally—or opponent, depending on what the future brought.

Duke Vedet and the First Hesperus Guards, though, were nowhere to be seen, which concerned him a bit. His concern had nothing to do with wanting the duke next to him in a fight—Vedet was motivated by so many things other than pure strategy that it made him unpredictable and a liability on the battlefield. But there was no doubt in Alaric's mind that Vedet had once again held back a piece of information, something that would be to his advantage.

It was possible this information would have little meaning to Alaric. Maybe Vedet wanted to be the first to a particular landmark, something that had importance in Free Worlds League or Lyran history or other such nonsense. If that were the case, Vedet was welcome to his subterfuge. There were too many real concerns to deal with in battle—Alaric felt no compulsion to bow to the illusory demands of history and symbolic gestures.

However, there was a chance that Vedet had his eyes on a larger prize. If the duke had information that would allow him to get his hands on Captain-General Anson Marik first, then that was a concern. Alaric was not so blind to symbolism that he didn't see the value of parading a captured ruler before his conquered nation. As a way to break the will of what was left of the Marik-Stewart Commonwealth and the Silver Hawk Irregulars, the capture of Anson Marik was a move of critical strategic importance. As such, Alaric did not intend to leave it in the hands of a self-aggrandizing bungler like Vedet.

He had put two wings of aerospace units in the sky to serve as advance scouts. One had orders to stay to the north, keeping an eye on the highway that led to the DropShip port. If Anson Marik had any ideas about making an escape, Alaric's forces would be near enough to the highway to cut him off as soon as his scouts gave the word. The other wing was looking for Vedet, hoping to see whatever it was that the duke had kept to himself. He knew Vedet would show him where to look.

Alaric had landed nearly 120 kilometers away from New Edinburgh, making certain he would be clear of Stewart's air defenses and outside the minefields when he came down. He already had sent the minesweepers ahead while the rest of the forces prepared their advance, since the information from Duke Vedet showed that the mines were thickest on this side of the city to compensate for the relative thinness of the troops here.

The sun was rising behind him as his *Mad Cat* walked west. It would be nice if he could make the defenders fight with the sun in their eyes, but he wasn't likely to encounter any enemy troops until the sun was much higher.

He was walking on a road that bent and twisted along the bottom of small hills while skirting the edge of scattered farms. There was a small town ahead of him, a few old buildings sitting on the side of the road. A few streetlights glowed here and there, but the rest of the town was dark. There was a good chance every one of the few dozen residents of the town had fled, looking for some place that was more likely than their village to have some troops assigned to guard it, or maybe just some buildings with thicker walls. It was foolish, though. A town like this, with no strategic value, was perhaps the safest place they could be for hundreds of kilometers. People generally had two choices during a time of war—be strong or be ignored. Alaric had trouble understanding why people who were not the former could never content themselves with being the latter.

As he walked through the quiet town, voices came over his comm. "Star Colonel, this is Omega Two. I have spotted the First Hesperus Guards."

"Where are they?"

"South of the city."

"Heading and speed?"

"Due north for the most part, but slow. Around thirty kilometers per hour. One company is lagging and moving off to the west of the main body."

"Keep your eye on that company. Fly a bit ahead of them, see what is in their path, then double back and make sure they have not changed their heading."

"Yes, sir."

The speed of the duke's units surprised him. He thought Vedet would be making a more aggressive move toward the city, treating the battle as a footrace to the palace. Alaric had even been hoping that would be the case: he believed the defenders would have enough strength to repel a charge by Vedet, and he hoped to take advantage of the false confidence the Marik troops would feel from repulsing one part of the enemy force early on. But if Vedet was traveling as slowly as the scout plane said, Alaric would beat him to the city. So would Roderick Steiner. Whatever Vedet knew, whatever he was after, was over there with him. Alaric just needed his planes to see it.

It did not take long.

"Star Colonel, this is Omega Two. There is a tarmac approximately thirty kilometers north of the breakaway company with a hangar next to it. Both are large enough for a DropShip and look fairly new."

That was it, then. Simple enough. Vedet was not racing to get Anson Marik because he obviously thought Anson Marik would come to him.

"Omega One, Two and Three, you need to stay near the First Hesperus Guards until I tell you otherwise. Keep a careful eye on any roads leading to the tarmac. Omega Four and Five, while you are watching the palace, watch any routes leading south. When Marik leaves, he will be going south."

The chorus of "Yes, sir" was prompt and crisp. As it should be.

26

Trillian shouldn't be in the DropShip anymore. The craft had landed, and everyone else was out of the ship and on their way to New Edinburgh. The battle was going to be starting, and unless she got out of the ship she was going to miss it. But she couldn't find Klaus, and she was too used to bouncing ideas off him to watch the battle without him. But she couldn't find him anywhere.

She'd seen him just recently too. She'd been using him as a sounding board for negotiating the relationship between Roderick and Vedet. At the time she'd noticed that he'd been acting a little distant, but he'd continued to be his usual invaluable self. Now that she was ready to get down to serious business, Klaus was nowhere to be found.

She couldn't wait any longer. She'd left several messages on his comm, checked his berth a half dozen times and looked in all the common areas she could think of. He wasn't there, and no one could remember the last time they'd seen him.

She had to get out. If it meant going without Klaus, then she was going without Klaus.

*   *   *

Once Trillian was on the ground, she found Roderick's troops easily enough, mainly because he was the only commander who bothered to talk her in over the comm. He was moving slowly, which made him easy to catch. Because Trillian was in only a lightly armored vehicle, she stayed well back of his lines—she couldn't afford to catch so much as a single stray shell. But all she really needed to do was get within scanner range. Once she could see the movement of the units for herself, she'd be able to make sense of a piece of the battle without having to rely on the commanders.

Roderick's troops were moving slowly and carefully, not in any rush to charge into the outskirts of New Edinburgh. Trillian drove near the rear of his lines, then stopped the engine rather than slowing to a crawl or serpentining back and forth while the troops advanced. This gave her more time to sit and stare at her scanner, which showed her nothing.

She kept this up for a good hour before a voice came over her comm.

"Lady Steiner, I'm told you are using this channel for personal communication. Is that correct?'

Trillian stared at the speaker. Who was that? Then she recognized the voice—it was Vedet, of course. He'd lost a certain edge to his voice, that rough aggression she'd always heard. Maybe, when he was about to act violent, he temporarily lost the need to talk violent.

"That's correct," Trillian said.

"I understand you're currently behind the First Steiner Strikers."

"That's right," she said, and cursed Roderick for passing along information about her to Vedet.

"I think you'll find that you want to be watching my troops—things will get interesting there before the battle is over."

"What kind of interesting?"

"I'm afraid it wouldn't be wise for me to offer any more details at the moment. I'm doing you a favor, Lady

Steiner, by telling you this. What you decide to do with my generosity is up to you."

"Thanks. Where are you?"

"West-southwest of your position. Travel that direction for about fifty kilometers, then tell me where you are. I'll guide you to where you need to be."

She looked west-southwest and saw nothing but the outskirts of the city. "Should I be worried about being on my own out there?" she said.

"No. The defenders are keeping to the north. They don't want anything to do with us for the time being."

"All right. But if I get captured or killed on the way over there, I'm going to be really pissed."

Vedet didn't respond. That was fine, though—since Klaus wasn't around, she had to be flippant to someone, and it really didn't matter if her target responded or not.

It would have been nice to have Klaus there, though. She liked to talk things through, and she needed to decide on the best way to deal with Vedet and whatever secret he was guarding. When she finally tracked Klaus down, she would have to explain that being an aide meant being around when your boss needed aiding. But that was a matter for later. For now, she had to figure out who to tell whatever she found out and when she would tell them.

Trillian stared for a time at her scanner as if that might help her make her decision, but all it told her was that Roderick's troops were slowly moving forward.

She knew that by following Vedet's troops she'd be playing whatever game he had developed, and that held little appeal for her. But if he wanted to drag her into his scheme, it probably meant that he had an ace up his sleeve. To find out what it was, she needed to journey west.

"Roderick, do you need me around here at the moment?" she said over the comm.

"No, I don't think so," he said, then paused. "Who is this?"

"Shut up."

"Sorry, Trill. No, I'm sure we'll be fine. But keep in touch if any interesting information comes your way."

"You got it," she said.

It would at least give her an excuse to go faster than thirty kilometers per hour. She floored the accelerator and took her jeep over a field filled with grass and a few wildflowers. It was amazingly quiet here, considering the number of hostile troops that had just landed on the planet. There were a few puffy clouds in the sky, and it looked like it was going to be a beautiful day. If you ignored the several hundred tons of metal walking around and the supercharged bolts of energy that would soon be flying everywhere, it would be a perfect day for a stroll.

A few low-flying fighters and scout planes whined overhead, carving wide circles over New Edinburgh and the surrounding area. Trillian couldn't see the markings on the planes, so she wasn't sure which craft belonged to what army, but at least she knew none of them were Marik planes—she hadn't seen a single shot fired yet.

But she shouldn't be looking at the sky. She needed to find Vedet. The ground was level enough that she should be able to cover the fifty kilometers to his forces in less than an hour. She kept her eye on her vehicle's scanner, waiting for the first of his troops to show up.

The drive was uneventful. Too uneventful, in fact. This was the start of a battle that could completely crush the Marik-Stewart Commonwealth. She shouldn't be taking a peaceful drive through grassy fields. She should be . . . she should be . . .

Well, that was the question, wasn't it? What was acceptable behavior for destroying a nation? Burning down villages and smearing yourself with the ashes? Grabbing some sort of firearm, blasting it until you were out of ammunition, then grabbing another one? Writing individual notes to the billions of civilians in the nation to apologize for the inconvenience and welcome them into whatever nation they were now a part of?

She probably didn't need to worry about it. Conquest

was an activity that built its own justifications. Winners of these kinds of wars seldom had difficulty eventually making whatever they had been doing look good.

She was getting a headache. She stretched her neck this way and that, then decided it would be better if she tried to not think of anything for the next forty-five minutes.

When she caught up to the First Hesperus Guard, she was amazed it had taken her so long. They seemed practically stationary—tracking them down should have taken almost no time.

What kind of battle is this? she asked herself. *Doesn't anyone charge into the breach anymore?*

She called the duke on the channel he had used to call her, assuming he'd be listening.

"Duke Vedet? I somehow managed to catch up to your troops. Did they find any good picnic spots while they were tooling about the countryside?"

"I wish I could tell you more about why I asked you to be here," he said. "But it's too early. And I hope you'll understand that each and every one of my soldiers is under orders not to talk to you, so please stay out of their way."

"That's all you've got for me? No fighting, no information and barely concealed hostility? I'm so glad I'm here."

"Stay long enough," Vedet said, "and you will be." Then the comm was silent.

Trillian wasn't convinced of the truth of that statement, but since it was clear that Vedet was up to something, she decided to keep an eye on him and see what it was. Hopefully he'd show his hand before the battle started raging out of control.

She was drawing closer to the outskirts of the greater New Edinburgh area, and buildings were popping up with more regularity. They were plain but sturdy, brick and stone instead of the splintered wood that had been common on Helm. She thought she saw a face or two peeking out of windows at her, but maybe that was an illusion. Or wishful thinking.

She kept to the back of the lines, weaving back and forth since forward motion was so minimal. She raced through fields and over roads, skirting around small towns so she wouldn't have to deal with yards and fences and other minor inconveniences. On a few occasions she had to run parallel to small rivers and creeks until she found a bridge, but that just gave her the chance to look at the grassy banks and watch the water glisten in the sunlight. It was a shame that riverbanks just like these, if not these very spots, would soon be scarred with metal slugs and smoldering metal and maybe even wounded infantry looking for a drink. But then, there really was no way to make war environmentally friendly.

Her reverie was interrupted by something in the distance. It was a building with a corrugated metal roof, reflecting sunlight as she drew closer to it. She thought it was some sort of a barn, but then realized that was a trick of perspective—it was farther away than she thought, which meant it was significantly larger than she had first guessed. It didn't fit in with the landscape, and since she didn't have anything else commanding her attention, she drove closer to it.

The landscape changed as she drew closer. It took her a moment to place what it was she had noticed, and then she had it. There was an empty spot, a place where there were no buildings, plants or tall grass. It was right next to the metal building and, like the building, was quite large.

She drove closer, and she saw blacktop and plenty of it, a few hundred meters on each end. It was rough on the edges and not entirely even, like it had been hastily steamrollered. Though it was imperfect, it was still large and smooth, and Trillian probably could have enjoyed herself for a time accelerating back and forth and spinning a few donuts. But it wouldn't do to forget she was in a war zone, no matter how placid things were at the moment. Plus, there was the matter of the large metal building with the huge doors.

She rolled to a stop and looked at her scanner. It showed a large building, but nothing more. She didn't get any sign of active engines other than her own. Either there was nothing active in there, or the interior was well shielded.

As she sat, she became convinced that this was why Vedet was here. Once she'd found his troops, she'd found this place pretty easily, and she didn't think that was a coincidence.

It also wasn't hard to figure out what this was. There were not too many reasons to pave over a large field, and there was nothing in the immediate vicinity that required a parking lot this size. The tarmac wasn't the right shape for an airstrip—it was almost a square, not a long rectangle. It was, however, about the right size for a DropShip, as was the hangar. Duke Vedet had found a temporary DropShip port that wasn't on any maps she had seen or in any Loki reports.

She cut her engine and thought once again that it would be good to have Klaus around. She was now at the point where she had stopped being angry at him and started being worried.

While it would have been nice to bounce a few ideas off Klaus, she knew the decision she needed to make. This tarmac was something that could affect the way the battle was fought—who would go where and why. So the people who would be fighting should know about it.

"Roderick, this is Trillian. Find any bad guys yet?"

"A few. Saber Company is running around the suburbs and they've managed to scare up a few Silver Hawks. It's like beating the bushes for grouse. Hasn't been much in the way of fighting yet. The Silver Hawks let loose a few rounds and drop back. They're not ready to engage us head-on yet."

"All right. If anything pops up that demands your attention, feel free to cut me off immediately."

"No offense, Trill, but I'd do that even if you didn't say I could."

"Good. Look, I've found the First Hesperus Guards. They're about fifty kilometers west-southwest of you. And they've found something."

"Do tell," Roderick said.

"A tarmac and a hangar. Looks for all the world like a temporary DropShip port."

"Really?"

"Yup. And Vedet's in no hurry to leave it. He's acting like he's going to be keeping an eye on it for a while."

"Because he thinks there will be something to see."

"You got it."

Roderick was silent for a few moments. Trillian used the time to determine that the scanner had nothing interesting to show her.

Then Roderick spoke again. "What's the security presence at the tarmac?"

"Nonexistent."

"Get the hell out of here."

"I'm serious," Trillian said. "I've been sitting on the tarmac for a few minutes and haven't seen a soul."

"There's something wrong about this. There's got to be a DropShip sitting in the hangar—they're not going to haul one across the city for takeoff."

"Okay."

"So you're telling me they left a DropShip completely unguarded?"

She looked again for Marik units guarding the building and saw only blue sky, green grass and blacktop. "That's what it looks like. So what? It's not like someone's going to steal it and go joyriding."

"Steal it, no," Roderick said. "Blow it up, yes. If there's no security on a DropShip port, that pretty much means you don't plan to use it. A quick strafing by a few bombers, and the port is completely neutralized."

"Maybe they thought it wouldn't draw any attention. Since it's not on the maps or anything."

"Maybe," Roderick said, but he sounded dubious. "That's a big risk to take, though. My guess is that if they really have a DropShip stored there and they plan to use it, it's not for anything essential. Maybe to get some stragglers off the planet once the dust clears."

"Then why would Vedet care about it?"

"Beats me. I've got enough to worry about here without trying to figure out how that man thinks."

"So I guess this means you're not going to come over here and join him in watching an empty tarmac?"

"Thanks for the invitation, but no."

"Okay. Just thought I'd pass the information along."

"I appreciate it, Trillian. Be careful out there—the fighting looks like it's about to become a little more regular."

"You be careful too."

She looked northeast to see if she could see any signs of clashing troops, but any distant explosions were washed out by the brightness of the sun. *Give it time,* she thought.

She drove her jeep off the tarmac, steering herself back to safety behind Duke Vedet's lines. She thought Roderick's analysis of the situation was sound, but something about the situation still nagged at her. Vedet thought he had something here, but she couldn't put her finger on what it was.

27

The word came down from different spotters—scouts on the ground, scouts in the air—but each time the word was the same. "Some of the troops are missing," the scouts reported. "They've hidden them somewhere. They've got a decent-sized force on the ground, but it's not as big as it should be. We can't find the rest of them."

Roderick pushed back his neurohelmet and scratched his forehead. "What does the highway to the DropPort look like?" he asked the latest scout to give a report, the pilot of a Crow helicopter.

"Clear of traffic," the scout reported. "They have it locked down and heavily guarded. There isn't much activity at the DropPort either—it looks entirely shut down."

"Is there traffic on any of the roads?"

"The northern highway is pretty busy in both directions. It must be their main supply and reinforcement line."

"What's the first major city that highway hits?"

There was a pause as the pilot reviewed maps of Stewart. "MacDonald. A good four hundred kilometers away."

"And the traffic continues north as far as you can see?"

"Yes, sir, but I should say that we haven't gone very far. The main concentration of activity is clearly New Edinburgh."

So Anson and the Silver Hawks are still holding something back, Roderick thought. *Still not ready for that final fight.*

The remaining Silver Hawk Irregulars units had to be either hidden somewhere in the city or poised beyond the range of the scouts, waiting to make a charge later in the fight. If Roderick was making a bet, he'd put his money on the latter. It suited the Silver Hawks perfectly— they'd give ground while the Lyran and Wolf troops made their way into the city, then charge down from the hills or some other damned place and catch everyone in a long, drawn-out street fight.

He wasn't going to let that happen. In this battle, he could afford to be patient.

Out of courtesy he radioed this information to Vedet and Alaric. Alaric curtly acknowledged receipt of the information. Vedet made no reply.

We few, we happy few, Roderick thought. *We band of brothers.*

But he didn't have to think about them anymore. He had his battle to fight, and they could fight theirs.

"Saber One, are they causing any trouble for you up there?"

"Negative, not yet," Decker replied. "They're jumpy as cockroaches, scurrying away as soon as we shine a light on them."

"They're probably trying to draw you into the city. Don't let them. Not yet."

"Yes, sir."

Ahead of him artillery shells sped through the air, trying to fly all the way to the First Steiner Strikers but generally falling short. The big guns weren't doing much damage but they were slowing Roderick down and keeping him from putting his artillery where he wanted it. But that wouldn't last long.

He checked his clock, then looked in the sky. They weren't there yet, but they would be. They were coming from behind him, fighters escorting bombers, and their targeting computers were already set to the exact coordinates of the artillery emplacements, thanks to the hard work of Loki agents on the ground.

"Bombers coming in," he said. "I want to make a brief surge right behind the bombs. Give the Silver Hawks a little taste of what we have in store for them."

The various subcommanders signaled their assent, and Roderick pushed his *Rifleman* into a jog. It was the first actual charge of the battle for New Edinburgh, and each stride of it was a great relief. No more talking, no more negotiating, no more politics. Just fighting and winning.

He heard the fighters screaming overhead, intercepting the Marik planes that had scrambled to intercept them. Contrails and puffs of smoke rapidly filled the sky, and Roderick saw one plane turn into a ball of orange fire and black smoke and fall to the ground. While the fighters tussled with each other, the bombers got through, unleashing their payload on the city below. The ground shook with the impact of the bombs, and flames erupted.

Roderick broke into a run with the rest of his command lance flanking him. He was in the suburbs of New Edinburgh now, and the buildings were concentrated enough that he had to stick to roads for the most part. He pounded forward, closing on defenders that had been guarding the artillery emplacements until they were wiped off the planet. They were already retreating, but on the scanner their movement looked random and disorganized. Roderick edged west, cutting across a broad parking lot and zeroing in on a *Ghost* that was reeling away from the fire behind it. Roderick fired his autocannons and watched the rounds bore holes in the *Ghost*'s torso. The narrow body of the 'Mech looked unsteady, but its sturdy legs kept it upright.

Roderick charged forward, now relying on his laser as the *Ghost* tried to get off shots of its own. Its lasers fired, passing in front of Roderick, who had slowed down to draw a better bead on the Silver Hawk 'Mech. He hit the *Ghost* with his pulse laser, and the 'Mech stood still. He left it standing in the middle of the street, looking like a statue, a ready-made memorial to the battle raging around it.

Tanks surged forward in front of him, doing some of the street-level grunt work that urban fighting required. Roderick laid down autocannon fire to drive back some Silver Hawk vehicles and clear a path for his tanks.

The confusion of the Silver Hawk Irregulars was already dissipating. They were too well trained to stay disorganized for long, and Roderick saw on his scanner that their pullback was becoming faster and more cohesive. That was fine. He'd gotten what he wanted.

"That's it, everyone," he said to all of his troops. "Let them go for now. Get the artillery to this point and start firing on them as soon as possible. They'll either have to come out and get us or be killed by a million little blows. Maybe this'll draw their hidden troops into the open."

His troops circled back to him, rallying around one of the destroyed Marik artillery bunkers.

The Marik troops will die slow or die fast, Roderick thought, *but they'll never move beyond this point.*

Alaric did not regret any of the decisions that made this battle what it was, but he had to admit that it brought certain inefficiencies. Rather than being able to focus on enemy troop movements, his scouts had to keep an eye on the other invading armies to see what they might be up to and report back so Alaric could take their movements into consideration. If he had known their plans in advance, and if he could easily share information with the other commanders, his scouts could just watch the defenders. He had considered communicating with Roderick Steiner, as the man had certain qualities of a warrior. But talking to one Lyran commander and not the other would inevitably drag him deeper into their political games, and Alaric did not need any more distractions. The business of victory consumed him.

His scouts reported on the Lyran bombing of the artillery emplacements, a move that had involved elements of both the First Hesperus Guards and the First Steiner Strikers, showing that coordination was not entirely impossible. Now Roderick Steiner held a position near the borders of the city from which he could fire into it without worrying about return fire. While not as direct a plan as Alaric preferred, it was bold enough to set the defenders on their heels and perhaps force them into making an advance on Roderick's position, thereby forfeiting one of the prime advantages of defense. It was a sound move, and it would nicely complement what Alaric wanted to do.

He had deliberately steered clear of the highway to the city, but not because he intended to leave it alone. It would not do for the defenders to retain possession of a wide, secure road, especially one that led to a Drop-Port. He would make it his own.

Tanks and 'Mechs regularly patrolled the length of the highway, which was also controlled by a number of checkpoints. The largest of these was about five kilometers west of the DropPort, and that was the one Alaric targeted.

His forces were moving almost due north in orderly lines on suburban streets. A bystander might think they were nothing more than soldiers on a parade drill—though in about two minutes, that would all change.

The highway was elevated at this point, which suited Alaric perfectly. His scouts told him that his approach had been seen, and the defenders were massing to head off his army. That, also, was perfectly acceptable.

While tanks and light 'Mechs raced ahead, Alaric stayed back with the heavier machines. Their first shots were all metal, autocannon and gauss rounds battering ramps leading up to the highway. These were followed by missiles zeroing in on the same targets, peppering explosions up and down their length. Some of the advance tanks had a clear enough view to take their own shots. The barrage was intense enough to leave gaping holes in the ramps in short order.

Up on the highway, the militia defenders took advantage of their elevation, firing down on the approaching units. The waves of shells and lasers were intense, and a handful of vehicles stalled in their tracks, smoldering and smoking. But then the fire from the heavies came in, aimed at the center of the militia lines. Their attack fell off, and they staggered back. Alaric pressed his *Mad Cat* forward, relying mostly on the PPCs. With no ramps to scurry down, the militia troops had to separate, moving east and west as their former checkpoint started to clear out.

Then, right on cue without a verbal command from Alaric, Striker Trinary went on the move, running east next to the highway. Alaric edged east as well, keeping his fire on the eastward group, making sure they saw that if they fled, this part of the road would be his.

There was no room for maneuvering on his part—for now, the battle was point and shoot. The militia troops on the highway saw the damage he was doing and concentrated some of their fire on him. A laser struck just below his cockpit, and a volley of missiles exploded up and down his right leg. In response he stepped forward and added his lasers to the PPC barrage. He welcomed the heat that was building in his cockpit, the sweat that was running down his chest. Proof of life and a beating heart was always welcome.

While he drew the attention of the east group of defenders, Striker Trinary had maneuvered behind them. With a burst of jump jets, most of the trinary was on the highway and closing on the defenders.

The militia troops had already started to turn in anticipation of the new attack, but they could not prepare for its ferocity. 'Mechs and battlearmor troopers tore forward, charging straight into whatever fire the defenders could muster. Alaric could not see their charge clearly, but he saw some of the dots on his scanner stop moving or disappear completely. Stalker Trinary was taking damage, but it was not stopping.

The Wolf forces on the highway did not stop to engage the militia troops in close quarters. They ran right through them, disappearing into the covering fire from Alaric and the other big guns on the ground.

Most of the militia units did not bother to turn and attempt pursuit of the fast-moving troops that had cut through them. Knowing the fire in front of them would intensify, they kept pulling back to the east.

Alaric edged east with them. The Stalker charge had fully occupied the militia on the highway; he was not under any fire for the time being, leaving him free to pick out distant targets and send missiles twisting through the smoke and dust toward them. He also kept his PPCs firing to keep the pressure on the militia.

Stalker Trinary now held the former checkpoint. Alaric regularly glanced at his scanner to make sure the defenders that had moved west had not decided to come back and reengage. So far, they were staying away.

Alaric maintained his focus on the east group, keeping them on their heels. He watched them bunch together, trying to combine enough fire to threaten at least one of the heavy or assault 'Mechs on the ground. When their formation was tight enough, he gave the order.

"Striker, take them again. All other jumping units get on the highway."

The second charge was as sudden and fierce as the first. The Stalker units did not even have to select targets—they could fire at will into the crowd of militia units and have a very good chance of hitting something.

Behind them were reinforcements from the other trinaries. Still pinned back by fire from the units on the ground, the militia broke under this wave. They scattered, most fleeing due east but some trying to find some way, any way, off the highway.

"Do not chase them too far," Alaric said. "Stay near the checkpoint."

To the west, the other militia units kept edging away.

They knew they were now outnumbered at this position, making a full-on engagement suicidal.

This part of the highway now belonged to Clan Wolf, which meant no one would be making it to the DropPort without their approval. One part of New Edinburgh had been secured.

28

New Edinburgh, Stewart
Marik-Stewart Commonwealth
5 June 3138

Most of the generals were gone. Some were out in the field, but Anson had sent a good number of them north to MacDonald, hoping to get them off the planet. The field commanders that remained should be able to take care of what needed to be done without the higher-ups.

That arrangement left the situation room empty. During an invasion, this room normally would be bustling, but the plans for this battle were unusual. The customary maps were still being displayed even though there were few eyes to see them, and they showed nothing good. Wolves were on the highway to the east, one Lyran unit had the temporary DropPort well covered, another was pouring artillery fire into the core of the city with little interference from the planet's defenders.

As bad as it was, though, Daggert looked over the maps with an odd sense of relief. The situation was bad, but he had expected it to be bad. His relief was that of the condemned man who finally sees the headsman's axe swinging after long months of sitting in a cell and hearing metal bite into wood when others met their fate.

He had exchanged a few words with the various unit

commanders, but so far there was nothing that demanded a major departure from the existing plan. Things were going poorly, but that only meant events were following an inevitable course.

Daggert heard a quiet beep; then the door to the situation room opened. He didn't look up, assuming it was one of the officers who had been left behind and now was trying to occupy himself by taking an occasional glance at the maps. Sometimes, checking on the progress of a battle served as an acceptable substitute to being able to do anything about it.

"It's about time for the motorcade to leave," a low rumble of a voice said.

Daggert looked up to see Anson standing next to the big black table. The captain-general was wearing simple military garb, looking like any one of a number of troopers fighting outside the palace, except fleshier and older. But the look in his eyes said he would grab a gun and stand alongside them in a heartbeat.

Daggert looked at the maps. "Yes. It probably is."

"That thrice-damned Duke Vedet won't make the trip easy."

"No. He'll be waiting."

"And the others?"

"Some of them will probably come too. Though the Wolves just took over a highway checkpoint, and I imagine they'll try to keep that under control for a while."

"Okay." Anson looked around the room while one hand idly scratched the other. Daggert watched him for a moment, then returned his attention to the screen in front of him. It showed an overhead view of the city with real-time tracking info on the defensive units. He watched as several of the Silver Hawk Irregulars units moved to the south side of the city. They would attempt to defend the motorcade when it emerged. They would fail.

Anson cleared his throat. Daggert looked up, assuming the captain-general wanted his attention, but Anson was still looking around the room while taking a few aimless steps.

Daggert looked at his screen again, but once again Anson cleared his throat. Daggert raised his head, looked at Anson and waited.

The captain-general took a few more steps, then saw Daggert looking at him. He met Daggert's gaze, for a moment looking like the angry, defiant Anson of old, but then his eyes widened, and his face took on the slightly puzzled look that had become more common in recent days.

"Daggert," he said. "I want to ask you something."

"Okay."

"Why didn't you just leave?"

"My lord?"

"When you resigned. Or tried to resign. I said you couldn't resign, so you stayed. Just like that. But you had an idea, didn't you? You knew how bad this could get. So why not just leave? I would have been mad, I probably would have put a price on your head, but so what? It wouldn't last long. Then me and whatever revenge I wanted to collect"—he made a sweeping motion with his right arm—"would be gone. You'd be free. You wouldn't have to be in the middle of this."

Daggert leaned back. He cocked his head to the right, thinking. He scratched his temple. "I don't know. I guess I never thought of just leaving."

"Why?"

"Duty. Decorum. It's just not done—you don't run out on your assigned duty."

"Duty to what? Not to me. You hate me. For all I know, you've always hated me."

"Duty to the Commonwealth." Daggert paused, measuring his words carefully. "That's different from duty to the captain-general. Though I believe the two have often been confused."

Anson laughed, a short, barking noise. "By me," he said. "You mean they've been confused by me." He shook his head. "I did things the only way I knew to do them."

Daggert wasn't sure if Anson's voice carried pride or regret or both.

He glanced at his screen. "The Silver Hawks that were on the move have found their position," he said. "The motorcade should leave."

Anson nodded curtly, but he didn't move. His brow knitted, his mouth twisted. When he spoke, the words were forced.

"It's probably a good thing that you stayed," he said.

"Thank you," Daggert said, but Anson was already on his way out of the room.

Trillian had cut the jeep's engine a while ago, and she was leaning back with her feet on the steering wheel. Vedet's troops had moved a little north, but they were unwilling to put much distance between themselves and the broad tarmac. She heard reports that the Wolves and the First Steiner Strikers had been involved in some engagements, but the battle hadn't started yet for the First Hesperus Guards.

She had run a number of scenarios through her head while she was waiting. All of them involved victory for the invaders, of course—given what she had heard and seen, she didn't see how the Silver Hawk Irregulars and Stewart Militia could hold them off, even if the units that Roderick believed were hiding somewhere finally came into play. The real question, for her, was who would get the most glory from this battle, and part of the problem was that the commander most likely to look for glory was the one who really shouldn't have it. If Duke Vedet came off as the hero of Stewart, she would have plenty of work in front of her trying to keep him in check. Turning Roderick into the battle's hero was a much more enticing prospect—heaping glory upon the Steiner name wouldn't hurt the archon. But Roderick was so unassuming that anything he accomplished here could be easily overlooked. Unless someone made sure Roderick was front and center in any battle reports that went out.

He'd hate her for it, probably, especially if it meant he had to endure media interviews afterward. But it was all for the good of the archon and, by extension, the Commonwealth. He'd understand.

The real wild card was Alaric Wolf. He wasn't a glory hound like Vedet, but he was a relentless, fierce fighter who probably could win the battle on his own. He didn't seem to care much for publicity and wouldn't likely do anything to exploit his own personal accomplishments, but what would he do if he was the first into the heart of New Edinburgh? Would he claim the planet for his Clan, locking out Vedet and Roderick? If he did, this could devolve into a Wolf/Lyran grudge match all too quickly.

What made it worse was that she was powerless to affect Alaric, at least for now. He was in his element, and he would do what he did best. She could only wait and hope he did not accomplish too much too fast.

Duke Vedet's voice interrupted her reverie. "Lady Steiner, I'm pleased to tell you that it's started."

"What's started?"

"What we have been waiting for," Vedet said in a tone so smug it made Trillian want to hit her comm.

"And what is that?"

"You'll see. At this time, you should proceed back toward the tarmac. Don't get too close, though—there should be some fighting there soon. Go about two kilometers south of the tarmac."

"Are you going to tell me what this is all about?" she asked, but Vedet did not respond.

Cursing, she started the jeep's engine and drove back toward the tarmac. She didn't see anything on the scanner that would have gotten the duke's attention. What had he seen?

She'd ask Roderick. He had more eyes out there than she did.

"Roderick, are you busy right now?"

"What the hell kind of question is that?" Roderick snapped. "No, Trill, I'm just sitting in a lawn chair getting a tan. Of *course* I'm busy."

"Okay, okay, sorry, stupid question. But I thought you should know that whatever Vedet's been waiting for is happening."

"What is it?"

"I don't know. He won't tell me."

There was a pause. Trillian guessed Roderick was taking a moment to utter a few choice words about Vedet without broadcasting them.

When he spoke again, he was surprisingly calm. "So what do you want me to do?"

"My view of things from down here is a little limited. What's changed in the past few minutes?"

"Well, the Silver Hawk Irregulars that were north and northwest of the city have figured out we're not coming from that direction and have moved around to engage us. One group was coming pretty fast—I thought they were going to charge right into us, but then they kind of just stopped."

"Where?"

"Middle of the city, almost exactly. Northwest of me."

"Anything else?"

"Yeah. It looks like some of the rats are abandoning ship."

"What do you mean?"

"A helicopter said a motorcade came out from underneath the palace. A good-sized one, maybe a dozen cars."

"What kind of cars?"

"Nothing special. None of the big limos or anything, so it's probably not anyone important."

"Roderick, if anyone important is on the move, do you think they'd be dumb enough to go in a car that broadcasts where they are?"

"I would hope they wouldn't be dumb enough to leave at all. They should sit in a bunker somewhere, safe and sound."

"Where is this motorcade headed?"

"Ummmm . . . south-southwest. Right through the heart of town."

Trillian tapped the steering wheel of her jeep. "So it will go past the Silver Hawks that just moved down there."

"Yeah. Looks that way."

Then she saw it. It was like dropping a jigsaw puzzle on the ground and watching the pieces bounce around for a minute before settling into a perfect, interlocked position.

"Roderick, Anson Marik is in that motorcade!" she said.

"I don't think so," Roderick said.

"He is! He's coming to this temporary DropPort to get off the planet. Vedet found out that was his plan—that's why he's been hanging around back here. He wants to get his hands on Anson, and this is how he's going to get him."

"Wouldn't Anson know that Vedet and his boys are down there? I think that would make him think twice about leaving from there."

"How much choice does he have?" Trillian shot back. "Alaric's taken part of the highway, you're putting pressure on from the southwest—he's not going to have any better opportunity as this thing goes on. That's probably why the Silver Hawks came around, to give him an escort to punch through the Hesperus Guards."

"A DropShip can't take off quickly," Roderick said. "He climbs in, and it'll be bombed out of existence before it can take off."

"Unless he's got something more in that hangar. I can't get any sort of a reading on it, and Vedet's troops are staying away. Maybe Anson's got some trick up his sleeve."

Roderick took a moment to think it all over. "I don't know, Trill," he finally said.

"Roderick, there's a motorcade from the palace on its way here, and Vedet's camped out because he thinks it bears watching. If Anson's on his way here, Vedet intends to take him. And, Roderick—that can't happen. We can't have Vedet marching around with a captive Anson Marik."

"Okay. Okay, you've made your point. I'll send some units over."

"I don't need units—I need someone else who could take Anson Marik prisoner. I need *you*."

Trillian could only imagine what Roderick was saying in the few moments he left his microphone off, but she guessed it wasn't pleasant.

"All right," he said. "I'm on my way."

Roderick took his command lance southwest, leaving the rest of his units behind to harass downtown New Edinburgh. He didn't like this, since he still didn't believe Anson would take this big of a risk, and he didn't like having to play politics in the middle of a battle. But Trillian had been right—it would be disastrous if Anson fell into Vedet's hands. If the duke got what he wanted from this battle, he'd probably be challenging the archon for power before the year was over.

He hoped he would make it in time, since his *Rifleman* was relatively slow. The motorcade, though, had farther to travel and, from what Trillian had told him, they would not be able to take highways to the tarmac south of the city. They'd also be bringing the Silver Hawk Irregulars with them to keep Vedet back, which also would slow them.

He would be where he needed to be in about an hour. Hopefully by then he'd have some idea of what he would do.

Alaric had paid careful attention as his scouts told him of Silver Hawk Irregulars units coming around to the middle of the city. They had stayed put briefly, but then moved south again, apparently accompanying a group of cars that had emerged from the palace.

Alaric did not know what sort of foolishness the defenders were up to, but he was determined to make them pay for it. The Silver Hawk units moving south would soon be isolated from any other defenders, making them extremely vulnerable to an attack from behind.

He intended to deliver that attack.

"Striker Trinary, I want two Stars to accompany me. Everyone else stay by the highway, but accompany the First Steiner Strikers if they make a move forward. Move out."

It would not be easy. He would have to make an end run behind the First Steiner Strikers, then dash west. But it was worth the gain—if he executed properly, a significant portion of the defensive force would be utterly decimated.

He was already moving south as the Stars from Stalker Trinary ran to catch up.

Time went very, very slowly for Trillian. Vedet had essentially stopped moving forward and was shuffling his troops back and forth to keep them from being easy targets. The motorcade was making them wait, moving slowly as the Silver Hawk defenders traveled in front of it. She was impatient for something to happen, but she consoled herself with the knowledge that the slow pace gave Roderick more time to get into position.

She was still south of the tarmac, knowing she might need to move farther back if Vedet's troops had to give any ground or if the Silver Hawk Irregulars broke through.

She was keeping to a regular pattern, looking out her windshield at the sky, then the ground ahead, then at her scanner, then right side, then left. Then start over. Her movements were as steady as a metronome, but her heart was beating faster and faster. The battle had been mild to this point, but ahead of her it was about to explode.

It was coming. Everything was moving the way Vedet wanted it to. The motorcade carrying a panicked Anson

Marik was rolling right into his arms. Maybe Anson had enough misplaced faith in his Silver Hawk Irregulars to think they could fight their way through, but Vedet would show him the error of that idea soon enough.

The Silver Hawks were getting closer. It was time to stop milling around and get into formation.

"Everyone to your assignments," he said. "Be ready."

Stalker Company, which had been doing little more than running in place, now dashed west, preparing to flank the approaching Silver Hawks. Tiger and Dagger companies drew even with each other, forming a wall a few kilometers north of the tarmac, with Vedet's command lance buttressing it from behind.

"Prepare to charge on my command," he said. They would meet the Silver Hawk Irregulars head-on, then take them apart, piece by piece.

Roderick was close enough to see the flashes and smoke when the firing started. He could see how Vedet had his troops lined up, and their formation looked firm. The Silver Hawks, in contrast, looked disorganized, shuffling this way and that as the motorcade moved south. It appeared that this was something they hadn't planned for, some duty they had drawn in the last minute and didn't know how to execute. Which Roderick thought was odd—it was his impression that the Silver Hawks drilled for every possible situation.

He came at them from the east, running into their left side. He didn't want to get in front of them, so that he would have a chance to sneak behind and get to the motorcade if the opportunity arose. Low houses and shops gave him a little cover, and it helped that the First Hesperus Guards were moving forward. The pressure from Vedet's troops made it tough for the Silver Hawks to devote any attention to Roderick and his lancemates.

The first unit Roderick saw was a *Condor* tank, a hover vehicle that seemed barely large enough to hold the arsenal of weapons piled on top of it. It turned toward Roderick as he approached, and it let loose a volley of missiles. Roderick responded with his autocannon, rounds ripping into the side of the tank while sparking off the guns on top. Roderick moved to his right, taking shelter behind a two-story brick building to avoid fire from the much shorter tank. He stopped behind the building, counted to eight, then moved back south.

The tank had started to move north to try to head him off, but had turned when Roderick started moving, and it was waiting for him. Hot metal flew out of the large gun at the front of the tank, but Roderick had been expecting it. He was already slowing before he emerged from the cover of the building, and the shot passed in front of him. Roderick triggered his pulse laser and it beamed into the tank, catching it right on the missile launcher. A series of explosions lit up the rear of the tank, and it backed up, retreating before Roderick finished it off.

Roderick let it go. There was a *Spider* in front of him, and it looked like it was itching for a fight.

Vedet believed his charge was stately and beautiful. The Silver Hawk Irregulars had not looked that organized to begin with, and the pounding fire the First Hesperus Guards greeted them with slowed them to a crawl. His *Atlas* took steady steps forward, relying mostly on its PPC to push back the Silver Hawks. The defenders mostly rode the smaller, quicker machines they generally favored—*Ocelot*s dashing this way and that, *Blade*s doing the same thing only faster—with a few bigger 'Mechs, like the *Warhammer* that had been harassing Tiger Company, thrown in for good measure.

The only weakness to Vedet's charge, as far as he could tell, was that he personally was not landing too many hits. But that was not his role. Not yet.

Then it happened. Stalker Company came in from the right, blasting the Silver Hawks at will. Fire poured through the streets and 'Mechs took shuddering steps backward. Vedet saw a *Stinger* reflexively move away from the Stalker charge, putting him right into the duke's line of fire. A combined PPC and laser blast blew into the *Stinger*, and the impact melted away most of the 'Mech's left side. The *Stinger* didn't have much left in it, and its last few staggering steps took it back into the line of fire of units from Stalker Company, who did their job thoroughly. The remains of the *Stinger* smoked as Stalker units made their way past.

Then the voice of one of Vedet's scouts came over the comm and ruined the battle's perfection.

"Sir, we have units joining the battle from both the east and north."

"Who? Defenders?"

"No, sir. Roderick Steiner's command lance is engaging units on the east."

Vedet smirked. He wasn't surprised that Steiner was here. Trillian had undoubtedly passed word that something was going on here, and her cousin had come to get his shot at glory. It didn't matter, though—four 'Mechs would not be enough to allow the First Steiner Strikers to play any significant role here.

"And from the north?" he said.

"Clan Wolf units. At least three Stars, and it looks like Alaric Wolf is part of it."

Vedet's good mood disappeared. The damn Wolf had slipped in the gap and was now the closest invader to Anson Marik! This couldn't be!

He switched to his units' general channel. "All units, we are changing plans. We don't have time to grind this out. We're going for the motorcade and going *now*. Move!"

His *Atlas* punished the ground as it moved ahead. His energy weapons cut through the Silver Hawks, who looked more confused than ever. But he wasn't looking at them. He was looking north.

Anson Marik would be *his* captive. No one else's.

The explosion to Roderick's left blinded him for a moment, filling his vision with yellow and red dots. He kept firing even though he couldn't see, knowing that the pilot of the *Spider* would be just as stunned.

His shots were wild, but it didn't matter. A 'Mech from the First Hesperus Guards, a *Firestarter*, was plunging ahead, and it caught the *Spider* off-guard, practically pushing it over as it charged past, weapons blazing. When it passed, the *Spider* did not move again.

Roderick looked at his scanner. Vedet's troops were on the move, charging fast. They were going straight for the motorcade.

Roderick stomped on his pedals and his *Rifleman* moved too. It was a footrace now, but one that would pass through fire and bullets and laser blasts. Reaching the finish wouldn't be easy.

The lack of discipline in the Silver Hawk Irregulars lines surprised Alaric. He had not seen any units in formation yet, and they were doing little if anything to help each other out. This made them porous, easy to run through.

It was different from the Silver Hawk units he had fought before, especially on Gannett, where their discipline and teamwork made them difficult to track down. Perhaps what was happening here was an echo of the discipline breakdown on Helm that had led to the attempted surrender of some units. Alaric, though, had seen too many tricks and deceptions from the Silver Hawk Irregulars; he would not be caught underestimating them.

He radioed all the units that had accompanied him to the middle of the city. "If they offer you a breakthrough, do not take it," he said. "There is no reason to overrun them yet. Stay in formation and pick them off one by one—we do not have to kill them all at once."

This style of fighting suited his *Mad Cat* quite well. He could herd the Silver Hawks as they scrambled around, pushing them back and mercilessly turning on anyone who was foolish enough to run too far from the main body of defenders. A battlearmor squad paid the price when Alaric's lasers caught them trying to flee west, incinerating the group of them. A *Stinger* found itself backing away from one of the Stalker Stars only to be hit by Alaric's pulse lasers. He had startled the pilot enough to freeze him, which allowed his other 'Mechs to move forward and finish the job.

The Silver Hawks were penned in now, attacks coming from all sides. The assault would be exactly as devastating as Alaric hoped. He was satisfied.

The pace of fire became faster the closer Vedet came to the motorcade. The Silver Hawks were falling back in their last, desperate effort to protect their leader. His *Atlas*, big as it was, drew a lot of the fire, lasers and shells seeming to bend corners just to find him. Fighting through this was like walking underwater, and alarms and warnings had started to flash all over his cockpit. But so far everything was functional, so he stomped ahead. The goal was close—once he had that, all the damage he had absorbed would be worth it.

The streets were filling with smoke, and smoldering wreckage seemed to be on every block. Vedet heard nothing except for gunfire and heavy metal footsteps. But he was only a kilometer away.

Roderick was pinned down, fire coming from two directions. He edged behind a building, looking for cover. He knew he should charge, but the way this battle was going, he could afford to wait.

Sure enough, in less than a minute the weapons fire died down. The Silver Hawks were on the move, responding to fire from some other attackers. Roderick moved, charging down the street, laying down autocannon fire to keep the path ahead of him clear. There were blips all over his scanner, but he kept his eye on one— the one he was pretty certain was Duke Vedet. The duke was moving quickly toward the spot where the motorcade was supposed to have stopped. Roderick had to get there too.

He sprinted through the streets, and beams of energy grazed him as he went by. He slowed, getting ready to turn right, when a barrage of fire poured down toward him.

Vedet was almost there, his 'Mech's firepower keeping the path clear for him. The Silver Hawks were tiring—even though he was almost on top of the motorcade, the defenders seemed to be pulling back from him. They had probably had enough.

Vedet was mostly relaying on his pulse lasers now, melting the windows of nearby buildings at least as often as he hit an enemy 'Mech. But he was keeping the path clear in front of him, which was all that mattered.

It was close now, very close. He scared away a tank that dared show its face, then turned left. And there it was.

A string of black cars, stopped in the middle of the road. Waiting for him.

"Get some infantry here!" he bellowed. "Get these people out of their cars!"

"Roderick, he's there! He's at the motorcade!" Trillian's voice was calm, but Roderick could hear the urgency in her tone.

"Little busy right now, Trill," he said. He was being pushed back by two 'Mechs, a *Vulture* and a *Locust*, and was waiting for help from one of his lancemates. He'd moved back nearly two blocks to find cover tall enough to protect him.

"Take care of yourself," Trillian said. "But hurry!"

Roderick waited, then watched the Silver Hawks make a mistake. They wanted to flush him out from his spot, so they split up.

Roderick made sure they got far enough apart, then charged toward the *Locust*. It couldn't react quickly enough, and his autocannons practically ripped it in half.

The *Vulture* turned to engage him, but Roderick was already gone, moving north. The motorcade was not far away.

Infantry filled the block ahead of Vedet. He had secured the area with 'Mechs at each end keeping an eye on things, and the Silver Hawks were still keeping their distance. Part of this, Vedet had to grudgingly admit, was due to the efforts of Alaric Wolf and his attack from the rear. Vedet would never speak those words aloud, though.

An infantry squad was at the door of the first car. But they weren't doing anything. They were just looking.

"What's going on?" Vedet demanded.

"Sir, it doesn't look like there's anyone in the car."

"What the hell are you talking about?"

"We don't see any—"

Those were the last words the squad commander spoke. There was a flash, and a roar, and the first car was nothing more than shrapnel. Hot yellow fire exploded outward, shattering windows. The impact of the explosion bent the beams of nearby buildings.

Vedet was blind and deaf, or at least he thought he was until he heard another roar. Then another. The whole world was exploding around him. Alarms were growing more and more urgent, but he couldn't read them. He couldn't see anything.

The sound was unearthly, so deep Roderick felt it rather than heard it. He saw a globe of fire erupt, towering over buildings less than a kilometer in front of him. Then the impact hit, and his *Rifleman* staggered backward. The gyros kept him upright, giving him a good look at the next explosion. Then the next.

"What the hell is going on?" he yelled over the comm. He didn't check the channel, so he had no idea who he was talking to.

"I don't know!" It was Trillian. "It looks like—oh God, the entire motorcade is going up! The motorcade is exploding!"

Roderick checked his scanner. The remaining Silver Hawks—few as they were—were already running in full retreat to the center of the city. They had pulled off one more deception.

"*Damn* them to hell!" Roderick said. He stepped forward, moving closer to the burning rubble where the motorcade had been.

"Vedet was right there," he said. "Is he all right?"

"I don't know," Trillian said. "It looks like everything near those cars was flattened."

It was the roaring of a surf that only rolled in, never out. Ocean water on a black night, black black, with no stars.

But then there were stars, a few of them. Pulsing stars. Stars that didn't twinkle; they flashed, red and yellow. And beeped.

Beeped? Beeping stars? What the hell kind of stars were they?

". . . will keep trying. Need to get him away from the fire," a voice said. "Duke Vedet, can you hear me? Are you there?"

Stupid bloody question, he thought. *I'm right here.*

But where was here? Maybe things weren't as simple as he thought.

He opened his eyes and saw blue sky. With a few clouds. So it wasn't night after all. So what were all those stars?

Lights. Lights flashing around him, telling him that almost nothing was working properly. He might be able to move if he really put his mind to it, but that was about it.

He was flat on his back, lying in the middle of a New Edinburgh street.

"What the hell happened?" he said. He hoped his hand was turning on the comm, but he couldn't be sure. He wasn't really aware of his body yet.

"Duke Vedet! Is that you?" a relieved voice said, which meant that Vedet had gotten the comm to work.

"It's me. What happened?"

"Booby traps, sir. The cars weren't carrying anything but explosives. They . . . they did a lot of damage."

"Anson Marik . . ."

"Probably at the palace still." There was a pause. "Unless he left on the DropShips."

"DropShips?"

"We have reports of several DropShips lifting off from MacDonald."

Vedet could feel his hands now. Both of them. They were shaking. His fingers curled, clenching into fists, digging sharply into his palms.

"The palace," he said. "Get to the palace. Find Marik. Find him!"

"Sir, there may be more DropShips preparing to take off from MacDonald. Perhaps an effort to stop them—"

"The palace!" Vedet screamed. "Rip Anson Marik's goddamned throat out!"

29

The screen showing the location of ships orbiting Stewart winked off. Then the continental overviews—Lanarkshire went off, then Aberdeenshire, then Argus and so on. One by one, they all went dark.

Daggert watched them all until the walls of the situation room were blank. He should leave now. This would be a good time. But instead he stayed and stared at nothing.

"Daggert, get the hell out of here." Anson had been in the room for a few minutes, watching the screens as the fake motorcade went up. Neither he nor Daggert had spoken when it was happening. "I didn't buy you enough time for you to sit on your ass."

"Yes, my lord."

"They'll be coming here next, and they'll be howling mad."

"Did the bombs work?" Daggert asked.

"They bought us time, and they got them where we wanted them to be. Plus, we took a few of them out." Anson almost smiled. "Yeah, they worked."

Daggert nodded.

Then Anson really did smile. "Did you see? The goddamned duke was right there when they went off. Almost on top of them. I wish I could've seen his face when they went off. I wish like hell."

"Did he . . ."

"His 'Mech's down. But he might have survived. He had plenty of protection around him." Anson shrugged. "Cockroaches survive almost anything."

Daggert nodded again.

"All right, quit bobbing your damned head up and down and get out of here," Anson said. "Duty calls and all that shit."

Daggert stood. "Maybe you should come too," he said.

"We've been through all this! You know what we're doing as well as I do, and you know what happens if we turn into pussies now. I'm staying. You're leaving. Get out."

Daggert thought he should say something, but he had no idea what. He searched for words while watching Anson's face grow redder and redder.

Finally, the captain-general erupted. "Damn it, Daggert, we don't have time for you to stand there trying to put some fancy words together. There is a vehicle waiting for your ass! You better be *in* it! Get moving or I will drop-kick you in front of the car, tell them to run you over a few times and then drag whatever's left of you behind them when they go to MacDonald!"

"Yes, si—"

Anson's roar approached epic volumes. "Don't 'yes, sir' me! *Move!* Get out the door and have enough guts to follow your own goddamned plan! Run through the hallways like your ass hasn't turned to oatmeal sitting behind a desk for so long!"

Daggert moved, and Anson was right behind him.

"You can move faster, you bastard! Get those rickety stilts you call legs into a run and get the hell out of my palace! Get out! Get *out*!"

The captain-general stopped walking behind Daggert at some point, but he never stopped yelling. As Daggert walked out of the palace, he could still here Anson's shouts echoing through the halls. It seemed a fitting exit.

That was it. It was done. The motorcade had done its job. The DropShips were launched, at least most of them were. Most of the Silver Hawk Irregulars were off the planet, and Daggert would be right behind them. They'd go to New Hope. Then they would see what they would become.

The hard parts were over. Anson Marik had only one thing to do, and it was a task he had been looking forward to ever since he finally understood just how this fight would go.

He had picked a spot. It hadn't been difficult. He didn't want to hide in the palace, cowering like a dog. He wanted a room he knew, a room he would typically use. A big enough room so he and a few other people could move around.

The formal throne room was the obvious choice. That was where he was going to be.

Most of the other rooms of the palace had been emptied out. His office, his personal quarters had been stripped bare, his belongings either taken off-planet to people who might want them or packed away in hidden rooms. His new office, however—the forgotten room he had briefly made his own—he left mostly as is. There didn't seem to be a need to dismantle it.

The throne room was also left mostly intact. Marik regalia hung from the ceiling, purple silk adding color to the black stone overhead. His steel and oak throne had been cleaned and polished, and the dais it sat on was spotless.

Most of the other furniture in the room, the chairs and tables for counselors and visitors, had been cleared away, leaving an empty black floor with a red and purple rug running down the middle of it.

The walls were lined with guards. Not the ones Anson would have picked—most of his elite personal guards had already shipped off the planet. These were younger troops, a little more raw, but they would not need polish for their assignment. They were all volunteers, and Anson appreciated their presence.

He walked past them toward his throne and felt their eyes on him. He was used to it, so it didn't bother him in the least. His footsteps were the only sound in the room, so he consciously stepped harder, making a pounding echo. Then he climbed the steps to the throne and sat down. He put a case he had been carrying on the floor next to him.

The guards in the room were still looking at him. *You should be looking at the door, you idiots,* he thought. *That's where they'll be.* But his silent order went unheeded.

They wanted a speech. They wanted him to inspire them, to give this moment some meaning. Damn them to hell.

So he spoke.

"I don't know if anyone will ever remember you," he said. "I don't know if history will record your names, or tell your stories, or sing your goddamned praises, or any shit like that. And I don't bloody *care.*

"This isn't about *history.* This isn't about anything noble. This is about Lyrans and Clanners on our soil. They will be coming through that damned door. And they will try to kill each one of you.

"This is simple. You are Marik troops. They are invaders. You will make them pay. Right now, there is nothing, *nothing* else besides this room. There is no massacre on Helm. There is no Commonwealth, no planet, no city. There is this room. This is our land. They are invaders. And they will damned well *pay!*"

A roar went through the troops, and they lifted their weapons in the air. Anson waved his arm to silence them, but they decided to yell some more. He scowled, and let them shout themselves to silence.

"Now let's watch the show," he said.

There had been an addition to the throne room, two large screens above the entry door that would let Anson track the progress of the battle, right up until it came to his door. Looking at it now, Anson could see the invaders pounding toward the palace on three sides. The most relentless advance was from the forces to the east, the Clan Wolf troops on the highway. They had troops on the road as well as alongside it and, like gangrene, they were slowly moving down this artery toward the city's heart.

The most aggressive assault, though, came from the troops to the south. Vedet's troops. They had been hit the hardest by the motorcade bombs, and if his luck held, they were incensed. Their anger would probably make them the first to Anson's door. Which was how he wanted it.

Time passed slowly. Rapid advances that gobbled up blocks at a time became slow blinks on the screens. There were fewer dots than there used to be as the defenders threw everything at the invaders, knowing it wouldn't be enough. What had been inevitable from the beginning was taking place.

Then it happened.

"We have troops at the gates of the palace," the chief of security reported over a comm. "Infantry and a tank. Fire is heavy."

Anson didn't bother to reply. There were no orders to give.

The next update was not long in coming.

"The front gate is down!" the chief reported. "We have disabled the tank, but Lyran infantry is in the perimeter, with more arriving."

Anson pressed a button on the armrest of his throne. One of the screens flickered and then displayed a floor plan of the palace. Pulsing red dots indicated spots where guards had pressed alarm buttons. There were four flashing now, all positions near the front gate. Then a fifth, then a sixth. The invaders were through the front entrance.

Anson couldn't hear anything yet. The walls were thick

enough. But since the Lyrans were close enough, it was time to get ready.

He reached into the case next to the throne and pulled out three pieces of metal. One was a Mydron pistol. The other two were a barrel and a stock that, when assembled, was a Rorynex submachine gun. Then he pulled out an ammunition belt that was long enough to fit around his generous waist, which meant it could hold plenty of clips and rounds.

The guards in the room were all looking at their weapons—polishing this, nudging that—making sure everything was just right. The wait was almost over.

The pulsing lights on the screen now numbered ten. The infantry had split up, marching down two separate hallways. One of them was only about a hundred meters from the throne room. For the first time, Anson heard the distant clatter of gunfire.

He stood, pistol in one hand, SMG in the other. The Lyrans couldn't get here fast enough.

A light flashed on a guard post only fifty meters away. There was an explosion outside that shook the doors to the throne room. The gunfire was louder, and now there were shouts. Anson bared his teeth.

There were two guard posts outside the throne room. The lights for both started pulsing at the same time. Another explosion, this time denting one of the doors. There was a scream. The noise grew briefly quieter, then louder, louder, a surge forward toward the doors. Metal slugs fired into the doors, clack-clack-clack. Voices yelled without forming words.

Then the doors flew open with a bang.

Smoke blew into the room on the heels of troopers wearing Lyran blue and helmets with glass faceplates. Anson pulled the trigger on his SMG and held it, sending a burst of fire into the troopers. The metal tore through their armor, and the first soldiers through the door fell down on the edge of the red and purple carpet.

Bullets came through, scattering some of Anson's guards and bringing one of them down. Then a larger round flew through, burying itself in the wall. It exploded, sending black rock flying across the room. A shard struck Anson's cheek, but he didn't move. That was as close as they would dare get to him with an explosive—they didn't want him dead. Not yet.

Now more troopers came in, concentrating their fire on the sides of the room. Guards pressed forward, pushing the Lyrans back, but leaving some of their own dead on the floor. If this was a fight of attrition, the Lyrans would win it easily.

Anson came down from his throne, jumping to the floor instead of taking the stairs. He ran ahead, squeezing off pistol rounds, keeping the Lyrans from the door. The clattering from the hallway was constant now.

More faceplates appeared. Anson fired the SMG, moving it left, then right, then left, sending a spray across the doorway. The pile of troopers there was making it tough for others to come through. Good.

Then a sustained burst, heavy fire from outside. The air seemed mostly metal, the heat from the rounds a hundred trails of fire. Anson felt a stabbing pain in his leg, followed by cold numbness, and he knew he'd taken a round. That was one.

He tried to move ahead of his guards, but they wouldn't let him. They closed ranks, moving toward the Lyrans, coming so close to some of them that they swung their guns at them instead of firing them.

Another explosion, close enough to send Anson to the ground. There was no one standing in the room. The smoke was so thick he couldn't see the ceiling. Bullets were flying through the air. It wasn't safe to stand.

Staying prone, Anson moved back. He scurried behind his throne, then stood. His right leg almost gave beneath him, but he willed it to hold him up. He fired both guns until they were empty. It was enough. The doorway was clear again.

He dropped back down to the floor and reloaded. When he stood, he saw one of the bodies in the doorway moving. Not by itself—it was being dragged. They were clearing the doorway. They were preparing to come through in force.

He'd be damned if he'd wait for them. If he would go out cowering behind the throne. If he'd let them take him prisoner. He would make them kill him, and he would do it with a charge.

He moved in front of the throne. His breath came in staccato bursts. He narrowed his vision until he saw nothing but the doorway and the bodies sliding away.

Then he ran. Pain shot through his right leg with each step, but that only made him charge ahead faster. He didn't fire yet. He was at the doorway when he saw a conscious Lyran, and he fired the pistol, cracking the faceplate. He fired a round, then another, with the SMG to his right, keeping anyone on that side on his toes.

Another bullet came, this time into his side. That was two. He turned toward it and let go an SMG burst, then ran on. He passed another Lyran who had been hidden by the smoke, trying to swing his gun at Anson to knock him out.

Never, thought Anson. He swung his meaty left arm and caught the soldier in the midsection, doubling him over. A shot from the SMG in his right hand finished him off.

But there were more troopers down the hallway. Bullets fired. One caught his right leg, one his arm. Three and four. He walked like a drunk. He fired, but he couldn't aim the SMG correctly. The shots were wild. But at least there were a lot of them.

Lyrans moved forward, rifles and their soldiers. They weren't firing. But they would. His left arm was still good. He fired five rounds at once and two soldiers fell. The others paused. He raised the SMG toward them, lifted it.

You have no choice, bastards. You have no choice.

He fired, never intending to let go of the triggers. Rounds came at him, seemingly from all directions. Stabbing pain here, and here, and here. The color drained from the world until it was all smoky gray. Gunfire still clattered, and he knew some of the shots were his because his arm jumped with recoil. Jumped and jumped and jumped.

His neck, pain in his neck. Air wasn't coming. He struggled to open his lungs, but a giant fist squeezed him.

Then his head, a stabbing sharpness in his—

Epilogue

New Hope Herald, 10 June 3138

ANSON MARIK DEAD, COMMONWEALTH IN SHREDS

New Edinburgh, Stewart—Captain-General Anson Marik is dead, killed in battle by invading Lyran troops. He fought the invaders to the end, engaging them in a fierce firefight outside the doors of the throne room of the New Edinburgh Palace.

With his death and the fall of Stewart, the Marik-Stewart Commonwealth has fallen into chaos. Calls have gone out for an emergency session of Parliament, but most ministers have fled to their home planets and are not likely to gather.

The remains of the captain-general are being held by Lyran soldiers, who have said they will bury them. The martial government imposed on Stewart by Duke Vedet Brewster of Hesperus has forbidden any public mourning of Anson Marik and, with the exception of one or two small gatherings on street corners, the order has been obeyed.

While his administration had fallen under heavy criticism in recent days, Captain-General Anson Marik was the face and the driving force of the Marik-Stewart Commonwealth. His drive to restore the luster of the Marik name and the glory of the Free Worlds League brought him many supporters—though his bullying nature and occasional self-aggrandizement often caused those he brought to his cause to later fall away.

Perhaps his most lasting legacy will be the reformation of the Silver Hawk Irregulars, a unit that is rumored to have partially escaped the carnage on Stewart. . . .

Tharkad Patriot, 13 June 3138

TRIUMPH OF THE ARCHON! MARIK-STEWART COMMONWEALTH FALLS, ANSON MARIK SLAIN

The captain-general of the Marik-Stewart Commonwealth has fallen in front of a spirited charge by Lyran Commonwealth soldiers. With his death and the capture of the planet Stewart, the Marik-Stewart Commonwealth now becomes a ghost of the past. A menace on our border has been eliminated, and the archon has secured one of the greatest victories for the Commonwealth in recent memory.

The aggressions of all Mariks against the Commonwealth are well known, and Anson Marik was certainly no exception. Brutish and vengeful, Anson Marik's entire reign was marked by incidents of cruelty and hostility toward his neighbors, with Lyran neighbors bearing the brunt of his aggression. His death can only bring peace to the Commonwealth and stability to the Lyran economy. . . .

Zeke Carleton was still in a bit of a haze when he heard the news. Someone told him Anson Marik was dead, and it took him a while to remember why that mattered to him. But then he remembered. And when he did, it made him sad.

He had never met Anson Marik. He had talked to a few people who did, and they didn't have much good to say about him. Carleton also had plenty of friends who could go on at length about the shortcomings of Anson Marik's government, about how he provoked wars he couldn't finish. Carleton didn't know enough about politics to say if they were right or wrong.

But Zeke Carleton was a member of the Silver Hawk Irregulars because of Anson Marik—his unit wouldn't exist without him. And even though painkillers had dulled his senses, Carleton knew there wasn't much in the universe that gave him more pride than his membership in that elite corps.

Even though he wasn't much of a student of politics, Carleton knew that the Marik-Stewart Commonwealth wouldn't survive Anson's death. There was no replacement, no heir, no one who would step forward to hold this battered nation together. It was done.

But the Silver Hawk Irregulars were not finished. Each time Carleton saw a ranking officer, they talked of a future, of a purpose and of their cause. They thought there was still something out there to fight for. Carleton wasn't sure what that was, but he was glad to know it was there. He'd be better soon. And when he was, he'd find out what that thing was, and he'd fight for it.

There had been a time when it was perfectly acceptable—to some people, at least—to drag the body of a vanquished leader through the streets. Vedet fervently wished he could do that.

He felt a small twinge of regret that his troops had killed Anson instead of capturing him, but it did not bother him much. Victory was victory. The Marik-Stewart Commonwealth was eliminated as a threat—and a nation, as well. He was due significant accolades, and he'd make sure he received them.

For now, he would rest in the finest hotel left standing in New Edinburgh, receiving care for the wounds he had received from Anson's last gambit. He would recover, Anson would not. That was all the satisfaction he needed.

There were stories circulating about Anson Marik, branding him a coward, a bully and anything else Trillian could come up with. It was part of her job. It wouldn't do to have his people make a martyr out of the man, though she suspected they didn't like him well enough to do that. She hoped that dragging his name through the mud would make the people of Stewart accept the archon more willingly.

Now that the gunfire was over, the longer fight, her fight, could begin. Negotiating the future of the conquered planets, consulting with Roderick to see which planets might need her attention and, most of all, keeping Vedet in line would occupy her. Hopefully, she'd be busy enough to think only about what she had to do instead of why she had to do it.

Roderick had lost the race to the motorcade, and it might have saved his life. He hadn't been able to keep up with Vedet's push to the palace, as he did not have the fast-moving ground troops that the duke had at his disposal. All he had done in the battle was obtain a good position, pummel the defending troops and make it possible for the final advance to happen. But since he hadn't played the political game of Capture the Anson well enough, he didn't know how much all the rest of it mattered.

He wanted to leave. There had to be other jobs for him. He never turned down combat assignments, but there had to be a way to find a new one. Anything other than this.

Though finding a new assignment might require playing the game and falling right into line with the rest of them.

Nothing was clear to him now. He didn't know what

to do, where to go. He just knew that Stewart had become possibly his least favorite planet in the Inner Sphere.

While he was here, he had no choice but to have his men join Vedet's forces in patrolling the city and keeping the peace. Occasionally, this meant assigning his men to guard pro-Lyran demonstrations (arranged and paid for by Duke Vedet and Trillian) and to make sure no Marik sympathizers caused trouble. He'd seen some of the duke's men at these events and had noticed how much they enjoyed beating down any of Anson's supporters they got their hands on.

Roderick made sure his men were not as aggressive. While he had no love for the late captain-general, when he compared Anson's last actions to Melissa's recent movements, he didn't feel certain that the Marik supporters' cause was groundless.

Klaus Wehner was on the run, but he still heard about Anson Marik's death before most people who weren't on Stewart. It was his job to hear things, and that didn't change just because he was no longer in his former position.

It helped that he wasn't far from New Edinburgh. He would have liked to join those leaving for New Hope, but he hadn't made it to MacDonald in time. And it seemed like Stewart would be an interesting place to be for a time, and he could find a way to be useful here.

As he listened to stories about the battle of New Edinburgh and gained a better understanding of the present situation, he started to grasp the big picture better than he had when he fled from his role as Trillian Steiner's aide. It was a comfort—his first reaction when he heard of Anson Marik's death was that he had failed, that his effort to alter the Lyrans' intelligence had not done any good. But now he had a better understanding of what the whole fight had been about, and he could see it had been a success of a kind. A terrible, expensive success, but the best result that could be hoped for.

There would be more fights to come. He would stay away from any large cities for a while, doing whatever he could to destroy Klaus Wehner and build a new identity. Hopefully Trillian would leave before he was ready to return to active life, but it did not matter much. By the time he was ready to emerge, she would be unable to recognize him.

The Silver Hawk Irregulars had left Stewart so they could fight another day, so the nature of the battle here would now be different. It was the type of fighting Klaus was well prepared for. When he came back into action, he would poke around and find others like him, people who were not willing to be Lyrans and who wanted to do something about it. Then the battle for Stewart could continue.

In the end, Alaric Wolf was inclined to view the whole invasion as an interesting experiment. While it demonstrated the futility of trying to deal with spheroids on an honorable level, it showed him that a warrior could still fight honorably in their presence—as long as he ignored most of what they were doing. He could go into the holes they opened and exploit their movements for his own gain without going to the trouble of communicating directly with them and playing their games.

It would be valuable information to know going forward. Inner Sphere armies were generally poor allies, but they could still provide opportunities for Alaric to advance the interests of Clan Wolf.

He knew the situation in the former Marik-Stewart Commonwealth would deteriorate rapidly. Anson Marik had surprised him by not fighting an all-out war on Stewart, but it did not matter—the end result was the same. The Marik-Stewart Commonwealth was gone. The Lyrans would try to claim as much space as they could and deny Clan Wolf the spoils of their efforts. It was possible, even likely, that the Lyrans would be dishonorable enough to withhold the rewards Alaric had earned, and that he might have to resort to force to obtain his due.

He had no concerns about that prospect. The things he had learned when fighting alongside the Lyrans would be quite useful should the time come to fight against them.

Archon Melissa Steiner received the news of the death of Anson Marik and the fall of the Marik-Stewart Commonwealth with relief. As the press would have it, she felt the relief of a ruler who had made her realm safer and more prosperous. While that was part of it, she also took comfort that the long odds she had played had paid off. Sending Duke Vedet Brewster and Alaric Wolf to fight side by side was like sending two rabid dogs after a piece of meat in the hope that they would devour it all without turning on each other.

So far, it had worked. But the long history of warfare had taught Melissa this: taking territory is not the same as holding it. And someone who fights at your side is not necessarily an ally for life.

Victory was a blessing. It was also only a beginning.

Protocol probably demanded that Jessica Marik show some sort of sadness or regret at the news about Anson Marik. After all, this was another noble of the former Free Worlds League, a man with whom she shared a name if not any actual blood relationship.

But she could not bring herself to do it. Thank God for functionaries—they would be able to draft a statement of vague sentiment that she would not feel bad about attaching her name to; then she could let Anson Marik drift into the dustbin of history.

What the statement wouldn't say was the truth, at least as she saw it. The death of Anson Marik was not a tragedy, not even really regrettable. It was an opportunity, and she was fully poised to take advantage of it.

Really, her only regret regarding Anson's death was that he would not be around to see what she would do with his former realm. Oh, how he would hate it.

*   *   *

There would be no accurate account of Anson's end. Daggert knew there wouldn't be, but he kept reading every media account he could find. They inevitably contained limited info, but Daggert was not surprised. How could anyone say what really happened there? It had been chaos to begin with, and the survivors didn't have much interest in telling the truth. Almost before fighting had stopped on Stewart, the Lyran propaganda machine was at work, saying Anson Marik had begged for his life at the end. That he had died like a coward.

There had even been a weak attempt to claim he had been a suicide, with Anson giving in to despair at the end, but that story faded quickly. Suicides don't usually take a dozen bullets.

There were enough people, though, who knew the truth. Daggert would make sure of that. If Anson had been a coward, he wouldn't have stayed behind. He would have landed on New Hope with Daggert and the remnant of the Silver Hawk Irregulars that he had sent away.

But if he had done that, then the plan wouldn't have worked. When he conceived it, Daggert thought there was a way they could execute the plan without sacrificing the captain-general, but Anson had known better. If he had escaped with Cameran-Witherspoon and the other Silver Hawk Irregulars, the Lyrans would assume the war was still going on. If the Marik-Stewart Commonwealth had a leader, then it was still a nation. So the Lyrans and Wolves would have continued chasing down the Silver Hawks until there was nothing left.

By staying on Stewart, by dying, Anson Marik had also killed the Marik-Stewart Commonwealth—and by killing it, he had given a portion of it a chance to survive. The Silver Hawk Irregulars would retreat to their home planets and defend their people, following Anson's instructions to Cameran-Witherspoon. Anson's nation would die, but his military unit would fight another day, to see what the future held for the former Free Worlds League.

It was the best they could have done.

Now, as a bureaucrat without a government, Daggert would retire. He would find a place somewhere and hope it would remain quiet. He would not miss anything. He would not miss the pressures and stresses of battle, the demands of moving an army and getting them into position and, least of all, the experience of working for a loud, demanding, angry, cruel boss. He would not miss that at all.

He would find a house with a porch that looked toward the sunset and he would sit there every night, alone, and watch whatever world he was on rotate. He would breathe slowly and evenly. He would have expensive bottles of wine shipped to his house and choose one each night and pour a single glass. He would find a few moments of peace in an Inner Sphere that generally didn't offer any.

And at least once, when he was alone, he would raise his glass in a silent toast to Anson Marik.

About the Author

Jason M. Hardy has bad hair and a beard, which in most states is all you need to become a science-fiction writer. He is the author of two previous *MechWarrior: Dark Age* novels, *The Scorpion Jar* and *Principles of Desolation* (with Randall N. Bills), and a Shadowrun novel, *Drops of Corruption*. He is also a regular contributor to the Battlecorps Web site and has other various fictions and game-related writings that pop up here and there. He lives in Chicago with his wife and son.

MECHWARRIOR: DARK AGE

A Battletech® Series

THE ULTIMATE IN
SCIENCE FICTION AND FANTASY!

From magical tales of distant worlds to stories of
technological advances beyond the grasp of man, Penguin has
everything you need to stretch your imagination to its limits.

penguin.com

ACE
Get the latest information on favorites like
William Gibson, T.A. Barron, Brian Jacques,
Ursula K. LeGuin, Sharon Shinn, and Charlaine Harris,
as well as updates on the best new authors.

ROC
Escape with Harry Turtledove, Anne Bishop,
S.M. Stirling, Simon R. Green, Chris Bunch, Jim Butcher,
E.E. Knight, and many others—plus news on the
latest and hottest in science fiction and fantasy.

DAW
Mercedes Lackey, Kristen Britain, Tanya Huff,
Tad Williams, C.J. Cherryh, and many more—
DAW has something to satisfy the cravings of any
science fiction and fantasy lover.
Also visit dawbooks.com.

Get the best of science fiction and fantasy
at your fingertips!